SUNFLOWER STREET

SUNFLOWER STREET

Pamela Grandstaff

Books by Pamela Grandstaff:

Rose Hill Mystery Series:

Rose Hill

Morning Glory Circle

Iris Avenue

Peony Street

Daisy Lane

Lilac Avenue

Hollyhock Ridge

Sunflower Street

Viola Avenue

Pumpkin Ridge

ISBN-10: 1519193440
ISBN-13: 978-1519193445

For Terry

CHAPTER ONE

G igi O'Hare slammed the back door behind the catering crew and took a deep breath, trying to compose herself. How dare those rude girls come into her house without her permission? She didn't care if they were just doing their jobs. She would call their supervisor and report them, just as soon as she calmed down.

Bunny and Chicken, her white Teacup Pomeranians, danced around her feet, begging for attention.

"Oh, hush," she told them, but then immediately apologized and stroked their little heads.

She walked through the kitchen and dining room to the front foyer and opened the front door. She stood on the front porch, surveying the lawn. Her brother had cut the grass, but she noticed he had not edged along the walkways. Such a lazy, good for nothing lay-about. She'd be damned if she'd pay him a nickel for doing the work. She dead-headed a few petunias while she was out there.

Well, that would have to do.

She thought she heard a door slam in the house. Surely, Eugene Junior hadn't disobeyed her. She went back inside and called his name, but he didn't answer. She called down the basement stairs, but, other than the panting of her tiny dogs, the house was quiet. For once, it seemed, he had listened to her and did what he was told. She didn't want him anywhere near the ladies who were coming to lunch. All that boring talk about rocks and they'd be polite about it, but she could just imagine what they'd be thinking.

She loved her son, but he was her cross to bear, and no one could deny that.

She went through the kitchen to the mudroom and checked the back door. It was closed but unlocked, so she locked it. When she slammed it earlier, it must have popped back open. It had been known to do that. A window was probably open somewhere in the house, and the wind had banged it shut. That must have been what she'd heard.

Her stomach growled, and she realized she hadn't eaten anything all morning. She opened the refrigerator, where she found a bowl of cold chicken salad. It looked delicious. She took a spoon from a drawer, ate several bites right out of the bowl, and then several more. It really was good. She ate until she felt full, then put a spoonful on a china saucer, and carried it upstairs.

"Come with Mama," she said to the dogs. "Mama's got a treat for her precious little babies."

The tiny dogs hopped up the stairs and followed her down the hall to her bedroom, where she put the saucer down and watched them gobble up the chicken.

"Now, that will have to hold you until after lunch," she said. "Mama has important ladies coming, so you'll have to stay in the bedroom."

Gigi looked in the mirror. Her hair looked good, thanks to Claire Fitzpatrick. She might have to consider making a permanent change of hairdressers, and if Claire was willing to make house calls, all the better.

She sniffed her wrist, but couldn't smell the perfume she'd put on just that morning. As expensive as it was, it should last longer than that. She reached for the bottle and for a moment, couldn't believe her eyes.

It was gone.

She knew she had put it back on her dressing table after she put some on this morning when Claire was there. Surely Claire would not ... but who else? Gigi didn't want to believe it. She looked down at the floor around the dressing table and then went to her en-suite bathroom.

There it was, on the vanity counter. She could not remember putting it there.

"Mama's losing it," she said to Bunny and Chicken, who were now cuddled up in the middle of her bed.

She took the stopper out and tipped the bottle. She was more liberal in her application of the perfume this time, and put a generous amount behind each ear, on each wrist, behind each knee, and down in her cleavage. Was it too much? Oh well, it would have faded a bit by the time the ladies arrived.

She tried to focus on what to do next.

The check, of course.

She sat down at her vanity and took her checkbook out of the top drawer. She wrote the date, the committee name, and signed it. She was trying to decide how much to make it out for when she began to feel ill.

She felt dizzy, and her heart was racing. Her skin began to itch like it was covered with a million mosquito bites. She looked at her wrist and was surprised to see a welt there. She slid up her jacket sleeve and found a hive. An inspection of her other arm revealed the same.

'Oh dear,' she thought. 'What have I got into?'

She went to the bathroom and searched the drawer where she kept her epi pen. It wasn't there. She looked in the mirror and was frightened to see her lips and eyes were swelling, and a mottled rash was coming up on her neck.

Panicked now, she searched her walk-in closet, went through all her handbags, but couldn't find the damn epi-pen.

It had to be here somewhere!

3

Her chest felt tight, and she began to have trouble breathing. It had never got this bad this fast before. It had been so long since she'd had an attack that she'd gotten lazy about carrying one with her.

Where was it?

She felt light-headed, and her breathing turned to gasping. She looked across the room at the telephone on her nightstand. She'd call her son, and he would help her, bring his epi-pen, and then call the ambulance only if absolutely necessary. It would be so embarrassing, and on the day of her luncheon, too.

She got as far as the end of the bed when the lights faded and everything went black.

Gigi was having the weirdest dream.

She was a child again, sitting on the front porch of the dilapidated house where she grew up. It was a holler house, as the cruel children at school often reminded her. There was nothing cozy, pretty, or warm about it. It sheltered them from the worst of the weather, although the roof leaked when it rained, and the cold winter wind seeped in around the cracked window frames.

She was sitting on the rickety front porch steps, holding her Raggedy Ann, which her mother had purchased from their church's annual tag sale. She held it tightly and rubbed its worn, mitten-shaped, muslin-covered hand against her upper lip, just like she used to.

She had never had a more vivid dream.

She could feel the hot sun shining on her dirty bare feet. She could smell the manure from the cows that lived at the farm up at the end of the road. There was a wood smoke smell from the still her father had hidden in the corn crib behind their house.

A robin was sitting on the sagging fence, chirping and twitching its tail feathers. There was a light breeze

4

blowing through the green leaves of the twisted apple trees, full of bright green little apples she knew would be sour to taste but made wonderful pies when they could afford the sugar.

The soft, worn cotton of her pinafore felt good against her tanned, freckled skin. Her mother had sewn red rik rak ribbon trim on the top of each pocket, and it had come loose on one side, where it was hanging by a thread.

She had a scrape on her knee, so she picked at the scab a little. Her hair was pulled back in pigtails so tight they pulled at the small hairs on the back of her neck, fell down over her shoulders in dark golden braids.

It didn't feel like a dream. The other life, where she was a grown-up, now felt like a dream.

"Gertie!" she heard her mother call. "Gertrude, where are you?"

It had been years since anyone had used her real name; not even her husband had dared.

Her mama.

Her mama, who had died of pneumonia the winter Gigi was seven, leaving her and her brother at the mercy of her short-tempered, perpetually tired father.

"Gertie, my girl," her mother called again, as she came around the side of the house. "There you are. I've been looking all over for you."

Her mama, still young enough to turn a stranger's head and not yet so careworn that she looked older than her years. Her golden hair was pulled back in a sensible knot at the back of her head, with tendrils escaping to frame her pretty face, her soft brown eyes.

Her mama, dressed in a cotton housedress and apron that were worn when she bought them, at the same tag sale where she'd purchased the doll.

Gigi got up, ran down the steps, leaped into her mother's arms, and breathed in the smells of her, the feel of her, all of which she thought she'd forgotten.

"Oh, my Gertie," her mother said. "I love you so."

"I love you, Mama," Gigi said.

"Come and see the new kittens up at the farm," Mama said. "Papa says you can pick out one to keep."

"Is this a dream?" Gigi asked her, through her tears of happiness.

Her mother laughed, set her down, took her hand, led her up the path to the dirt road, and then on toward the farm at the end of the holler.

CHAPTER TWO

I'm afraid for my son," Gigi O'Hare said.

"I'm sorry," Claire said, as she switched off the blow dryer. "I couldn't hear you; what did you say?"

"I'm worried about Eugene," Gigi said. "Who's going to take care of him when I'm gone?"

Claire hesitated, because what could she say?

Rich widow Gigi O'Hare had called Claire in a panic just an hour before. She had an important luncheon that day, and her regular hairdresser had canceled her appointment.

"Kidney stones," Gigi had said. "Probably from all those supplements she takes; that woman is a walking health food store."

Claire, who recently had taken to sleeping late in the morning, since she was currently unemployed, had reluctantly agreed to come up the hill to the O'Hare's stone mansion on Morning Glory Avenue to do Gigi's hair.

When she arrived, Gigi had been in the dining room with her attorney and his assistant, going over some papers. Gigi had asked Claire to wait in the front parlor. Claire was still admiring the paintings and vases on display in that room when Gigi came to fetch her.

"I'm signing some papers, and I need a witness for my signature," Gigi said. "Would you mind signing as my witness?"

"I don't mind at all," Claire said.

In the dining room, the attorney and his assistant were still seated at the table. The attorney, a gray-haired man with glasses, was impeccably dressed in a three-piece suit and an expensive watch, the kind certain men collect like others collect sports cars. He stood up when Claire entered the room. His assistant was a pale, mousy-looking older woman who spoke so softly Claire could not hear what she said, so she just smiled and nodded.

Gigi introduced the attorney to Claire as Walter Graham and ignored the assistant. Walter introduced the assistant, Claire instantly forgot her name, and everyone shook hands.

"It's a pleasure to meet you," Walter said. "We've heard so much about you."

Claire was a little surprised to hear this, but she smiled to cover her confusion with congeniality, which was a talent she'd developed working in show business.

They asked to copy her IDs, so she fished out her driver's license and social security card, and the assistant ran them through a small portable scanner before returning them.

The assistant pushed a document across the table toward Gigi, who signed on one line, and pointed to another line next to it.

"You sign there, Claire," Gigi said.

"You do understand what you're being asked to do?" the attorney said to Claire.

"Sure," she said. "I don't mind."

Claire signed on the line Gigi indicated, and then the assistant wrote on the document beneath their signatures, signed it, and used a self-inking stamp next to her signature.

This process was repeated two more times, with Claire following Gigi's signature with her own, followed by the assistant notarizing the document beneath their signatures. When they were done, Gigi patted Claire's shoulder.

"Thank you, Claire, you're a godsend," Gigi said. "Go on upstairs to my room, and I'll be there in a minute."

Claire went up to the second floor and opened the door to the sumptuous master suite, which was decorated in tones of ivory and peach. Gigi's two little dogs ran to greet her, and she ruffled their fur. They looked like small white puffs with bright brown eyes and tiny pink tongues.

"You're too cute," she told them.

Gigi had joined her before too long, and shortly afterward offered her son's hand in marriage.

Claire had known Gigi's son, Eugene Junior since she was a little girl, and she was fond of him, much like she was fond of her neighbor's ugly, ancient, three-legged dog, which suffered from seizures and constant flatulence. That is to say, from a safe distance and seen infrequently.

And Eugene was an unfortunate fellow, indeed. He suffered from a severe stammer, a lisp, various odd allergies, and a tendency to throw up and faint when stressed. Any single one of these, alone, would be considered a challenge; put together in one person they seemed like a curse.

In grade school, Claire's male cousins had taken him up as a sort of a pet and protected him from being bullied. She could still recall him trailing along behind them as they got up to their typical mischief, which Eugene would watch with awe while he giggled from behind his hand. Behind his hand because, oh yes, she had forgotten, Eugene's teeth had come in darkened due to a medication his mother had taken while pregnant with him. Nothing could ever be done about them because of his allergy to Novocain.

Claire pitied poor Eugene as well as the mother who raised him.

"What will he do when I'm gone?" Gigi asked Claire.

"Sometimes when people have to do for themselves they can," Claire said, as she wrapped a section of Gigi's fine, apricot-colored hair around a hot curling iron. "Eugene may do just fine."

9

"If he isn't reminded to eat, he won't," Gigi said. "He has to take so many medications, and on such an exact schedule. He has at least one doctor appointment per week, and he can't drive himself because he might have a seizure."

"I'm sorry to hear that."

"What he needs is someone to manage him, someone to take care of him," Gigi said. "He's going to be a very rich man after I pass away ..."

"There are other family members," Claire said.

"There are," Gigi said. "But I've recently discovered something rather unpleasant about them, and I've decided not to put Eugene's fate in their hands. That's why the lawyer was here this morning."

"I'm sorry to hear that," Claire said. "That must worry you."

"If you married Eugene, I know you'd take good care of him. I've never forgotten how kind your family has been to him over the years, and he is so fond of you. If I knew I had you to watch out for him, I could die in peace."

Gigi had made this offer to Claire before. Claire wondered how many other single women in Rose Hill had also been on the receiving end of this pitch. She suspected it was all of them.

"You know I'm seeing Ed," Claire said.

"Ed Harrison is a fine, upstanding young man, but his future earning potential is very limited," Gigi said.

"It's true the newspaper doesn't pay much, but he's also teaching journalism at the college."

"That's a perfectly acceptable vocation, and Eldridge is a fine school, but they don't pay much, either."

"Money isn't everything," Claire said.

Gigi ignored that statement.

"I know there aren't many single men in your age group left in Rose Hill," Gigi said, "but a girl as pretty as you could have her pick, surely."

Claire, who was about to turn forty, didn't mind Gigi calling her a girl, but she did mind the implied criticism of Ed. In the interest of continued friendly relations, she decided to ignore it.

"Maybe Eugene will meet someone he likes," Claire said.

"If he'd ever leave the basement," Gigi said. "Which reminds me … excuse me a minute."

Claire withdrew the curling iron as Gigi stood up. This immediately excited her two small, fluffy dogs, who had to be bribed with treats to return to their napping spot on the bed. Once they were settled again, Gigi went to an old-fashioned-looking intercom attached to the wall next to the door to her bedroom. It squawked and gave some feedback when she pressed a button.

"Eugene!" she barked. "Can you hear me?"

Claire was so startled by the vehemence in the woman's voice that she flinched.

"Eugene," she barked, again. "What are you doing down there? Answer me this minute."

"Yeth, M, M, Mother," eventually came a meek, barely discernable reply.

"Come up to my room," she said. "Claire's here, and she wants to see you. Bring the clean laundry up with you as you come; it will save Gail a trip."

Gigi turned and smiled brightly at Claire.

"He'll be right up, and then you two can chat while I get dressed."

Claire dreaded this at a level right up there with spider removal and dental work, but she smiled in return and said, "That'll be nice."

Gigi reseated herself on the carved mahogany chair placed before a matching vanity and looked at her nails.

"You don't do manicures, do you, Claire?"

"No, sorry," Claire said. "Just hair."

Claire was actually very good at nails and did her own manicures, but she was wary of becoming Gigi's full-time beauty consultant.

"I'll just have to do it myself," Gigi sighed. "When my husband was alive, I never went down to breakfast until I was dressed in my best with perfect hair and nails."

"You must miss him."

"I do miss the social whirl," Gigi said. "What with Eugene Senior being CEO of Pendleton General Hospital, we were out almost every night, to fundraisers, cocktail parties, formal dances, country club functions, and dinners with our gang. Most of them are dead or living in Florida now. A new generation has taken over, and they don't have much use for an old woman like me."

"But you're having lunch with friends today," Claire said. "Who's coming?"

"Marigold Lawson was invited but says she has a previous engagement. I don't blame her, really. Since the scandal, she's not seeing anyone. I feel sorry for her now that she's dropped out of the mayoral race. It's a pity; she could have done some real good in Rose Hill. Someone needs to chase out the riffraff and enforce some standards of appearance for people's properties. I don't think your friend Kay has the spleen to do it. That reminds me ... excuse me a moment, won't you?"

Claire gathered up wet towels and tidied the en suite bathroom while Gigi made a call she couldn't help but overhear. The two little dogs followed Claire around as she tidied, and took turns begging for treats, even though she kept telling them, "Sorry, guys, I don't have anything."

"Chester," Gigi said. "You were supposed to come up here and mow this morning. I've got ladies coming in two hours, and the lawn is a disgrace."

There was a lull before Gigi spoke again.

"I'm not paying you anything," she said. "I've given you enough money this summer. Get up here in fifteen minutes or don't bother asking me for anything ever again."

When Claire came back in the room, trailed by the two little dogs, Gigi's face was flushed. She sat down at her vanity and moved some things around on the top. She picked up a bottle of perfume that Claire knew the cost of and was impressed by. She took the stopper out and rubbed some on her wrists and behind her ears.

"I love that scent," Claire said.

"It was a gift from Chip's wife, Jillian," Gigi said, gesturing at a photo on her vanity.

There were several framed photos of her and her late husband, and a wedding photo of Jillian and Chip, but no photos of Eugene Junior.

"What were we talking about?" Gigi asked as she picked up both dogs and settled them in her lap.

Claire didn't feel like arguing about politics with Gigi, so she focused on teasing and smoothing the hair on the crown of her head, which she then sprayed so heavily it couldn't be moved by a gale force wind.

"You were telling me who is coming to lunch," Claire said.

"Your cousin-in-law, Ava," Gigi said. "You know she's been seeing that man who's buying up all the available properties in Rose Hill; he bought the old Rodefeffer glassworks and is putting a bicycle manufacturing business in there. I can't imagine that's a good business, but it must be. The man's rich as Croesus and everything he touches turns to gold."

"I had heard that," Claire said.

"Is it true he rented every room in Ava's bed and breakfast so no one else could stay there but him?" Gigi asked.

"He has a staff," Claire said. "He did rent the whole place, but there are more people than just him staying there. He's staying there while he builds a house."

"I heard he bought everything on the other side of the Little Bear River, and he's going to build a private bridge at the bottom of Pine Mountain Road."

"I don't know about that," Claire said.

"He's so unusual looking," Gigi said. "One of those long beards all the young people are wearing nowadays, and a handlebar mustache."

"He seems like a nice man," Claire said. "I've only met him briefly."

"Well, Ava certainly landed herself a live one," Gigi said. "His father is a millionaire many times over, quite possibly a billionaire. It's new natural gas money, of course, but it still spends, nevertheless."

"Who else is coming?" Claire asked.

"Gwyneth Eldridge," Gigi said. "She inherited family money, of course, and thousands of acres of property between here and the state park. She's on the Eldridge College Board of Trustees. She'll lower herself to hobnob with the other board members, but the rest of us aren't good enough for her, so I was amazed she agreed to come."

Claire was well-acquainted with the snobby Gwyneth Eldridge, who was still hounding her to set up and manage a spa in the basement of the Eldridge Inn. Gwyneth just couldn't be made to understand that waving her checkbook around like a magic wand didn't immediately cause everyone to leap to do her bidding.

"You know Candace, don't you?" Gigi said. "She and her husband have built the most beautiful home out at Eldridge Point."

"Candy and I went to school together," Claire said.

"It's Candace now, she's quite firm about that. She's the chair of the fundraising committee for the Children's Hospital," Gigi said. "She's after me to underwrite the whole thing so they'll put my husband's name on it."

"That would be nice," Claire said.

14

"Oh, I'll give them something," Gigi said, "but I'm not giving them near as much as that."

"Giving anything is good, I guess," Claire said.

"This lunch is supposed to be celebrating Candace's appointment as chair," Gigi said, "but it's really a way for her to ask me for the money. She needs my expertise, of course; I was chair of the same committee when we built the Cancer Center. Candace wants to cultivate Ava, now, before she marries her millionaire, so she'll be in good after the wedding. Gwyneth will be good for a donation or to host an event in her home. Marigold can't really afford to give anything, and she has no political clout anymore, but we felt sorry for her, so we invited her just to cheer her up."

"Anyone else coming?"

"My nephew's wife, Jillian," Gigi said with barely concealed contempt. "Do you know her?"

"I only know Chip," Claire said. "He was in school with us as well. Back then he was called Chippie."

"Small town, small world," Gigi said. "I'm surprised you haven't met Jillian."

"I can't say that I have."

"Chip is a vice president and the Director of Information Systems at the hospital. My husband paid for his schooling and then created the job for him. He and Jillian are part of the new guard; Candace and Jillian are very close."

"I see," Claire said.

"Jillian's a bit of a social climber," Gigi said. "There's nothing wrong with aspiring to better social standing, of course, but I often have to remind her not to be so blatant about it."

"Is that everyone?" Claire asked.

"Yes," Gigi said. "It's just a small gathering. I'd invite you, Claire, but you'd probably be bored by all the shop talk."

"I have plans," Claire said, "but thank you for thinking of me."

Eugene arrived in the doorway, wheezing and red-faced, holding a large straw basket full of folded peach-colored towels. The two little dogs jumped down and ran to him, then jumped up and down, begging for his attention.

"About time," Gigi said. "Bunny, Chicken, stop that."

"I h, h, h, h, had t, t, t, t, to ..."Eugene said.

"Never mind why," Gigi said. "Just set the basket on the bed."

Eugene flushed at the sight of Claire. He nodded to her, and she smiled at him, which caused him to duck his head in shyness. He set the basket on the bed, pulled an inhaler out of his pocket and used it.

"You've done a wonderful job," Gigi said to Claire, as she admired herself in the mirror.

She opened her purse, took out her wallet, withdrew a twenty-dollar bill as if it were a hundred, and handed it to Claire. They hadn't discussed a price, and although Claire had charged many times that when she worked in Los Angeles, she accepted the bill with grace and gratitude, and decided then and there that she wouldn't do this again.

"Eugene," Gigi said, "I'm having some ladies in for lunch, so I want you to go somewhere and not come back until dinner time. Can you do that?"

He nodded, glanced at Claire, and his face flushed again.

"I'm also having a meeting at eleven," Gigi said, as she looked at her watch. "You have thirty minutes to get yourself out of here, and you're not to return until at least five o'clock. Do you understand me?"

Eugene nodded again.

"Good," she said. "Now, be a good boy and walk Claire to the front door."

He started toward the door as Claire said, "You don't have to do that."

He then stopped, unsure of whom to obey.

"Nonsense," Gigi said. "In this house gentlemen have manners, and Eugene will escort you to the door, shake your hand, and thank you for coming. Even *he* is capable of doing that much."

Eugene seemed to shrink into himself. Claire wanted to put an arm around him, to shield him from the contempt his mother didn't even try to hide and wasn't embarrassed to display in front of someone else.

"C'mon," Claire said to him. "I haven't seen your latest rocks, and I bet you have some beauties."

"Rocks in the basement, rocks in his head," Gigi said. "Thanks, Claire. See you next time."

With a wave of dismissal, Gigi walked toward the en-suite bathroom, her little dogs following along in her wake.

Eugene fairly ran down the stairs, then remembered Claire, and waited for her, albeit without making eye contact. She didn't really want to see the rocks, but she'd felt she wanted to say something kind to him in the face of his mother's blatant disregard for his feelings. She followed him down the steps to the first floor, and then back through a hallway to the stairs that led to the basement.

He looked at his watch, and Claire realized he was worried about the time.

"I'll just take a quick look," Claire said. "We'll get you out of here in time."

The basement was dark, cool, and smelled like dryer sheets. At the bottom of the stairs, Eugene flipped on bright fluorescent lights to reveal row after row of shelves, built from floor to ceiling. There was a label on each shelf with tiny, precise handwriting on them, denoting the contents of the white box on that shelf.

"Onyx, Jasper, Coral, Lapis," were some of the labels she read. "This is amazing."

When Eugene smiled this time, he forgot to hide his teeth.

He took her on a tour. There was a packing and shipping area, with stacks of broken down white boxes of various sizes, tape, labels, a postal scale, and a neat office area with a computer. The labels were printed with "O'Hare Minerals and Gems" and their home address.

"This is a real business," Claire said.

"Ith th, th, th, thertainly thomething," Eugene said.

"It is," Claire said. "It's something great."

Fifteen minutes later, as Claire held the next in a seemingly endless supply of polished rocks, and tried to think of a new way to say 'this is so pretty,' the intercom squawked and Gigi barked, "You better make tracks, young man, if you know what's good for you."

Eugene, who had seemed to expand as he showed Claire his business, and had spoken with very little stuttering the whole time, shrank and trembled.

"I have to go, anyway," Claire said. "Thank you so much for showing me your work. It's quite an accomplishment; you should be proud."

Eugene took something from a box marked "Special one-offs" and offered it to Claire.

"I couldn't ," she said.

"P, p, p, p, p, pleathe," he said.

Claire accepted the polished rock, which was colored teal, green, and indigo, with swirls of white. It reminded her of photos of Earth taken from space.

"It's beautiful, Eugene, thank you."

As Claire left the house, she saw a man in the driveway unloading a lawnmower from the back of a rickety pickup truck. When he saw Claire, he stopped what he was doing and leaned against the bed of the truck. He then raised his ball cap in a greeting and looked her up and down in a speculative manner.

There was a cigarette dangling from one corner of his mouth, his raggedy pants hung low off his flat behind, and his dirty wife-beater shirt was spotted with a buffet of food stains. He took a length of pipe and a can of oil from the bed of the truck and held them up.

"Hey, pretty lady," he said. "How much would you charge to grease my pole?"

Claire, who had worn her tennis shoes, took off at a trot but was running before she got to the bottom of the driveway.

"Can't take a joke, huh?" he called after her. "Snotty bitch."

Hannah Campbell was chasing her three-year-old son, Sammy, around the outside of their three-story farmhouse, when the phone he had stolen from her began to play "Brown-Eyed Girl," which was her work ringtone.

"Sammy, dammit," she said. "Give me that. It's my work calling."

"You hafta gimme a dollar, Hannah," he said as he ran. "You cussing."

He finally stopped long enough to answer the phone and Hannah caught up with him.

"Hi," he said into the phone. "Hannah cussing, so she hafta gimme a dollar."

Hannah snatched the phone away.

"Hannah Campbell, Animal Control," she said. "How can I help you?"

Fifteen minutes later, Hannah arrived at Gigi O'Hare's house, and parked at the bottom of the hill, on the street. Up the hill, several people were standing on Gigi's front steps and walkway. The driveway was full of expensive cars and SUVs parked in a line behind a catering truck.

Hannah's cousin-in-law, Ava, who had called her, walked down the driveway as Hannah got out of her animal control truck.

"Thank goodness," she said. "We can't catch Gigi's dogs, and we're afraid they'll run into the road and be killed."

There were two tiny white dogs running in circles on the front lawn, with two women in dresses and heels trying in vain to catch them. The dogs were obviously having a great time; the women, not so much.

"No one seems to be at home, although we have a luncheon scheduled," Ava said.

Hannah took a plastic baggie out of her waist pack and pulled a raw hot dog out of it. She put two fingers of one hand in her mouth and whistled, which got the dogs' attention. She then tore off a couple of tiny pieces of the hot dog and tossed them toward the dogs.

"Bunny! Chicken! Come and get your treats," she called out in a high-pitched voice.

The two little dogs made a beeline for Hannah, and two minutes later she was walking up the steps holding them.

"Hi, Gwyneth," Hannah said. "Hi, Candy."

She knew Candace and Gwyneth, and she recognized Jillian, whom she knew by sight but hadn't formally met.

"Thank goodness you caught them," Jillian said. "I'm Jillian McClanahan, Mrs. O'Hare's niece. We're so worried about her. We were supposed to have lunch at noon, but when we arrived, the dogs were outside, and no one's answering the doorbell. I've called and called, but no one answers. I'm so afraid she's fallen and broken a hip or something."

Members of the catering staff were standing around on the sidewalk, holding boxes of food and equipment. Hannah handed one dog to Ava and the other to a very put-out Gwyneth Eldridge.

"You have got to be kidding," Gwyneth said, as she held the small, squirming dog at arm's length. "This is silk."

Hannah tried the door, which was locked. She then pulled up the doormat to reveal a key. She handed the key to Jillian, who used it to open the door.

"Aunt Gigi," Jillian called out.

There was no response.

"What should we do now?" Jillian asked Hannah.

Hannah took the small dogs the women were holding and set them on the floor.

"Follow them," she said.

The little dogs took off up the stairs, and Jillian turned to the other women.

"Maybe I better go up first, in case Aunt Gigi's not dressed."

"Knock yourself out," Hannah said. "I'll wait to make sure she's all right and then I'll be on my way."

The caterers passed through the waiting throng and headed back toward the kitchen. No one stopped them or suggested they wait. The remaining women tapped their feet, looked at their watches, and checked their phones for messages.

Jillian screamed.

Hannah bounded up the steps and followed the sound to a large bedroom. There, on the floor, was Gigi O'Hare. Her glazed eyes stared at the ceiling, and her mouth hung open. Her face was blue, her lips and eyes were swollen, and there were red, raised welts on the backs of her hands. Even though there was no doubt in Hannah's mind that she was dead, she checked for a pulse on the underside of her wrist, which was just starting to feel cool.

The little dogs were nosing around Gigi's body, whimpering.

"I'm so sorry," Hannah said to Jillian, who was hyperventilating.

Ava arrived next and put a consoling arm around Jillian.

One by one, the other ladies appeared in the doorway and gasped at the scene. The little dogs curled up next to Gigi's body and tucked their noses down between their paws.

"Don't come in," Hannah warned the women. "This is a crime scene."

"It looks like an allergic reaction," Ava said.

"May God rest her soul," Candace said.

"Shouldn't someone call an ambulance?" Gwyneth asked in an exasperated tone.

Hannah took out her phone and tapped the shortcut for 911.

"There's been a murder," Hannah said into the phone, and then gave the address.

"Why would you say she was murdered?" Jillian asked when she completed the call.

She was making a big show of being upset, but Hannah noticed her eyes were dry.

"Because of the dogs," Hannah said. "Gigi loved these dogs; she would never leave them outside unattended, and they would never leave her side. Someone else accidentally let them out when they left or put them out on purpose."

"Eugene," Jillian said.

"Don't be silly," Hannah said. "Eugene wouldn't hurt a fly."

"I'm not so sure," Jillian said, and then turned a meaningful look toward the women in the hallway.

"Everybody should go downstairs and wait in one room until the police get here," Hannah said. "I'll guard the crime scene."

Ava led a protesting Jillian out of the room, and all the ladies went downstairs. Hannah could hear Gwyneth complaining as she went.

"I don't see why we all have to stay here. We're not witnesses to anything. I'm going home. The police can call me if they want to ask me anything."

Hannah made a quick survey of the area. There was a basket on the bed, filled to the brim with folded towels. Gigi's ivory silk robe was draped across the foot of the bed, and there were damp towels draped over a towel bar in the bathroom. All the drawers in the bathroom vanity were pulled open as if someone had gone through them. In the huge walk-in closet, all Gigi's handbags were on the floor in a pile, as if someone had gone through them, as well.

It looked as if Gigi might have surprised a burglar, but what had caused the allergic reaction?

Back in the bedroom, she looked at Gigi's body. She was dressed in a pale blue linen suit jacket and skirt, with a white silk blouse tied at the neck. Around her neck hung a double rope of pearls, and she wore pearl earrings to match. She was wearing stockings, like the older ladies still did, but her shoes were sitting neatly paired by the seat to her vanity as if she had taken them off there or set them there to put on before she left the room.

Looking closely, Hannah could see more red welts on Gigi's lower legs.

There were tubes and cases of make-up out on the vanity top. Hannah looked at Gigi's face, which, although swollen, was neatly made up. Her lipstick was on, but the lower lip was missing a crescent of pink. Hannah looked for a cup that would have the missing pink crescent on it. She found a fine china saucer, painted in a delicate floral pattern, on the floor by the vanity, but no matching cup.

23

"Aha," she said. "Where is that cup?"

She crawled around on the floor, flipped the bed skirt up, and stuck her head under there, using the flashlight setting on her cell phone to look around. When the little dogs started yapping furiously, Hannah backed out from under the bed skirt.

"Find anything interesting?"

Rose Hill Chief of Police Scott Gordon was standing in the doorway.

Hannah got up and explained what she was looking for and why. Scott bent down to look at Gigi's face, checked her pulse just as Hannah had, and then looked back up at Hannah.

"Sarah's on her way," he said. "Go downstairs and keep an eye on all the suspects."

"They were all locked out of the house together when I got here," Hannah said. "I could start the questioning for you. Jillian was the only one alone with the body; I'll start with her."

"Just please go downstairs and at least act like I have some sort of control over this crime scene," Scott said. "Leave the questioning to Sarah."

"Yes, sir," Hannah said, as she clicked her heels together and saluted.

As she pivoted on her heel to go, Scott said, "Good detective work, Hannah. I think you're right about the lipstick and the cup."

"Thanks, man," Hannah said. "I left Sammy at the library with Dottie; I'll just call her and tell her it'll be a little while."

"Could you take these dogs with you?"

Hannah scooped them up and put one under each arm.

"Poor little orphans," she said. "Come along with Auntie Hannah to the kitchen, and we'll find some expensive appetizers to feed you and me."

Downstairs, Jillian and Candace were in the dining room, whispering, while the caterers set up for lunch. Ava was sitting on a bench in the foyer, watching with polite interest but barely concealed boredom.

"Someone needs to find Eugene and tell him," Hannah said.

"Not me," Jillian said. "He might have killed her."

"I didn't know he was violent," Candace said. "Here I thought he was just this pathetic, timid little man."

"He has these seizures," Jillian said. "He has rage attacks afterward. Aunt Gigi was very worried about them."

"Had they been to a doctor?" Candace asked.

Jillian shrugged.

"I just know what she told me," Jillian said. "She was becoming frightened of him."

"That's bullcrap," Hannah said. "Eugene wouldn't hurt anybody."

Jillian looked down her nose at Hannah's wrinkled shorts, tanned, unshaved legs, fallen wool socks, and work boots.

"I hardly think you'd be in a position to know my family better than I would," she said.

"I've known Eugene for thirty-five years," Hannah said, "How long have you known him?"

Jillian rolled her eyes, smirked at Candace, and ignored the question.

"Since you're such a close family member, I guess you won't mind taking the dogs," Hannah said. "I'll put them in a travel crate for you."

"No, I'm sorry," Jillian said. "We have two large dogs at home that can't be trusted around small dogs."

"I'll get the crate," Hannah said. "We can figure out some arrangements later."

25

Hannah handed off the dogs to Ava and Candace and went down the hill to her truck to get a crate. She called her cousin, Maggie, as she walked.

"Hey, Watson," she said when Maggie answered. "The game is afoot."

She began to explain what had happened, but Maggie interrupted her as soon as she told her Gigi was dead.

"Eugene is here, in my store," Maggie said. "He's been here since before lunchtime. What should I do?"

"Do you know the exact time he got there?" Hannah asked. "You might be his alibi."

"I think a little after eleven," Maggie said. "Kirsten starts her shift at eleven, and she was working."

Hannah ended the call with Maggie and then called Scott to report Eugene's location. He said he would have Deputy Skip or Frank go round him up.

A siren could now be heard in the distance.

"Constable Cat Litter has arrived," Hannah told him.

"Try not to make her mad," he said.

"Like that's possible," Hannah said.

A county car followed an ambulance up Morning Glory Avenue and parked behind it in the middle of the street. The ambulance crew took a gurney up the driveway while Sarah Albright got out of the county car, approached Hannah, and stuck out her hand

"Ms. Campbell," Sarah said, "I understand you're running for city council."

Hannah shook the proffered hand and smiled at the woman for whom she and her cousin Maggie took delight in making up names. Maggie was married to Scott, but that didn't stop Sarah from trying to get in his pants every chance she got.

"Oh, I've got that seat locked up," Hannah said. "The election is a mere formality."

"I'm sure," Sarah said. "Why are you here?"

Hannah explained what had happened, but did not mention her detecting activities at the scene of the crime. She showed Sarah the crate.

"I'm going to take the pups home with me until we can figure out what to do with them."

"That's kind of you," Sarah said. "I'll call you later if I have any more questions."

"Hey, Sarah," Hannah said, as they walked up the driveway. "You're gonna hear Jillian in there bad-mouthing Gigi's son, Eugene, but he's really a harmless little guy. Take it easy on him; he's got a lot of health problems, and he scares easily."

"I'll keep that in mind," Sarah said.

The city's police cruiser pulled up behind the county car, and Eugene was out of it and running before Deputy Skip could get completely stopped. Hannah later thought that as long as she lived, she would never forget the terrified look on Eugene's pale face. As he pushed past them, Sarah put her hand on her gun and shouted, "Stop!"

Hannah didn't know what possessed her, but she put her hand over Sarah's on her gun.

"That's his mother in there," Hannah said. "She was the only person he had in the world. Let him go to her."

"Understood," Sarah said. "But if you ever put your hand on my gun like that again I will shoot you."

"Understood," Hannah said, withdrawing her hand.

"It was awful," Hannah was telling Maggie and Claire, later.

Maggie was sitting at Hannah's kitchen table, drinking a root beer and eating chips and salsa. Claire was drinking water with lemon and refusing to even look at the chips. Hannah was at the stove, preparing chicken enchiladas for dinner.

Gigi's little white dogs were in the sunroom, fighting over a large rawhide bone that belonged to Hannah's big dogs. Sammy was sitting on the kitchen floor, building a death ray out of snap blocks.

"As a punishment, I took away his toy weapons, so he builds his own," Hannah told them.

"Pew pew," Sammy said, as he aimed it at Claire. "Me kilt you dead."

"That's too bad," Claire said, "cause I was going to let you play games on my tablet."

"Pew pew," he said, as he aimed at her again. "Now you no dead."

"Thanks," she said and reached for her handbag. "You can play the games we already have on it, but don't buy anymore without asking me."

"Them's a deal," he said.

"You know he's gonna buy more games," Hannah said.

"The last time he spent thirty bucks, so I put a password on it," Claire said.

"How is Eugene now?" Maggie asked. "I thought he was gonna faint when Skip came to get him."

"He knows Skip so that probably helped," Claire said. "Better than if some County Mountie he didn't know came for him."

"The sound he made," Hannah said with a shudder. "It was like a wounded animal howling."

"Poor Eugene," Claire said. "If you had heard how Gigi talked to him."

Claire told them about her morning spent with Gigi and her son.

"It couldn't be easy being Eugene's mother," Hannah said. "You should hear how I talk to Sammy sometimes."

"Hannah always says cussing," Sammy said. "Now she hafta gimme a million dollars."

"I'll put it in your piggy bank tomorrow," Hannah said. "I don't have any cash right now."

"Nuh uh," Sammy said. "You hafta gimme a dollar for my box on this day."

Claire took a ten-dollar bill out of her wallet and handed it to Sammy.

"Put this in your box, Sammy," Claire said. "We'll probably all do some more cussing before the evening is over."

Sammy ran off to get the tin box he kept all his treasures in.

"Poor Eugene," Claire said. "What will happen to him now?"

"Once Sarah's done questioning him he'll probably hang," Hannah said.

"When are they doing that?"

"When they carried Gigi's body out, he got so upset he vomited, passed out, and hit his head on the stairs," Hannah said. "They're keeping him at the hospital overnight for observation. Scott's going to pick him up tomorrow and bring him to the Rose Hill station for questioning. He convinced Sarah that would be better than a place he doesn't know."

"What time do you think?" Maggie asked.

"Ten, I think they said," Hannah said. "Why, what are you going to do?"

"Stand on the back of the couch in Scott's office and press your ear against the heat vent?" Claire asked.

"Yep," Maggie said.

"What can I do to help?" Claire asked.

"Snoop," Hannah said. "Find out what the story is on that Jillian. I didn't like her, not one little bit. You should've heard her talking trash about Eugene when his mother's body wasn't even cold."

"What's Scott say?" Claire asked.

29

"They don't know how she died," Maggie said. "The medical examiner will have to say."

"I think she was poisoned," Hannah said and told them about the swollen face and red welts on her body. "Did he tell you about the missing cup?"

"No," Maggie said.

Hannah told them about the lipstick and the saucer on the floor.

"We need to get back in there and look at her china," Maggie said. "If there's not an even number of cups and saucers, we'll know why."

"You think the murderer poisoned her and then took the cup with him?" Claire asked.

"I think Jillian took it," Hannah said. "Gail Godwin cleans that house, so you know it's immaculate. Why else would there be a lone saucer underneath her vanity?"

"We should call Gail," Maggie said. "She can count the cups for us."

"If it's a crime scene, they won't let her in," Hannah said.

"She's sleeping now," Maggie said, as she looked at the clock on the wall in the kitchen.

"I'll catch her when she cleans the bank tonight," Hannah said.

"I'll do it," Maggie said. "You've got Sammy to look after."

"Where's Sam?" Claire asked, about Hannah's husband.

"He's down at the community center, same as always," Hannah said, and Maggie gave Claire a "drop it" look.

"Who is Gigi's next of kin?" Claire asked.

"She's got a slimy brother named Chester McClanahan who lives just down the holler from us," Hannah said. "His nickname is Cheat."

"People call him 'Cheat' because that's what he does to the out-of-town property owners who hire him to manage their rental properties," Maggie said.

"He calls himself a property manager," Hannah said. "As soon as he gets the keys to a place he strips it of every valuable thing, takes it all to Pendleton Pawn, and then reports a break-in to the owners. They collect the insurance payout and Cheat half-asses the repairs."

"You hafta gimme a dollar," Sammy said.

"Make a mark on this paper for every cuss word you hear," Claire told him, as she handed him a notepad and pen. "When you get to ten, let me know."

"I heard Gigi talking to her brother on the phone," Claire said.

She recounted the conversation as best as she could.

"I think I met him in the driveway as I left," Claire said, then covered Sammy's ears and told them what he'd said.

"Ew," Hannah said.

"Me mark a cuss on you," Sammy said after Claire removed her hands from his ears.

"They don't count if you can't hear them," Claire said. "And I didn't cuss."

"You think after you left, maybe Cheat K.I.L.L.E.D. his sister?" Hannah said.

"Hannah's talking 'bout candy?" Sammy asked Claire. "Me never gets candy."

"She said she had a meeting with someone before the lunch," Claire said. "She wanted to be sure Eugene was gone by eleven."

"Was he?" Hannah asked.

"I left at ten till eleven," Claire said. "I don't know how soon Eugene left after I did. He was worried about leaving on time, though. He kept looking at his watch."

"I'm pretty sure he was at the café just after Kirsten started her shift at eleven, and Kirsten is never late."

"I'm willing to help, but I'm not willing to go near that slimeball, Cheat," Claire said.

"I can handle Cheat," Hannah said. "You get the dirt on Jillian."

"Is 'sign ball' a cuss?" Sammy asked Claire.

"No, honey," Claire said. "But don't worry, the night is young."

Scott and Ed showed up in time for dinner.

Ed kissed Claire hello.

"Ew, kissing," Sammy said. "Go to you's room."

"No, Sammy," Hannah said. "It's 'get a room,' not 'go to your room.' You try to teach a kid basic manners ..."

Scott sat down with a sigh and thanked Hannah for the beer she placed in front of him.

"Tough day?" Maggie asked him.

"Eugene went berserk at the hospital," he said. "They've placed him on a 72-hour psychiatric hold."

"Oh no," Claire said. "That's terrible. He must be so scared."

"He's in a secure psychiatric ward," Ed said. "I tried to see him, but they wouldn't let me in. I know one of the nurses, and she said they're going to keep him restrained until they're sure he doesn't have a concussion. Then they can give him a sedative to calm him down."

"That's not going to help his case," Claire said, and Scott shook his head.

"Sarah thinks he did it, doesn't she?" Hannah said.

"Afraid so," Scott said.

"That Jillian," Hannah said. "I'd like to put her through what he's been through and see how she likes it."

"When will you have the medical examiner's report?" Maggie asked Scott.

"Within 24 to 48 hours if it's natural causes," Scott said. "If it's more complicated than that, it could be weeks or months."

"So, they can't have the funeral right away."

"If the coroner determines it's a possible homicide," Scott said, "they hold the body an additional 24 hours, and extract what tissues and fluids they need to do further testing. Worst case scenario, they'll release the body to Machalvie's Funeral Home in three days."

"Do you think Eugene will be well enough to attend the funeral?"

"I'm not sure Eugene will ever recover from this," Scott said. "I've never seen anyone have a total nervous breakdown; it was scary."

"Psychotic break, they called it," Ed said.

"It's just too much for him to process," Claire said. "He's been sheltered his whole life. Everything's regimented for him. He needs to be back at home where everything's familiar, where he can get back on schedule. With time, I'm sure he can come out of it."

"But who's going to advocate for him?" Ed said.

"Not Jillian, that's for sure," Hannah said.

"I will," Claire said.

"That's nice of you to offer," Ed said. "But only his next of kin will have the opportunity to petition for a conservatorship. If they get a judge to grant them medical and financial control over his affairs, no one else can do anything."

"Gigi said she'd found out something disturbing about those people," Claire said. "She had a lawyer there at the house when I got there. I think she changed her will."

"What do you know about Chippie?" Maggie asked Ed.

"We called him Chippie," Ed said. "But his real name is Chester McClanahan, Junior."

"He's Cheat's son, then," Claire said.

Ed nodded.

"After his mother died, Gigi basically took him to raise, paid for his college tuition, convinced her husband to hire him on at the hospital," Ed said. "They treated him like a son."

"Probably more so than Eugene," Claire said.

"He goes by 'Chip' now," Ed said.

"The better to fit into high society," Hannah said.

"What passes for high society in this county would be laughable anywhere else," Maggie said.

"It's a small pond," Ed said. "At one time, Eugene Senior and Gigi were among the biggest fish."

"She had photos of Chip and Jillian on her vanity table," Claire said, "but not one of Eugene."

"Jillian's a committee junkie," Maggie said. "She's got her fingers in every nonprofit pie in the county. She's always trying to put donation cans on my counters or get me to sponsor something."

"Hah!" Hannah said. "Maggie's so tight she makes Scrooge look good."

Maggie threw a chip at Hannah, which she caught and ate.

"Their son goes to Pineville County Consolidated," Ed said. "He's the same age as Tommy and Charlotte."

Tommy was Ed's adopted son, and Charlotte was Ava's daughter; both were sixteen.

"Talk to Ava, ask her what Charlotte says about him," Hannah said to Claire.

"There can be no more investigating," Scott said. "You need to let me handle it."

"Yeah, like that's gonna happen," Hannah said.

Scott sighed and looked at Ed, who grinned.

"It's pointless to boss us around," Claire said.

"He knows," Maggie said.

"Just please don't break any laws," Scott said. "I can only protect you as long as you don't do anything illegal."

34

"We'll tell you everything we find out," Hannah said. "You need us to help figure this out."

"It's Sarah's case," he said. "I'm just the local errand boy."

"Constable Cougar doesn't care unless it gets her name in the paper," Hannah said. "If we don't look into it nothing will happen."

"Please be careful," Scott said. "If someone murdered her, you could be next on the list just for being nosy."

"We'll be careful," Maggie said.

"Thanks for backing me up," Scott said to Ed.

"I'm planning to pick my battles very carefully," Ed said, with an affectionate look at Claire. "This is not going to be one of them."

Claire leaned over and kissed Ed.

"Get a room!" Sammy said.

"That's my boy!" Hannah said. "You all really need to cut that crap out. It's demoralizing for us old married people."

"Me marking you," Sammy said.

"What are we up to?" Maggie asked him.

"Eleventy-four," Sammy said.

CHAPTER THREE

Claire woke up tangled in the sheets, sweating, her heart pounding. It took her a few moments to figure out where she was. In the dream she'd been having, she was in the house Scott owned, up on Sunflower Street, fooling around in bed with Laurie Purcell. It had been so real, so intense, and so, well, enjoyable that she awoke disoriented and confused. Her first inclination was to go back to sleep, with the hope that they could take up where they left off.

She heard the front door close, and it broke the spell. There was no escaping the fact that she was in her childhood bedroom in her parents' house, and Laurie had died three weeks previously. With that realization, her emotions zoomed downward, and the tears came. She covered her face with her pillow and cried until it was over, and then the numbness of the new day settled in its place.

"Claire," her mother said softly at the door. "Are you awake, sweetie?"

"Just getting up," Claire said. "I'll be out in a minute."

"I'm going to the IGA to buy groceries," her mother said. "Your dad's at the station."

"The station" meant her Uncle Curtis's gas station, where her father spent most of his mornings. He had vascular dementia, and could not be left alone for even a minute, lest he wander off or set the house on fire. He had attempted both in the past week.

Claire had been back in Rose Hill since spring, having quit her job working for a famous actress. Her career may have only amounted to twenty years of catering to an abusive boss, but it included high wages and fabulous first-class travel. She had every intention of making her trip home a short visit, but events had conspired to keep her here, and here it seemed she was doomed to stay.

Claire dragged herself out of bed and checked her phone. It was noon, and she had twenty-four text messages. They were all from her cousins, Maggie and Hannah, whom she loved, but not enough to participate in their ongoing text conversation, augmented by phone calls, which they started at the break of dawn and concluded some days after midnight.

It was exhausting, for one thing. Maggie was perpetually irritated by everything and everybody. Hannah was hilarious, but her constant refusal to take anything seriously could also be annoying. Those two had had twenty years to build their relationship as adult friends, and Claire was still trying to catch up.

Claire avoided the mirror as she left the bedroom and made her way to the bathroom. After a shower and some serious makeup and hair maneuvers, only then would she allow her thirty-nine-year-old face to be seen in public.

Which would be forty, come Saturday. Ugh. Forty and living at home with her parents was more than anyone should have to bear.

The doorbell rang as she came out of the bathroom, and it was Ed Harrison.

Ed was the closest thing Claire had to a boyfriend, but that term seemed too lighthearted and juvenile to describe what he was to her. He was her best friend, first and foremost. He knew her better than anyone; her checkered past, her conflicted feelings about being back in Rose Hill, and her current paralysis when faced with what to do with the rest of her life. Ed saw her for who she really was, and he loved her with all his sweet, loyal, honorable heart.

He was also her lover, a few times per week when they could find the time and a place where her parents and his son, Tommy, were unlikely to show up. Claire refused to do it in a car, like a teenager, so Ed's office after hours had become their unofficial love shack.

A couple weeks earlier, Ed had started a new job with the local private college, Eldridge, as their journalism teacher.

"I'm their whole journalism department, actually," he had told Claire. "It's a dying liberal art these days."

He was enjoying the challenge of introducing students to the newspaper business, via the *Rose Hill Sentinel*, of which he was owner and editor. As part of the deal he had with the college, the students were learning the day-to-day functions of creating and managing a small town weekly paper, with Ed as their teacher, mentor, and editor-in-chief. They, in turn, were showing Ed ways in which he could utilize social media to communicate with a broader, younger audience.

Ed seemed so happy and excited about this new adventure that Claire sometimes had a hard time being around him. It only exacerbated her rootless feeling of not having anything to do, or anywhere to be every day. Three days per week she did volunteer at the hospice in nearby Pendleton, but that was just a way to keep busy and take a break from her self-pity, guilt, and grief.

"Good morning," he said, as he came in.

He wrapped his arms around her. He felt warm from having been out in the sunshine. He had grown a beard and mustache over the past few weeks, and it was coming in reddish. He rubbed his beard against her neck, and she pushed him away.

"That beard's getting full," she said. "You look like the mandolin player in a folk rock band."

"I'm considering a handle-bar mustache," he said, as he looked in the entryway mirror and twirled the ends of his mustache. "What do you think?"

"I think your students will love it," she said.

"I have forty-five minutes left for lunch," he said. "We can grab a bite to eat or fool around, but not both, so make your decision and make it snappy. I'm hungry and horny, but I can't be late."

Claire flashed back to her dream of the morning, and piano music began to play in her head. It was "The Very Thought of You."

"I can't," Claire said before she'd thought of a reason why she couldn't.

"Too bad, your loss," Ed said. "I'm going to run up to the diner and get something to go. I'll see you tonight, then?"

"Sure," she said, feeling guilty about lying. "I'll come by the office."

He kissed her quickly and sailed out the door and down the sidewalk, whistling.

'I could never abide a whistler,' Laurie said in her head.

He'd taken up residence in there since his funeral, and Claire couldn't decide if she was crazy or haunted.

'Not now,' she said to him in her thoughts.

'That beard is ridiculous,' he said. 'He'll have an owl tattoo and a porkpie hat by the end of the semester.'

'He's happy,' she said. 'Leave him be.'

"It's perfect for him,' Laurie said. 'Teaching an antiquated profession to spoiled, rich hipsters. They'll have the printing press back to work before you know it. They can make the paper, too, out of their canceled trust fund checks.'

'At least he has a job.'

40

'You don't have to work, you know,' he said. 'If you'd quit buying enormous handbags and insanely elevated footwear you could live off your dividends.'

'I'll thank you to stay out of my financial affairs,' Claire said.

'Can't be helped,' he said. 'Your consciousness is like a house full of thin-walled, drafty rooms, and your money worries are like wallpaper.'

'I don't know what to do,' she said. 'I'm stuck.'

'Just enjoy being alive on Earth, why don't you?' he said. 'Go outside and lie down in the green grass, look up at the blue sky, feel the sunshine on your face and the wind in your hair, take a swim in the river. You're living like a dead person, Claire Rebecca Fitzpatrick; you might as well be here.'

'Shut up,' Claire said.

The piano music started again. This time it was, "Cast Your Fate to the Wind," by Vince Guaraldi.

As Claire got dressed, her phone rang.

"We're going down to the pond," Hannah said. "Sam's got Sammy, so we're putting the tubes in the water and the beers on ice."

"I just did my hair and make-up," Claire said.

"Criminy, you're prissy," Hannah said. "Here, Maggie wants to talk."

"Get your ass out this holler and play with us," Maggie said. "We have maybe two days per summer when we can do this, and I know for a fact you don't have anything else to do today."

"The water's too cold," Claire said.

"Wah, wah, wah," Maggie said.

She could hear Hannah saying, "Give me the phone."

"Listen," Hannah said. "I'll give you a dollar."

"We shouldn't have to pay her to have fun," Maggie said in the background.

41

"I'm going to start smoking again, I can just feel it," Hannah said. "If you don't come out here and stop me, I'm going to take up smoking again, and it will be all your fault."

"I don't have an appropriate bathing suit," Claire said.

"Where were you raised, Paris, France?" Hannah asked her. "Put on some tennis shoes, shorts, and a T-shirt. This isn't the Fountainhead in Miami, Florida."

"The Fontainebleau," Claire said.

"Whatever," Hannah said. "Come on, Claire. I've got cigarettes hidden in lots of places, and I'm starting to remember where."

Claire had a sudden inspiration.

"I'm going to go see Eugene in the hospital," Claire said.

Silence.

"What'd she say?" she heard Maggie ask.

"She's going to go see Eugene," Hannah said.

"I'm worried about him," Claire said. "I think one of us should go, and since I don't have anything to do it might as well be me."

"All right," Hannah said. "Permission granted. Hey, Maggie and I have some things we want to send with you for him; we'll leave them on the kitchen table."

"Okay," Claire said. "I'll catch up with you guys later."

Per the directions of a cheerful gray-haired volunteer at the information desk, Claire followed the yellow stripe painted on the gray linoleum floor as it wound through the labyrinthian hallways of Pendleton General Hospital, to where it ended as an arrow at a nurse's station. There, an irritated-looking woman in green scrubs with a stethoscope draped around her neck glanced at Claire, frowned, and then summoned up a semblance of a smile.

"Can I help you?" she asked.

"I'm here to see Eugene O'Hare."

"Are you family?"

"I am," Claire said.

"Just a moment," the woman said.

She typed something on a keyboard and studied a flat screen monitor. A brief look of concern flashed over her face before she covered it with a bland, give-away-nothing expression.

"I need to call somebody; do you mind to wait?"

"Not at all," Claire said, as she set her gift bag, which contained some comic books picked out by Hannah, a new Tolkien bio provided by Maggie, and a purloined bag of Claire's father's favorite butterscotch candy, on the counter.

"Someone is here to see Mr. O'Hare," the woman said into the phone. "Says she's family."

She listened for a brief time and then hung up, saying to Claire, "The doctor will be right with you."

A few minutes later, a short man in a white lab coat approached Claire. He was dark-eyed, with a friendly, elf-like quality about his features. Claire half-expected to see pointed ears sticking out from beneath his dark, curling hair.

"I understand you're here to see Eugene?"

"Yes," Claire said. "I'm so worried about him. I'm afraid no one will understand what he's been through and why he's acting like he is."

"I'm Dr. Schweitzer," he said and held out his hand.

"Claire Fitzpatrick," she said as she shook it. "For real, that's your name?"

He laughed and showed her his I.D.

"At least my parents had the good grace not to name me Albert," he said. "Are you related to Eugene?"

"Not really, not by blood," Claire said. "But I've known him my whole life, I was a good friend of his mother's, and he's very dear to my family."

"I can't talk to you about Eugene's medical condition, but I would like to hear what you have to say. Would you mind coming to my office?"

Claire followed him through more maze-like hallways until they reached a tiny office in a corner intersected by two hallways. There was barely room for the desk and two chairs, but there was a wrap-around window with a beautiful view of the neighboring mountains.

"You see why I put up with this small space," he said, gesturing to the view.

On one wall, from floor to ceiling, shelves were filled with books and stacks of papers, and his desk was covered in medical file folders. Multiple coats and a messenger bag hung on the back of the door. A bicycle was parked in the minuscule bathroom, its front wheel sticking out through the doorway.

Claire handed him the bag of gifts, and he gestured as if to ask if he could look.

"Of course," Claire said.

He took out the comic books, the Tolkien bio, and the candy.

"This is interesting," he said. "I've learned a little bit more about Eugene just from these thoughtful gifts."

"How is he?"

"I have to be very careful not to violate HIPPA laws," Dr. Schweitzer said, "but I can say I'm concerned about him. Please tell me anything you think might help me understand him a little better."

Claire took a deep breath and let it out.

"Do you have time for this?" she asked.

"I'm making the time," he said. "His psychiatric hold will expire the day after tomorrow, and I'll need to make a decision."

Claire started with her earliest recollection of Eugene on the first day of kindergarten, when he clung to his mother and then wept inconsolably when the teacher finally pried him out of her arms.

Hannah had made friends with him first, mostly because she was curious about this sobbing, prostrate creature, but soon she adopted him as her own, just like all the stray animals she collected.

"Hannah has always had a soft spot for lost causes, both two-legged and four-legged," Claire said. "After we started elementary school, Hannah and Maggie's brothers took to him as well, and no one was allowed to bully him when any of us were around."

Claire told him as much as she could remember about Eugene throughout their school years, when he suffered from so many strange allergies and ailments, and spent many days at home sick. Permanently excused from gym class due to his asthma, Eugene spent that time in the library, which was where you could most often find him.

"When he was out for an extended time, one of us would take his homework to his house, and if he was well enough, we could visit with him for a bit."

Gigi was so grateful to any child willing to be friends with Eugene that she would shower them with candy and sodas when they visited the house and gave each of them a gift on their birthdays and Christmas.

Eventually, however, as they all grew up and became self-centered teenagers, Eugene was mostly forgotten.

"Still, no one dared pick on him," Claire said. "But he got left behind a lot, and I'm sure that hurt. He never acted bitter or resentful about it; he just seemed grateful for any attention he received."

"I moved away soon after high school," Claire continued. "I don't think I saw him more than a handful of times over the years. I moved back this past spring, and now I see him at least once a week. Hannah is really the closest to him. They like the same comics and video games."

"Do you know what happened the day his mother died?"

"I was up there, actually, that morning," Claire said. "He was fine then."

She told him what had happened while she was there.

"His mother was very domineering, the way you tell it," he said.

"She was," Claire said. "Although it couldn't have been easy to live with Eugene. She was disappointed in him, but she wasn't in any way afraid of him; I want to be clear about that. She was worried about him, but definitely not afraid of him."

"What about later that day, after her body was found?"

"Hannah was there when they found her," Claire said. "She saw him fall apart when he came home and found out what had happened."

"I'd like to talk to Hannah," he said. "Do you think she would call or come in?"

"I'll ask her," Claire said. "I know she's worried about him."

"I appreciate you coming in," he said, as he stood up. "I'd like to speak with Hannah as soon as possible. No one in his family has been to see him or called."

"His cousin, Chippie, works here," Claire said. "I guess he's called Chip now. I heard his wife, Jillian, has been saying awful things about Eugene, so she probably won't visit. Chip's father is a slimeball who shouldn't be allowed anywhere near him."

"He's closely monitored," the doctor said. "No one gets in to see him without my approval."

"I'm glad to hear that," Claire said. "Now that his mother has passed, Eugene is a rich man, and I'd hate to see him get taken advantage of."

The doctor raised an eyebrow but did not comment.

"One more thing," Claire said.

"What's that?"

"Could you give me a map or something? I don't think I can find my way out."

"I don't want to go down there," Hannah said when Claire called her from the hospital parking lot. "I hate, hate, hate hospitals."

"But you want to help Eugene, don't you?" Claire said. "They're going to decide what happens to him when the 72 hours is up, and we need to convince them he's not a danger to anyone."

"Ugh, the smell of that place," Hannah said. "It reminds me of having Sammy. The food is horrible, and you know I'm not picky. Plus, Sam just dropped off Sammy, and there's no one to watch him."

"I'll watch him."

"Hah!" Hannah said. "It isn't like babysitting, you know. You can't take your eyes off of him for even a second."

"I can handle it."

"Famous last words," Hannah said.

Silence.

"Please," Claire said. "He's in real danger."

More silence.

"He's our friend," Claire said. "We're all he has now."

Silence.

"Hannah," Claire said. "Remember kindergarten? Remember what the first day was like for Eugene? What just happened to him is like that times ten billion."

47

"Oh, all right," Hannah said. "Meet me at Megamart, and bring your cash money. Sammy needs some new swimmies, but do not under any circumstances give him sugar. I don't care if he's climbed the highest rack they've got in the warehouse and is threatening to jump."

"You're exaggerating."

"You'll see," Hannah said. "They have a code at Megamart for when we're spotted in the store; you'll hear it announced. It's CODE SAMMY, and it means all hands on deck."

Later that afternoon, a red-faced Claire, surrounded by stern-looking security personnel, lifted a soaking wet Sammy out of the huge goldfish tank at Megamart. She apologized over and over as the manager escorted them out of the store.

"He's been banned for over a month," the woman said. "Please tell his mother not to send anyone else in here with him, or we'll call Children's Protective Services."

In the parking lot, she held on tight to Sammy as water continued to stream out of his clothing onto hers. As she reached her car, Claire spotted her old friend, Candace, dressed immaculately in an expensive yoga ensemble, getting out of her large, shiny, black SUV. Claire pretended not to see her as she struggled to get Sammy secured in the battered child's safety seat Hannah had provided.

"Yoohoo, Claire!" she heard Candace call as Sammy fought her with all his might, which was considerable.

"Listen," Claire hissed at Sammy. "If you sit still, be quiet, and don't embarrass me while I talk to this fancy lady, I'll buy you the biggest, bluest Moonshine Slershy you have ever seen."

Sammy considered the offer and then held out his hand, which Claire shook.

"Them's a deal," he said, with an exaggerated nod of the head.

Claire turned around and Candace, who had been about to hug her, took one look at her soaked clothing and grimaced.

"What happened to you?"

"A slight accident in the store," Claire said, feeling her face get hot. "I'm watching Sammy for Hannah."

"You're a wild one, aren't you?" Candace said as she looked in at Sammy.

Sammy put a finger up to his mouth and shushed her with a frown.

"He's a stitch," she said to Claire. "I had him in Vacation Bible School last month, and your mom had to come with him just to make sure he didn't escape."

"I understand you were at the O'Hare's when they found Gigi," Claire said.

"Oh, that was awful," Candace said. "That poor woman. I just had the briefest look at her, but she was covered in a bright red rash and had all these welts; it looked as though she'd been stung by bees."

"Eugene's still at the hospital under a mental health hold," Claire said. "I just went over to see him. They're not letting anyone but family in."

"I doubt Jillian will go," Candace said. "Gigi told her that Eugene had recently become violent toward her."

"I know Gigi pretty well," Claire said. "I was with her on the morning before she died. She was worried about him, but she wasn't scared of him."

"You never know, I guess," Candace said, looking as if she was done talking and anxious to be on her way.

"What's Jillian like?" Claire asked.

"She's all right," Candace said. "She's very involved in everything and anxious to move up if you know what I mean. Sometimes a little too anxious, but she means well. They own a house near us at Eldridge Point."

49

"How did she and Chippie meet?"

"She was a nurse and met Chip while working at Pendleton General. He was engaged to another friend of mine, Sophie Dean, at the time."

"Why did he and Sophie break up?"

"I don't really remember," Candace said. "She owns that Trashy Treasures store over by the farmer's market in the old train depot; do you know the one? It's a little too funky for my taste. I have an aversion to rust as a decorative finish if you know what I mean."

"I do," Claire said. "Well, it was good to see you."

"Let's do lunch sometime," Candace said, as she air-kissed Claire near one side of her head.

"I'll have my people call your people," Claire said, and Candace laughed as she walked away.

Claire got in the car and looked back at Sammy, saying, "Well done, kiddo."

Sammy held up a fat goldfish, desperately gasping for water.

"Gots me one," he said. "He's name's Bert."

Claire met Hannah in the hospital parking lot and handed her the fish, now swimming around in a slershy cup full of clean water.

Hannah took one look at her damp clothes and the grin on Sammy's slershy-blue stained face and cackled.

"You don't even need to tell me," she said. "I can piece it together on my own."

"Hey, Hannah," Sammy said. "Me's gots mine own goldfish; he's names Bert."

"That's a mighty fine goldfish, son," Hannah said. "Well done."

"You didn't tell me he was banned from Megamart."

"It was strongly suggested that Sammy wasn't welcome, but I don't think they used that exact term."

"How was your visit?"

"I like that doctor," Hannah said. "He's cute. Single, too."

"Not interested. What did he say?"

"Not much, really, just asked me to tell him about Eugene."

"Did you get a sense of which direction he's leaning?"

"They're not going to keep him," Hannah said. "He said they'd probably let him out as soon as the cuckoo-hold is over."

"You got a lot more out of him than I did."

"He's fun-sized like me," Hannah said. "There's a hidden network of elite petites who all work together to better the world. We hide in plain sight while righting wrongs and saving humanity from the terrible tall tyrants."

"Uh huh."

"He thought you were pretty cool; I think he'd like you to tyrannize him a little."

"Please stop," Claire said. "When can we see Eugene?"

"I saw him just now," Hannah said.

"You did?" Claire said. "I thought only family could see him."

"We told the nurse I was his stepsister," Hannah said. "The doctor thought it would do him good to see a friendly face."

"I have a friendly face."

"But you're one of them, you see."

"The tall tyrants."

"Uh huh," Hannah said. "Plus, I could pass as his sister, and you could only be a visiting supermodel working for a charity that cheers up crazy people."

"How was he?"

"Loved the comics and the book; did not, unfortunately, like the candy you sent."

51

"Is he okay?"

"He's sedated, but just to the point of calm, not oblivion. He made perfect sense. We talked about his business; he's worried about orders backing up."

"Did he talk about his mother?"

"He said someone should call her attorney; he has all her paperwork."

"Sounds really sane to me."

"Here's the funny thing," Hannah said. "He didn't stutter, hardly at all. Other than the lisp, he talked just as plain as you or me."

"How is that even possible?"

"The doc says it's one of the medications he's on. They developed it for people with Parkinson's and turns out it works on people who stammer."

"Can he stay on it?"

"I didn't ask."

"This is all good news," Claire said. "I'm so glad you went to see him."

"Me, too," Hannah said. "I have a new prospect for my matchmaking hobby. We gotta get that tiny doctor a nice tiny woman before some tall gold digger nabs him."

"Mama, I gotta wee," Sammy said. "Real bad."

"That's what happens when you drink a gallon of blue sugar water," Hannah said. "I'll take you to Noodleheads for lunch, and you can wee there. Care to join us?"

"No, thanks," Claire said. "I'm going junk shopping."

Trashy Treasures was one of several stores now residing in the old train depot warehouse down by the river in Pendleton. A bustling farmer's market anchored it at one end, and a deli restaurant at the other. In between, under a long corrugated metal roof, several small shops spilled their wares out onto a wooden walkway made of railroad ties. There were chalkboard signs on easels, small vignettes of tables and chairs, and a healthy crowd of sunburned tourists milling around, emptying their pockets in a gratifying manner, as evidenced by the number of shopping bags they were carrying.

There was a huge metal Texaco star affixed to the wall on one side of the door to Trashy Treasures, and on the other side a lit-up neon gas station sign promised "full service." Inside, Claire could see that all the shops were separated by wooden partitions that rose up ten feet into the air, leaving the area upwards to the peaked roof open. In that space, among the new steel beams and old wooden rafters, a few chirping birds flew. The voices of many happy shoppers spilled over from space to space, and the sound system that served all the shops was playing funky Texas swing music.

The ambiance was definitely junk-inspired, and everywhere Claire looked she saw another cool thing she wanted but had nowhere to put.

A bouquet of Mason jars had been transformed into a pendant light, an old rusted piece of gate was now an art piece on one wall, and a pealing white birdcage was filled with yarn balls in many different colors. An iron bed, distressed from sage green to ivory, had a cheerful little iron bird attached to the gracefully curving headboard and footboard. A worn cotton quilt made up of faded feed sack fabric was draped over it, topped with many pillows made from vintage floral handkerchiefs.

"I could swear I'm in Austin, Texas," Claire said to the woman behind the counter.

"Thanks!" she said. "I'll take that as a compliment."

She had curly golden-red hair tamed by two short braids and a bright red bandanna, and multiple silk necklaces dripping down the front bib of her denim overalls. From her bright blue eyeglass frames and green

T-shirt to her bright pink tennis shoes, her look was all funky, friendly charm, just like her shop.

"Are you Sophie?" Claire asked her.

"One and the same," the woman said.

Claire introduced herself, saying, "We have a mutual friend, Candace, who told me about your shop."

"Candy's a dandy," Sophie said. "My stuff's not her style, but she sends me lots of clients."

"I love your shop; how long have you been here?"

"I was just about to go for lunch, care to join me?" Sophie said. "We can have an uninterrupted chat."

Leaving an equally interestingly dressed employee in charge of the shop, Sophie led Claire a couple doors down to a bakery she had smelled earlier.

Sophie greeted the owner, introduced Claire, and when their food came, led her back out to a two-top table in a shady spot a little way from the crowded boardwalk.

"This is my favorite table," Sophie said. "It gives me a break from customers so I can catch my breath."

"Business must be good."

"It's good all summer, great during leaf peeper season, and fabulous during ski season," she said. "There's a distinct drought from March to June, though, and I'm the only employee most of the time."

"How long have you been doing this?"

"They renovated the depot about five years ago as part of an economic development plan, and at that time they were offering insane incentives to get people to open small businesses. Being a single mom, I was able to get a small business grant. I negotiated a long-term lease because I knew it was going to be great; other people weren't so lucky. I'm one of the few original tenants; everyone else either couldn't afford to renew at the going rate or closed up when they realized how hard it is to run your own business."

"You have kids?"

"One daughter," she said. "She's away at college."

"Have you always worked in retail?"

"Heavens, no, or I wouldn't have been foolish enough to do this," she said. "I was a nurse at Pendleton General, in the NICU."

"I'm sorry, what's that?"

"Neonatal intensive care unit," she said. "Sick babies, very sad some of the time, but also very meaningful work."

"Oh, my goodness," Claire said. "I don't think I could handle that."

"I loved it," Sophie said. "I miss it."

"Do you ever think of going back?"

Sophie shook her head, with a brief, bereft look quickly replaced by a sunnier kind of weary good nature.

"What do you do?" she asked Claire.

"Ugh," Claire said. "I hate that question."

"I'm sorry," Sophie said.

"I'm not mad at you for asking it," she said. "I'm mad at myself because I don't know what in the heck I'm doing right now. I'm volunteering at the hospice three days a week while I try to figure out what to do when I grow up, even though I turn forty this Saturday. I'm a hairdresser by trade, worked in the film industry for twenty years, and just recently moved back to Rose Hill to help my mother take care of my father. He has stroke-related dementia."

"That's tough," Sophie said.

"I love your shop, and I intend to relieve you of many items when we go back, but I also have an ulterior motive," Claire said.

"I wish I could afford to hire you," Sophie said. "All I can afford are minimum wage teenagers at the moment."

"I'm not looking for a job," Claire said. "I'm investigating what may be a crime, not officially of course, but unofficially because a friend of mine has been accused of something he didn't do, entirely because someone has been badmouthing him to anyone who will listen. I'm trying to find out more about this wretched woman, and I think you might know her. Jillian McClanahan."

Claire was surprised to see the color drain out of Sophie's face, and her mouth narrow into a tight frown. She shook her head.

"Keep your voice down," Sophie said, looking around. "I don't want to remind her I'm alive, let alone find out I was talking about her behind her back."

"What did she do?" Claire whispered.

"Not here," Sophie said.

She gathered up the remains of her lunch and dumped them in the nearest garbage can. She took off toward the parking lot and it was all Claire could do to keep up with her. She finally stopped at the side of a vintage pickup truck, painted deep, shiny green. She got in on the driver's side and gestured for Claire to get in on the other side.

After the doors were closed, she gripped the steering wheel and took some deep breaths.

"That bad, huh?" Claire said.

Sophie fixed Claire with a stern stare.

"I don't know you from Adam," she said. "Candace and I were good friends before Jillian put an end to it, and I can't afford any gossip about me to get back to her from any direction."

"I understand," Claire said. "I just want to know why Jillian is trying to frame my friend."

"What does he have that she wants?"

"Money, I guess," Claire said. "A big house that her husband would inherit if Eugene goes to jail."

"I know Eugene," Sophie said. "Is this about Gigi's death?"

Claire told her all she knew.

56

"I'm willing to help you know Jillian better," she said. "But only because you're helping Eugene. But please, please, please, don't let anything I say blow back on me."

"I won't mention you," Claire said. "I promise."

"I was engaged to Chip," Sophie said. "We met at the hospital when he was just starting out in the IT department, and I was still in pediatrics. He wooed me over terrible coffee in the cafeteria. He was working really hard, trying to prove that it wasn't just nepotism that got him his job, but he was overshadowed by his uncle, who wanted him to be important and successful. Chip was just a sweet, honest guy who'd been raised in a terribly abusive home. His mother was a mean alcoholic, and his father is the lowest scum of the Earth; he used to say the vilest things to me every time Chip left the room. It gives me the chills just thinking about it."

"I've met Cheat, and he's a sleazeball," Claire said. "Amazing such a nice guy could come from such a terrible family."

"That was all Gigi. She rescued him. His mother died in a car accident, and Gigi took him in. She adored him. She and Eugene Senior lay the world at his feet; wherever he wanted to go to school, they would pay for it. They bought him a car and a house to live in while he went to college; anything he wanted. They treated him like a son."

"The one they thought they were owed, apparently."

"Chip was never mean to Eugene; he treated him like a brother. They were close the whole time I knew him. Eugene was supposed to be the best man at our wedding."

"What happened?"

"Jillian happened," Sophie said. "She started in pediatrics right after I left to go to the NICU; she took my old position. She hated being compared to me. That crew was like my family, and it was hard to step into my shoes;

57

I'd been there for ten years at that point. She was always fake sweet to me; do you know what I mean?"

"I do."

"Someone who had worked with her before even warned me about her. He said she was let go from her previous job because she liked to stir up so much drama. I didn't give her a second thought. Then she decided she wanted my job and my man, and she didn't stop until she had both."

"What did she do?"

"It was subtle at first. She told people I was rude to her, that I was spreading rumors about her. No one who knew me well believed it, but a hospital is like a small city; there were lots of people there who didn't know me, who did believe her. I even got called into Human Resources to address this issue I didn't know I had. She had accused me of bullying her, and they take that very seriously. I said I didn't know what she was talking about, but there the accusation went, into my file in HR. I had my previous and current supervisor vouch for me, but that only riled her up.

"She slit my tires. There's barely an inch of parking lot around that place that isn't covered by video cameras, but I was dumb enough to park in an area that was not monitored. She'd followed me out into the parking lot the night before and threatened me. It was my word against hers, but nobody could believe she was that crazy."

"What happened?"

"Chip reviewed the video coverage from that night, and even he didn't believe she did it. I got written up and was advised not to get within ten feet of her. That's hard to do when you work in the same place. I started feeling isolated and paranoid, and withdrew from people."

"What did she say to you that night in the parking lot?"

"She said that Chip had been seeing her behind my back and that he was working up the nerve to break up with me to be with her."

"Was that true?"

"He said it wasn't true, but it was the thin end of the wedge she'd driven between us. The more things she did to me the more paranoid I became, and to Chip, she became more sympathetic."

"What else did she do?"

"She was trying to get me fired, so any rule violation she thought she could pin on me, she did. Through gossip, she accused me of accessing patients' confidential information, and of sharing that information. She told parents of patients on the pediatrics floor that I was suspected of neglecting the patients, that they shouldn't leave me alone with their children. It went on and on."

"And no one ever believed you?"

"It was just too far out there, you know? No one wanted to believe this sweet little nurse in pediatrics would do such a thing. It was more likely I was the crazy one, and I soon looked like it. I couldn't eat or sleep, so I got really thin and had dark circles under my eyes. Eventually, it started to affect my work. When I realized I couldn't give one hundred percent to the babies in the NICU, I resigned."

"Did it stop, then?"

"She came to my apartment one night when Chip was at a seminar out of town. She spray-painted "child-killer" on my garage door."

"That's horrible."

"I know. Luckily my next-door neighbor caught her doing it and called the police. He and I went to the police station, and I told them the whole story. Finally, someone believed me. I agreed not to press charges if she stayed away from me. I swore out a restraining order that still stands today. She isn't allowed within 100 yards of me; no contact in any way."

"That's awful," Claire said. "Surely, then Chip believed you."

"Unfortunately not. Jillian told him I wrote the message on my own garage door and got the neighbor to back me up because I was screwing him behind Chip's back."

"Why would he fall for that?"

"She'd been manipulating him full time now that I wasn't working at the hospital. He said she showed him evidence that I was sleeping with this guy, had cheated with a bunch of guys. He was gullible, I guess, or blind in some way, when it came to her. When he came back from out of town, he broke up with me, we called off the wedding, and I don't think we've spoken more than one or two times since."

"That's a horrifying story."

"So, you see why, when someone comes and asks me about Jillian, I would rather pull my own teeth out through my nose."

"I can see why," Claire said. "And now she's after Eugene's money."

"Jillian does have a weakness," Sophie said.

"What is that?"

"She's a classic narcissist," Sophie said. "Textbook case."

"Having worked in Hollywood, I'm very familiar with the type."

"They need to feel important and admired at all times by everybody."

"Which is not feasible in the real world."

"And if they don't get the attention or respect or material things they feel they are due, it has to be someone else's fault."

"And that person must be punished."

"Poor Eugene," Sophie said. "Because I also think she's a sociopath."

"What's her Achilles heel?"

"Control," Sophie said. "Control of Chip, her son, and her social position."

"How can I use that to help Eugene?"

"If she has a choice between Eugene's money and control of everything else in her life, she will choose control."

"If she doesn't kill us all first."

Claire's phone rang.

"Sorry," Claire said. "It's my mom."

"Go ahead," Sophie said.

Her mother said there was a certified letter waiting for her.

"Go ahead and open it," Claire said.

It instructed her to contact an attorney, Walter Graham, the same one she had met at Gigi's home.

After Claire ended the call, she told Sophie what the call was about.

"His office is not too far from here," Sophie said. "Go ahead and call; I don't mind."

Claire called him and set up an appointment for the following morning.

"Can you tell me what this is about?" she asked him.

"You already know what it's about," he said. "You signed all the paperwork in front of me the day Gigi died. I bet you never thought that day would come so soon."

"I guess not," Claire said, confused.

After she hung up, Sophie asked what that was about.

"I witnessed Gigi's signature on some documents before she died," she said. "I guess I have to go to the lawyer's office to verify my signature or something. I don't know. No big deal."

"What in the hell?" Claire asked Mr. Graham the next morning, after being informed exactly how big of a deal it actually was.

"I asked you if you understood before you signed," the attorney said, in an irritated tone. "She said she had discussed it at length with you."

"She wanted me to marry him, and I declined," Claire said. "I thought I was just witnessing her signature."

"Well, unless you want to back out now, which would be a huge headache for me, by the way, you are now more or less in charge of Eugene and his fortune."

"Doesn't Eugene get a say in this?"

"He signed as well."

"But this is crazy!"

"Listen, Claire, just take some time to get used to the idea," he said. "I'll help you with the legal aspect, and Gigi's broker and accountant do the financial management. If you decline this, it opens the door for Chip and Jillian to get him declared incompetent and take control."

Control.

The thing Jillian wanted more than anything and Claire had it.

"I'll do it," Claire said. "But only to protect Eugene, and only if you can protect me from Jillian."

"I've met Jillian," he said. "She's a social climber and kind of tactless, but essentially harmless."

Claire told him the story Sophie had told her. He made some notes on a pad.

"You're my attorney now, and that was privileged," she said. "If Jillian finds out Sophie told me about her who knows what she'll do."

"I'm just going to verify a few things, discreetly," he said. "Jillian's been calling my office every hour since Gigi died, and I've been ignoring her calls."

"As soon as she knows I'm in charge, I'm done for," Claire said.

"I'll work on that. We can appoint several successor custodians; she can't eliminate everyone."

"That doesn't comfort me, Walter."

"Leave it to me. We Irish must stick together. Meanwhile, we need to form a plan for when Eugene gets out of the hospital, and arrange for Gigi's funeral. I have her preferences here in her file, and I've made an appointment this afternoon at the funeral home in Rose Hill. I'll take you to lunch first."

"I can't believe this is happening."

"You're from Hollywood, Claire. It's like one of those movies where a relative dies, and you suddenly get their little kid," he said.

"Only he's forty years old," Claire said. "And somebody may be willing to kill him *and me* for his money."

Claire warmed to Walter over lunch, where he regaled her with tales of crazy clients past, and she reciprocated with crazy Hollywood behavior, and by the time they had made Gigi's funeral arrangements, she considered him a friend.

Back at his office, he walked her to her car.

"Uh oh," she said.

Her tires had been slashed.

"How could she know already?" Walter asked as he took out his cell phone.

"I hope you're calling to hire me a bodyguard," Claire said, "or an elite task force of Irish Seals."

"I'm calling the police," he said. "In this town, that's the same thing."

Police Chief Shep Shepherd was an old friend of Claire's father and remembered Jillian's attack on Sophie. Claire was sitting in his office, where Walter had dropped her off.

"I thought you were going to retire this month," Claire said.

She tried to push away the thought that before he died, Laurie had intended to take over as chief, but a little piano music started to play in her head. It was "If I Should Lose You."

"I've been chief of this town's police force for over twenty-five years," he said. "Until they find my replacement, I'll stay chief."

"They're lucky to have you," Claire said.

It was very distracting having a soundtrack in your day to day life, but Claire tried to ignore it.

"Walter's going to bring me the surveillance tape, and if Jillian shows up on it, bending down to do the dirty deed, I will arrest her with pleasure," he said. "Once in a while you come across a wolf in sheep's clothing, living among the flock, and you never quite take your eye off of that one. Can't afford to. I've been waiting for her to make a mistake, and I'd love to be the one to catch her."

"She made quite an impression, I see."

"Oh, she's quite popular with the suits that run that hospital, and with their wives," he said. "I see her in the newspaper, attending this gala and that charity ball, and on the committee for the children's hospital they're building. But there's a look some people have in their eyes, not pure evil, or anything supernatural, mind you, just a complete lack of regard for anyone but themselves, and the mistaken notion that they're fooling the world. She has that, our Jillian, in spades."

"How can I protect myself? And Eugene?"

"If we see her on that tape, we'll arrest her," he said. "Let's wait and see."

64

After Walter and Shep met alone with the tape, they called Claire in to see it as well. It was impossible to tell the identity of the perpetrator from the black-and-white videotape, only that he or she was of medium height, medium build, and wore a black hoodie on the hottest day of the year.

"So, that's that," Claire said.

"We'll ask around," Shep said. "Maybe someone saw her."

"I'll get better surveillance set up at work," Walter said. "You might want to do the same at home, Claire."

"Don't be alone with her," Shep said. "You might want to travel with one of those ornery cousins in tow for a while."

"Don't worry," Claire said. "I'm going to tell all my relatives. Jillian won't be able to make a move in Rose Hill without a Fitzpatrick breathing down her neck."

CHAPTER FOUR

Hannah picked up the trail of clothing left on the floor from the kitchen to the bathroom, where Sammy was singing "Old MacDonald Had a Farm" at the top of his lungs, while her husband, Sam, attempted to bathe him.

"And on he's farm he's had a chicken," he sang. "Bee eye, bee eye, bow!"

Downstairs, Hannah surveyed the wreckage that was the kitchen after feeding Sammy breakfast. He'd wanted "hots cakes," and it seemed as if Sam had used every bowl and pan in the cupboard to make them. There was syrup on everything, including Hannah's hair, and one of the cats was on the table licking a stick of butter.

Hannah shooed away the cat and started cleaning. After that, she had to take Sammy to daycare and hoped that he stayed long enough so that she could get some actual work done. There were squirrels in Father Stephen's attic, a possum in Dottie's garage, and a stray dog reported out Pumpkin Ridge Road.

She had just started the dishwasher as Sam came down the stairs carrying Sammy, who was dressed in red pajama pants, a green T-shirt with a superhero on it, and black tennis shoes worn over a gray sock and a blue sock. To overcome the getting-dressed tantrums, they had been letting him pick out his clothes. As long as he left the house with his feet and private parts covered, Hannah considered it a successful enterprise.

"Some woman called for you," Hannah told Sam, deliberately not looking at him as she did so, and trying to keep her tone casual. "It was the same one who called you last night and two days ago."

"Okay, thanks," Sam said.

"Can I ask who this woman is who calls you all the time now?"

"It's one of my soldiers, Hannah, you know that."

"She sounds more like a bimbo from a USO show," Hannah said. "Her voice is all breathy, like, *Helloooo, is Saaaam hoooome? I'd love to speak to him with my breathy, breathy, girlie voice.*"

Sam laughed.

"She's twenty if she's a day," he said. "I told you about her; she's the arm-below-the-elbow, leg-below-the-knee. Been back a month, and her home situation is not good. Her boyfriend broke up with her. She's had it rough."

"Well, you know what that's like," Hannah said.

"I do," Sam said. "That's why I'm letting her lean on me a little more than usual. Six months from now it will be 'Sam who? Oh, that old guy who works with the vets up at the community center.' She's just fragile right now."

"They're all fragile," Hannah said. "It's a never-ending stream of fragile, broken-down people you and Coach have to build back up piece by piece. It's wonderful what you're doing; I'm sure you'll get your wings when you get to heaven, but your wife is a little tired of having to get in line behind all the soldiers."

"It's what I do," Sam said. "That was part of our deal."

Before Sammy was born, Sam had agreed to move back to Rose Hill from their farm out on Hollyhock Ridge if Hannah would agree that he could sell his network security business and work full-time with recovering vets.

Full-time was an understatement. He was on call 24-7.

"We're having people over for dinner," Hannah said. "Will you pick up something to grill?"

68

"I told Vince I would go to his AA meeting this evening," Sam said. "He's getting his six-month chip tonight."

"Can't Coach do it?"

"I'm the one who mentors him, and occasionally I need to give him my undivided attention."

"When do I get your undivided attention?" Hannah asked.

"Tonight in bed," Sam said. "Provided our son doesn't have an earache or a toothache or a bellyache or a bad dream or a monster under the bed."

"You's fightin'," Sammy said. "Me no like it."

Hannah reached out and hugged her son between them.

"Sammy sammich," Sammy said. "Dat's better."

"Will you at least take Sammy to school?"

"I planned on it," Sam said. "I'll pick him up, too."

"Me no like school," Sammy said. "Me stay at Auntie Delia's."

"Auntie Delia is helping Auntie Bonnie at the bakery today," Hannah said. "Besides, Miss Suzanne is going to let you guys play with the water tables today. That reminds me, you need to put a change of clothes and shoes in his backpack."

"Already did," Sam said, patting the backpack. "I do listen to you, you know."

They left, and Hannah went upstairs to clean up the mess they had made of the bathroom. Sam hadn't even bothered to drain the tub. Hannah's hairbrush was in the toilet, which hadn't been flushed, and her bottle of vitamins was floating in the bathwater.

"Gross," Hannah said, as she threw away the brush.

The vitamins seemed to be dry, so she put them back up on the counter where she kept them.

She was picking up wet towels when she heard the dog door flap, and four dogs stampeded up the stairs.

Bunny and Chicken were unrecognizable with their muddy fur full of burrs and grass.

"No, no, you guys!" she cried, but they jumped on her and licked her face, their muddy paws all over her clean clothes.

"Out, out, out," she yelled.

They beat a hasty retreat back down the stairs and back out through the dog door flap.

Hannah looked at herself in the mirror. Her hair was sticky with syrup and lopsided from bedhead, her clothes were covered in muddy paw prints, and there were dark circles under her eyes.

"I wanna get married, I said. I wanna have kids, I said. I wanna live on a farm with lots of animals, I said. What was I thinking?"

A couple of hours later, out at the Pumpkin Ridge Organic Farm, Hannah was trying in vain to catch a wily, fast-moving border collie who had been trying to round up the groovy, free-range, grass-fed cows, when her phone rang.

"Hannah, it's your Aunt Delia," the voice said, but it was hard to recognize because of the crying. "Your Uncle Ian's missing."

Hannah threw what was left of the hot dog at the collie, explained what was happening to the farm owners, jumped in her truck, and put her foot down on the gas pedal until she was back in Rose Hill. She went to Delia's house first, where their friend, Kay was commandeering volunteers over her cell phone. Church ladies were making coffee, there were already dozens of baked goods in boxes on the kitchen table, and several casseroles rested on the counter.

Delia was sitting at the kitchen table, crying, with Hannah's mother seated next to her.

"Hi, Mom," Hannah said, and then bent over to hug her Aunt Delia.

"Did you even brush your hair this morning?" her mother, Alice asked. "You could have at least shaved your legs. You look like a hippie. Honestly, Hannah Jane, I don't understand you at all. It's like you don't even want to be a girl."

"We'll find him," Hannah told Delia.

"He was sound asleep in his chair," Delia said. "Usually nothing can wake him during his nap. I just ran out for a minute ..."

"He needs to be in a home for crazy people," Alice said. "He's going to burn this house down with everyone in it."

"Mom," Hannah said to Alice. "You need to go home and wait there in case Ian shows up looking for Dad."

"Well, I could do that, I guess," Alice said. "I'd go out and look for him, myself, but my sciatica is so bad today, and I've been trying to get a migraine. You know how sick that makes me."

"You go on," Hannah said. "Please hurry, he might be there now."

"I'll go, but I can't very well hurry. I have arthritis in my knees, and my plantar fasciitis is acting up."

Alice got up and left slowly, taking her cup of coffee and a doughnut with her.

"Thank you," Delia said to Hannah, laughing through her tears. "God bless you, child. If you do nothing else that can be your good deed for today."

"What's the latest word?"

"Kay's started the prayer chain, and everybody's out looking," Delia said. "I just don't know where he could have gone."

She started crying again, and Hannah squeezed her shoulder.

"Don't you worry," she said. "We'll have the whole town out looking for him, and someone will find him."

Hannah interrupted Kay on the phone.

"I'm going out to the farm," she said. "Ian's been wanting to go fishing; let's just pray he didn't put a boat on the pond."

Out at the farm, she met Ed and her father leaving the house.

"We're going to check the pond," her father said.

"Cal's getting a boat out on the river," Ed said.

"I'll get someone to go down to Turtle Creek," Hannah said. "He can't have walked that far, but someone might have recognized him and picked him up."

"Has anyone called Claire?" her father asked.

"I'm on it," Hannah said.

When Hannah picked her up at the police station, the first thing she said to Claire was, "Now don't panic, but your dad is missing."

"Oh, Hannah, no."

"The whole town is out looking for him," Hannah said. "Someone will find him."

"The river," Claire said, as her heart raced and her mind spun through several horrid scenarios.

"Cal and the rescue team from the fire station are out on the river looking."

"Oh, Lord help us," Claire said. "This is my mother's worst nightmare."

"She feels awful," Hannah said. "She's at home waiting by the phone."

"Go faster."

"Yes, ma'am," Hannah said.

"This will kill her."

"Please don't worry. We'll find him. Sam's helping, and you know that man has serious skills."

At the entrance to Rose Hill, traffic was backed up as cars were being stopped and people alerted to her father's disappearance. Hannah took a right down a steep, muddy alley that wasn't officially a roadway but eventually ended up on Peony Street.

"I wasn't kidding when I said the whole town is on top of this," Hannah said. "Tommy and Ed made the flyers they're passing out."

Hannah took Claire home, where her mother was weeping in a chair by the phone, and Kay was putting the casseroles in the refrigerator.

"I'm so sorry," Delia wailed when she saw Claire. "He was sleeping ..."

"It's okay," Claire said, as she hugged her mother. "You can't watch him every minute."

"Two nights ago he went outside at three a.m. because he thought there was a bear in the backyard," Delia told Hannah. "Luckily, the dog started barking, and Claire got up to see what was wrong."

"We took the guns out of the house earlier this summer," Claire said, "so he had taken a butcher knife with him."

"There's only so much you can do," Hannah said. "You can't lock him up."

"You're doing your best," Kay said. "Everyone knows that."

Delia snuffled and nodded, and Claire took a clean dish towel and wiped her face.

"You stay by the phone," Claire said. "Hanna and I are going to go look for him."

"I can't think where he went," Delia said. "Maybe the pond on Hannah's farm ..."

"My dad's down there now," Hannah said. "Don't worry, Aunt Delia, we'll find him."

Hannah followed Claire outside.

"Where to?" she asked.

"I don't have a clue," Claire said.

"It's a small town," Hannah said. "Someone will have seen him."

73

They started by going from business to business downtown, but everyone had already heard about it, and no one had seen him. As they went, Claire felt a rising panic in her body.

"The Catholic church," she said. "He was talking the other day about how Father Stephen and he were going to play chess someday soon, just like they used to."

They ran up the hill to the Sacred Heart Catholic Church, but the secretary informed them that Father Stephen and Sister Mary Margrethe were out looking for him. They searched the church, anyway. Claire was hoping to find him fast asleep in a patch of sunlight somewhere, like a lazy tabby cat.

As they left the church, Claire asked, "Where to now?"

"Let's think like your dad," Hannah said. "Where would he go?"

"Rose and Thorn, Service Station, Laurel Mountain Diner, Catholic Church, Frog Pond, Turtle Creek ..."

"Check, check, and check," Hannah said. "We've checked all those places."

"Maybe he went to the guard shack at Eldridge," Claire said. "He knows those guys."

Just then the town's only police car zoomed up Peony Street and made a left down Lily Avenue, below the Community Center.

Hannah and Claire took off running.

The dust kicked up by the squad car left a trail all the way around the back of the building to the old bus barn.

"Of course," Claire said.

Claire's father had driven a school bus after he retired from the police force.

When Claire and Hannah got there, Sam and Scott were standing outside the squad car. Scott was talking on his cell phone, and Sam stood with his arms crossed, sporting his usual hundred-yard stare.

Sam Campbell was Hannah's husband, Sammy's father, and had been, at one point many years ago, the love of Claire's life. No one besides Sam and she knew about that except Scott, whom Claire had confided in soon after she returned to Rose Hill. Claire's cousin Hannah was dearer to her heart than just about anyone in the world, and when she married Sam, Claire had buried those feelings. It didn't mean they stayed buried; she still occasionally kicked dirt over them.

As Claire and Hannah approached them, Scott was telling someone Ian had been found.

"He's with me now, Delia," he said. "We're bringing him straight home. He thought he was late driving the bus, and then when he got here, there were no buses, and he was confused. He sat down on the loading dock to wait for the morning buses to return and fell asleep. Sam thought of it, came to have a look, and found him."

Claire opened the door to the back seat of the squad car. Her father was sitting next to Sammy, each sharing half of what looked like a banana ice pop.

"Me finded him," Sammy said. "Uncle Ian's was lost and me and Daddy finded him."

Claire looked at her father, who was avoiding eye contact.

"Are you okay?" she asked him.

There was no point in asking why because dementia has its own reasons why.

"This is a good thing," her father said, gesturing to the ice pop. "It's an icy, candy, melty thing; what's it called?"

"Nanner pop," Sammy said. "They's called icy pops, and you gets them at the store in the cold part. Don't climb in there or they gets mad at you. Auntie Delia can gets them for you; me ask her to."

"We'll both ask her," Ian said. "I've never eaten anything that tasted this good in all my life."

Ian said this about everything he ate, as it seemed to him to be true, so this was a pretty normal statement for him.

"How're you doing, Dad?" Claire asked him.

"I don't know what all the fuss is about," he said. "A man can't take a walk in his own town whenever he feels like it, I guess."

"Not without letting his wife know."

"Me, too," Sammy said. "Me never gets to do nothing."

"Come on, Blues Clues," Hannah said to Sammy. "Let's take Daddy home and go for a swim. You should come over later, Claire Bear, and go for a dip with us. There will be plenty of beer, and you look like you need a few."

"Me likes beer," Sammy said.

"Root beer," Hannah said. "Always remember to say the 'root' part, Sammy, or mama will have to convince the nice judge she deserves to keep you."

"I'll be over later," Claire said. "Right after I install twenty locks, four video cameras, and one big alarm system."

After Sonny Delvecchio finished installing the alarm system, Claire wrote him a check.

"I'll order those cameras for you," he said before he left. "Be here in a few days."

"Thanks, Sonny," Claire said. "Tell Kay I said thank you, too."

"Our pleasure," Sonny said. "Just let us know what we can do, and we'll come running."

Claire's father was snoring in his recliner. Delia was reading the owner's manual for the security system.

"I think I've got it," she said. "Once you open a door or window, you have 30 seconds to enter the code, or the alarm goes off. Sonny also set it up to call the fire station if it detects smoke or carbon monoxide."

"Do you care if I go out to Hannah's?" Claire asked her. "I can stay home if you want me to."

"Of course not, honey," Delia said. "Just remember to use your code when you come in."

"What happens when we can't handle him anymore; when he doesn't know us?"

"I can't think about that," Delia said. "I just don't know."

Her mother's face had grown more haggard just in the few months since Claire had been home. There were dark shadows under her eyes, and Claire could sometimes hear her crying at night.

'I can't bear it,' she thought. 'I need to do something, but what?'

"Hannah suggested we tie a bell to him, like a cat," she said and was rewarded with a smile.

"Not a bad idea."

Out at Hannah's farm, Claire shucked her shirt and waded into Frog Pond, wearing tennis shoes, cut-off jean shorts, and a black sports bra. She hopped up on one of the large tractor tire inner tubes that were tethered to the dock and arranged her body so that her bottom was down in the water and her legs and arms were draped over the sides.

She leaned back and looked at the sky, just starting to darken over the mountains to the east. A crescent moon shared the sky with the setting sun. The air was warm, the sky clear, and the water cool.

"This is the life," she said.

"Two days out of the year," her cousin Maggie said. "It was eighty-five today, might get up to ninety tomorrow."

"That's the record," Hannah said.

Her two cousins were already in their tubes, which were lashed to a fourth tube, in which the beer cooler was secured.

"Where are Sam and Sammy?" Claire asked.

"Bath, books, and bedtime," Hannah said. "His turn."

"Let's set sail," Claire said, as she untied her tube and pushed off from the dock.

"There be dragons," Hannah said.

"Shouldn't that be sea serpents?" Claire asked.

They drifted out to the middle of the pond.

"I wonder what normal people are doing right now?" Maggie asked.

"Normal's overrated," Hannah said. "I'd rather be odd."

"Odd people have more fun," Claire said. "Because they care less what everyone else thinks."

"A funny thing happened today," Maggie said. "Floyd said someone notified the health department that they got deathly ill from eating in my coffee bar yesterday."

"What did they eat?" Hannah asked.

"The caller said it was chicken soup, but we haven't had chicken soup for over a week."

"Who's Floyd?" Claire asked.

"Pine County health inspector," Maggie said.

"That is weird," Hannah said.

"The woman said she got deathly ill, had to go to the emergency room with food poisoning, and she wanted there to be a report made against the bookstore," Maggie said. "Floyd checked at the emergency rooms of the closest hospitals, but there were no food poisonings reported at any of them in the past twenty-four hours."

"It's Jillian," Claire said.

She told them what Sophie had told her and what had happened with the attorney and her car.

"So, you're rich, now, huh?" Hannah said. "Sammy wants his own Moonshine Slershy machine. Sam wants enough exercise equipment to serve the entire veteran population of the tristate area. I only want a tiny, stately yacht for my pond. How about you, Maggie?"

"I want a new heating and air conditioning system for my building," she said. "The one I have is almost twenty years old; probably won't make it through this winter."

"It's not my money," Claire said. "I'm just the head of a sort of committee that takes care of Eugene and his money. There's me, Walter, the attorney, Gigi's broker, and her CPA. I'm going to try to get Dr. Schweitzer on board, too."

"On board the O'Hare gravy train," Hannah said.

"I'm not getting anything from it," Claire said. "I can get reimbursed for any expenses, but I can't imagine what they would be."

"Tickets for us to take him to Harry Potter World," Hannah said. "I need to be on that committee, in charge of leisure activities."

"Do you really think Jillian is behind the food poisoning call?" Maggie asked.

"I think as soon as she found out I got custody of Eugene she began her campaign of terror, yes," Claire said. "When Dad disappeared, I was afraid she had kidnapped him."

"That Sophie chick has made you paranoid," Maggie said.

"It's not paranoia when someone *is* out to get you," Hannah said. "It's common sense. It's self-preservation. Sometimes fear is a perfectly legitimate response to a very real threat."

"It makes me think Jillian may have killed Gigi," Claire said.

"Well, she's picking on the wrong people," Hannah said. "We will prove she killed Gigi and put her away."

"Did you go see Cheat today?" Claire asked.

"Now, don't nag me," Hannah said. "I meant to, but I got busy. There was a possum in Dottie's garage that had backed her cat into a corner, and neither one was giving in."

"What'd you do?"

"I took two trash can lids, sneaked up behind them, and banged them together. The possum fell over and played dead, and the cat flew out of that garage like its tail was on fire. I scooped up the possum and relocated it to the woods."

"Why doesn't everyone in town come out here and do this?" Claire asked. "I remember when we were kids, and Lily and Simon owned it, there was always a crowd out here. They had cookouts and set off fireworks."

"Sam doesn't like anyone he doesn't know on his land," Maggie said.

"It's true," Hannah said. "I started a rumor that the pond was infested with copperheads, and everyone quit coming out."

Claire felt something brush against her foot in the water and jumped.

"Ha ha," Hannah said. "Got you."

"You need to go question Cheat tomorrow," Claire said.

"All right, all right," Hannah said. "What do you suggest I ask him?"

"Ask him who might have wanted to kill Gigi, or what his daughter-in-law is up to."

"What if it was him?" Maggie asked. "What if he killed her?"

"Maybe I better go with you," Claire said.

"Damn straight," Hannah said. "Sending me in with no backup; not cool, Claire."

"All right," Claire said. "I'll come up and get you, and we'll go there together."

"I feel like we should warn the whole family," Hannah said. "If Jillian's coming after us, we need to be prepared."

"Don't be stupid," Maggie said. "These are all coincidences. Don't let yourself get all wound up or you'll start seeing Jillian around every corner, blaming her for every bad thing that happens."

Hannah had just got off the phone with Maggie when Claire arrived in the morning.

"Jillian strikes again," Hannah said. "Someone called the health department and claimed food poisoning from Aunt Bonnie's bakery; this time they said it was the corned beef pasties."

"It's a good thing you all know this health inspector so well," Claire said.

"He even told Maggie it seemed as if somebody might be out to get her family," Hannah said.

"Does she believe us now?"

"She's coming around," Hannah said.

"Maybe we should have a family meeting," Claire said. "Warn everyone."

"Well, I told my dad, and Maggie told her mom, so consider that done."

"I need to tell my mother," Claire said. "I will as soon as I go home."

"How's she doing?"

"She's exhausted," Claire said. "Uncle Fitz has him this evening; they're playing cards up at the Whistle Pig Lodge."

"Just tell me what I can do to help," Hannah said.

"I don't know," Claire said. "It's getting harder."

They were quiet for a moment. Claire knew Hannah would break the tension with a joke; she just waited for it.

"Are you ready to meet and greet Cheat?" she said. "I know you want him."

"I'm volunteering at Hospice today," Claire said. "We'll have to do it later."

"But Cheat would be so happy to see you," Hannah said. "If you play your cards right, I bet you could have your way with him."

"That man gave me the willies," Claire said. "I wish I never had to see him again."

"He digs you," Hannah said. "Use that to our advantage. Flirt with him a little. He'll probably incriminate himself just to impress you."

Claire was standing in the garden behind Pine County Hospice, watching a hummingbird sip from each cupped spike of a deep red Bee Balm flower. The sky was bright blue with a few decorative, puffy clouds lounging about. She closed her eyes for a moment and breathed in the scent of daisies, marigolds, and something she didn't know the name of, a profusion of little pink flowers with a wonderful, delicate scent. When she opened her eyes, the hummingbird was gone, and a man in a clerical collar had taken its place.

"I didn't want to disturb you," he said, "but I wanted to introduce myself. I'm Ben Taylor, the chaplain here."

Claire felt a little disoriented and faintly embarrassed, but she shook the hand he offered. He looked to be around her age, tall and fit, not with a handsome face, but a friendly, kind one with laugh lines. No wedding ring, she noticed, and then chided herself for looking.

"Nice to meet you," she said. "I've heard lots of nice things about you."

"And I about you," he said. "The director says you've brightened the lives of not only many patients and their families, but the staff members as well."

"That's kind of her," Claire said.

"Do you mind if we sit?" he asked. "I've been on my feet all morning, and I could use a rest."

They walked to a nearby bench and sat quietly for a few moments, admiring the view of the mountains in the distance.

"The director says you've been coming in to volunteer three days a week."

"I love doing it," Claire said. "It's very meaningful work, but I need a day off in between just to recover."

"I know exactly what you mean," he said. "There's a very real syndrome called 'compassion fatigue.' It plagues those who help people in a highly emotional environment like this. You have to take time away to recharge your batteries; to get a little distance between you and the drama."

Claire thought about the black cloud that had been following her lately, no matter where she was or what she was doing, and before she knew it, tears were falling.

"I'm so sorry," she said.

He handed her a handkerchief from his pocket. It was wrinkled but clean.

"No need to apologize," he said. "Maybe you need more than a day away."

"I need to do this," Claire said. "I need to be busy and stay focused on something other than myself. Otherwise, I'm just a walking pity party."

"Anything you tell me will be held in strict confidence," he said. "I'm really good at listening."

Claire looked in his kind, dark brown eyes.

"You're supposed to be resting," she said.

"I can rest and listen," he said.

"I lost someone recently," she said, and then had to pause while she shed fresh tears.

He was quiet and waited. Claire felt like she could take all the time in the world and he would just sit there like he would rather be there with her than anywhere else. That was a good quality in a clergyman, she decided.

"Laurie was a policeman, like my dad. He had a drinking problem, a bad one. He was kind of bitter but had a sense of humor about it. He was funny. He was sad. He was kind of lost and ... it wasn't exactly a romance, but it was more than a friendship," she said. "I actually didn't know him all that long, but the chemistry between us was instant and intense. I was with him when he died. It was very sudden, and I'm just not handling it very well."

Ben was quiet and gave Claire time to consider saying more before he spoke.

"The journey through grief can take a long time," he said. "You must be as patient and compassionate with yourself as you would be with a dear, old friend."

"I feel ill," she said. "I hurt all over, and I want to sleep all the time, but when I lay down, all I can think about are all the stupid things I did and said, and imagine all the things I could have done differently. I don't want to be around my friends, I'm neglecting my boyfriend, and I'm short-tempered with my parents. I feel like a complete mess."

"Have you talked to a doctor?" he asked. "Do you have one?"

"Doc Machalvie is our family doctor. I know what he'll say, that I'm depressed, and he'll want to give me a pill so I won't be sad. The crazy thing is I almost don't want to feel better. I don't want to move away from it. I don't want my memories of him to fade. It would be like losing him all over again."

"I'm not saying you need one, but I think you might find that an antidepressant would help you cope with your feelings, and make them more manageable, rather than make them disappear."

"I feel a little crazy saying this," Claire said, "but it's almost like he's hanging around, and he doesn't want me to move on."

"You could talk to him, explain that you need to get on with your life, but that you'll always remember him and love him."

"You don't think it's crazy that I talk to his ghost?"

"There are lots of ways our minds help us work through grief," he said. "It's very normal to feel visited by the deceased in your dreams or as a strong feeling of their presence when you're awake."

"After my friend Tuppy died, I heard him talk in my head for a while, too."

"When did it stop?"

"After I figured out who killed him, and got them arrested," Claire said. "I don't want to be one of those people who attracts ghosts. I used to watch that show, and I felt sorry for that woman. Most people thought she was crazy."

"It's completely normal; happens to lots of people," he said. "Ask your friend what it will take to make him go away."

"I kind of like him being with me," she said. "Isn't that bad?"

"Totally normal," he said. "But, is it keeping you from living your life?"

Claire looked away.

"Give yourself more time," Ben said. "Talk to his presence, tell him how you feel, and ask him to help you get on with your life. If he loved you, he wouldn't want you to suffer indefinitely."

"I hear his voice in my head," Claire said, "commenting on things that happen during the day, giving me a hard time, kidding me, just like he did when he was alive. I like it. It makes me feel better. It's like I get to be with him again."

"But you're alive, and you still have a long life to live," Ben said. "I'm sure there are people in your life who care about you. Reach out to them, let them know what you're going through, and let them support you while you go through it."

"There are people, but they have their own problems," she said. "Sometimes it seems like such an incredible effort just to be with people, let alone talk about this kind of stuff. I'm just so tired."

"Make me a deal," he said. "We'll meet here for lunch on the days you volunteer, and we'll keep talking about this."

"I don't want to make you work through your lunch," she said.

"We'll bring our lunches, then," he said. "We'll eat and talk. What you're going through is interesting to me. It's a compelling story, and I want to find out what happens. I'll help you if you let me."

"I'm not very religious."

"Not a prerequisite. We're just two people who met up at the right time. You're going through something you need help with, and I'm very good at helping people. It's kind of my jam."

"Did you learn that expression in youth group?"

"Not appropriate?"

"No, it's funny," she said. "I like it."

"Hang in there," he said. "Here's your homework assignment: tell your ghost friend what I said, ask him what has to happen for him to move on, and write down what he says. I'll be interested to hear what he has to say."

"He didn't believe in God," she said.

"Maybe he does now," he said. "Ask him. Meanwhile, I'll see you day after tomorrow."

He patted her arm and left.

Claire closed her eyes and felt the wind lift the tendrils of her hair from the back of her neck. In the distance wind chimes rang, leaves rustled, and a Mockingbird went through his repertoire.

'Complete bollocks,' she heard Laurie say. 'That's his *jam*.'

Claire smiled.

'About this God question?' she asked him.

'Privileged information,' he said. 'I could tell you, but then I'd have to kill you.'

'Did you hear everything he said?'

'Blah, blah, blah, feel your feelings when you feel them,' he said. 'Blah, blah, blah, take a pill.'

'Why are you still hanging around?'

'Nothing better to do,' he said. 'All the good concerts are sold out for months in advance. I'm on the waiting list for Amy Winehouse, Billie Holliday, and Patsy Cline. You can't even get on the list for Elvis unless you died before 1977. On the other hand, they can't give away Richard Wagner tickets. Fifteen hours where you are feels like fifteen years over here.'

'He wanted me to ask you what it would take for you to move on and let me get on with my life.'

'Just say the word,' he said. 'Tell me to scram, and I'll vamoose.'

Claire sighed.

'The truth is you don't want me to go,' Laurie said. 'And why would you? I'm better company than your erstwhile professor of journalism, Earnest McBoringstein. What is it with the beard, by the way? Is he having a mid-life crisis? He'll be riding a bike with a wooden crate tied to it before the week is out.'

'Leave Ed alone,' Claire said. 'He's been really nice about you.'

'Cause he's alive and I'm dead,' Laurie said. 'It's not exactly a level playing field.'

Claire heard someone pushing a squeaky wheelchair down the path, and when she turned to see who it was, she could feel Laurie's presence recede and disappear. One minute he was with her, in her head, talking to her just like he was sitting next to her, and then he was gone.

She knew she needed to let go of Laurie and focus on her real life, but when she thought about telling him not to come back, she got a pain in her chest.

'Not yet,' she thought. 'Not just yet.'

Claire went back inside the Hospice House, a long red brick building that looked kind of like a ranch house someone started building and just didn't know when to stop. The patient rooms were on the southeastern side, facing the extensive gardens and beyond that, a stunning mountain view. Across the hallway were the offices and treatment rooms, along with a large living room, recreational room, and a children's playroom for the families of the patients.

Walking down the hallway, Claire thought she recognized a woman dressed in scrubs walking toward her, but before she could come up with a name the woman gasped and, in that hushed voice that everyone spoke in so as not to disturb the peace and quiet, she said, "Claire Fitzpatrick!"

Claire smiled in recognition, but she couldn't come up with the woman's name. When they met in the hallway, she grabbed Claire and squeezed her way too tight.

"Oh my goodness," she said. "As I live and breathe. Come in here this minute."

88

She pulled Claire by the arm into the employee breakroom and shut the door behind them.

"Please forgive me," she said. "Do you have someone in here?"

"No," Claire said. "I'm volunteering."

"Thank goodness," the woman said and clutched her hand to her heart. "I love your family, and I would be devastated to hear something had happened to any one of them."

She motioned to the long table surrounded by chairs.

"Sit down," she said. "I just moved back a couple of weeks ago and my mother said you were back, too, but I've been so busy getting the kids settled and finding a job that I haven't had time to even take a breath."

"So, you're a nurse?" Claire asked, racking her brain to try to come up with the name.

She was picturing her back in high school when she'd been a very studious, shy girl with braces and glasses.

"Nope," she said. "Physician."

"I'm sorry," Claire said. "I shouldn't have assumed …"

"No worries, it happens all the time," she said. "I haven't quite got the hang of remembering to wear my ID."

She fished around in her pocket, came up with a laminated badge hanging from a lanyard, and slipped it on over her head.

'Thank goodness,' Claire thought, as she read the name.

"It's so good to see you, Jan; I don't think I've seen you since we were teenagers."

"A hundred years ago, at least," Jan said. "Mom filled me in on your exciting life; it must have been hard to move back to our bump on a log."

"I'm learning to love it," Claire said.

"I hope I can say the same, eventually," Jan said.

89

"Where were you living?"

"My husband and I were attending physicians at a hospice in Charlottesville, VA," she said. "Last year our only daughter died from a drug overdose and left us with her three children. Their father's in prison and unlikely to ever see the light of day again, thank goodness."

"I'm so sorry to hear about your daughter," Claire said. "I can't imagine how hard that is."

Jan shrugged her shoulders and stretched out her neck as if preparing to lift a heavy weight.

"As if that's not enough to deal with, my husband took up with a younger woman; he's with her in Hawaii now, playing resident physician at some swanky resort. He said he didn't want to go through raising kids again like we had a choice! I tried to do it all myself, but that's impossible. My parents are getting on, just like yours, but they offered to help, and I jumped at the chance. I tried to get them to move to Charlottesville, but you know how they are at that age. It's not my ideal scenario but when does life ever fulfill that fantasy?"

"Everyone here seems very nice," Claire said. "I've only been volunteering for a few weeks, but it seems like a well-run show."

"It is, I'm sure," Jan said. "I'm used to a much tighter ship, with more emphasis on bringing up the census and keeping the costs down, but that's the difference between a for-profit and a charitable organization."

"We'll have to get together," Claire said. "I'm living with my parents, too."

"Listen," Jan said. "How lucky are we to have them? I don't know what I would have done. I slept in last Saturday for the first day in over a year. It felt so good I cried like a baby; just the relief of having someone to help shoulder the responsibility."

Using her cell phone, Jan showed Claire pictures of her grandkids. They reminisced for a while until Jan mentioned that she had done her first medical internship at Pendleton General Hospital.

"Did you know Sophie Dean or Jillian ... it's McClanahan now, but I don't know what her maiden name was."

"Did I? Oh my goodness, you mean, as in, the big soap opera they had going on with Chippie McClanahan? That was crazy!"

"I've heard bits and pieces about it," Claire said. "What happened?"

"It was just like that movie, *All About Eve*," Jan said. "Jillian came in and boom, boom, boom; she took Sophie's job, her fiancé, and her friends. That Jillian was a piece of work, and you were either on her side or on her enemy list and, buddy, you did not want to be on that woman's bad side. I felt sorry for Sophie, but I was an exhausted intern, and I only heard about most of it from the intern in the NICU. She was on Team Sophie, of course."

"I've met them both, and I really like Sophie," Claire said. "Maybe we can all get together some time."

"That'd be great," Jan said. "Listen, I better get back to my rounds. Next time you volunteer, page me."

"I will," Claire said.

They said goodbye in the hallway and Jan was walking away when she suddenly turned back.

"I've just remembered something," Jan said. "I was taking a nap in my car one night in the hospital parking lot, and I heard a noise, looked up, and saw the weirdest thing. Sophie Dean was slitting the tires on her own car. She didn't see me, and I heard later she blamed Jillian for it. I never told a soul what I saw; I didn't want to get involved. But it just goes to show, doesn't it? Nobody's as innocent as they claim to be."

Claire thought about this on the way home.

Maybe Sophie had spray-painted her own garage, as well.

When Claire arrived at Hannah's farm, where she was supposed to meet Hannah and Maggie to go swimming in Frog Pond, they weren't there. Sam, holding Sammy, directed her down the hill.

"They're already down there," he said, chuckling. "They've been working on a project."

"Me's going to be a nastronut," Sammy said. "Me's going to the moon."

"Good for you, Sammy," Claire said and shared a friendly smile with Sam.

Claire walked down the hill to Frog Pond and stood on the gray cedar dock that had been there since she was a child. She shielded her eyes and looked far out toward the other side of the pond, where she could see something, but wasn't quite sure what it was.

"Hey!" she yelled and then whistled.

Hannah whistled back, and they began moving toward her. It wasn't until they were halfway across the pond that she could see what they were rowing.

"Oh my Lord," she laughed.

The flotation device was made up of five tractor tire inner tubes lashed to a sixth in the middle, so that the outer ones were like the petals of a big tractor tire flower. In the middle tube was an oversize tin washtub filled with ice, through the middle of which was stuck a large beach umbrella. Claire assumed the ice was chilling some good beer, and she couldn't wait to taste it.

"Avast, me Matie!" Hannah called out when they were close enough.

"How do you like it?" Maggie asked.

"It's genius," Claire said.

"Come aboard the dread pirate ship, The Black Frog!" Hannah called out. "We need a pirate flag, but I didn't have any black fabric. Maggie and I want to get your mom to make us one; do you think she would?"

"Of course she would," Claire said, as she sat back in one of the outer tubes. "This is officially the best boat ever, in the history of all boats."

Hannah had on cut-offs and a bikini top, and her skin was deeply tanned. Maggie, wearing leggings and a long-sleeved T-shirt, was shading her fair, freckled face under a wide-brimmed hat. Claire didn't own a pond-appropriate bathing suit, so she had worn her black sports bra and cut-off shorts again.

Claire leaned back and savored the chilly water and the warm sunshine. Hannah handed her a beer.

"Drink up, me hearties," she said.

"How was your second visit with Eugene?" Claire asked her.

"He's still got the lisp, but he's talking really well," Hannah said. "It's the weirdest sensation, like talking to an altogether different person living in Eugene's body."

"We thought he was slow because of his disabilities," Maggie said. "Turns out he's a smart person trapped inside a speech impediment."

"What did he say?"

"He's mad, so mad," Hannah said. "I told him it was okay to be pissed off, but if he wants to get out of there, he better start acting like a sane person."

"Are they treating him okay?" Claire asked.

"Seems like it," Hannah said. "I know a couple of the nurses, so I told them the whole story. Your boyfriend, Doctor Lovemuffin, thinks he'll be out tomorrow."

"I have to go to the hospital with the attorney to pick him up," Claire said. "I can't take him back to his house, he can't stay with me, and I'm certainly not going to suggest Chip and Jillian take him in."

"I already talked to him about it," Hannah said. "We're going to fix up the barn loft for him."

"The lab?"

When Simon and Lily had owned the farm, Simon had used the barn loft as a lab for his agricultural experiments, which mainly concerned developing an extra potent, drought- and pest-resistant marijuana plant.

"We cleaned it up today, and Ed and Scott are going to move some of Scott's mom's furniture up there this evening. It'll be nice for him. If we can get all his rocks out of his mom's house, we can set up his shop in the barn. First, Scott has to get permission from Chairman Meow."

"Any progress in the police investigation?" Claire asked Maggie.

"Scott won't tell me anything," Maggie said. "Skip and Frank are forbidden to talk to either of us."

"Skip will crack first," Hannah said. "I know how his tiny brain works. I have a plan involving beer and nacho-flavored chips."

Claire told them about meeting Jan at the hospice house.

"Poor her!" Hannah said. "She was such a brainiac. I copied off her all the time, and she was always so nice about it."

"Boo hoo, she's a doctor," Maggie said. "She'll be just fine. She can cry into a big bag of money."

"You're such a witch," Claire said. "Anyway, listen to what she told me about Sophie Dean ..."

After they rehashed their gathered evidence and went over various, increasingly ludicrous potential murder scenarios, they floated for a while in silence, Hannah and Claire sipping their icy cold beers, Maggie nursing her usual root beer.

Claire closed her eyes and listened to the classic summer sounds of her youth: the chirping crickets, the peeping frogs, the buzzing of the occasional locust, and Hannah's long, musical burps.

"If you could go back in time, knowing everything you know now," Claire said, "what age would you go back to, and what would you do differently?"

"Back to when I first met Gabe," Maggie said. "I'd punch him in the nose and throw him out of the bakery."

"Your mother would've loved that," Hannah said. "What about you, Claire?"

"The summer I was seventeen," she said. "I made so many life-changing mistakes that summer, and I would do everything differently."

"But then you would have missed out on your world travels," Hannah said. "You wouldn't have met all those movie stars and stayed in all those classy hotels."

"Wasn't worth it," Claire said. "It was all fake, every bit of it. I was wasting my time on a thrill ride instead of living a real life."

"You would've been bored out of your mind here," Maggie said.

Claire was remembering having a similar conversation with Laurie when he had expressed the same opinion.

'I always liked Maggie,' Laurie said in her head. 'She's a fierce amazon woman with a glorious Titian mane.'

Claire mentally batted him away like a fly.

"What about you, Hannah?" Claire said.

"I wouldn't change a thing," she said. "I've got it made."

"The funny thing is, Claire, she really means it," Maggie said.

"Whaddaya mean?" Hannah said. "I love my life. I wouldn't trade it for anybody else's for any amount of money."

"That's great," Claire said. "I'm glad somebody's happy."

"What's happy got to do with it?" Hannah said. "I'm only happy about twice a week for five minutes. I'm saying I'm glad I have what I have, that I'm grateful for it."

"Compared to most people in the world," Maggie said, "you're a rich woman, living in a rich country, with a healthy child who's been immunized, has plenty of food to eat, and clean water to drink."

"And Blue Moonshine Slershies," Hannah said. "Don't forget about those."

They could now hear the sound of male voices in the distance, laughing as they came down the hill toward the dock.

"Shiver me timbers!" Hannah said. "I hear the sons of a biscuit eater. Batten down the hatches, man the cannons, and prepare to fire!"

Hannah pulled a large, plastic water cannon out of the pond, where it was attached to her inner tube with twine. Maggie searched through the ice until she found a water gun.

"I'm unarmed," Claire said. "What'll I do?"

"Smile and wave," Hannah said. "You're the bait."

CHAPTER FIVE

laire took Sammy firmly by the hand as she led him across the hot cinders that covered the pool parking lot. He had his inflatable swimmies on his arms and was carrying a water gun.

Claire hadn't been to the Rose Hill Community Pool since she was a teenager. It made her cringe to think of the idiot she'd been back then. At the tender age of seventeen, she'd seduced her ex-husband Pip while hanging out there, where he was a lifeguard. Her face burned just thinking about what they had got up to in the women's shower room after hours. She'd been an inexperienced child in the body of an adult woman; Pip had been Pip, which is to say, an idiot child in a man's body, a condition that had never changed.

Claire paid for them to get in.

"Me wants a Moonshine Slershy," Sammy said. "Please, Claire, please, please, please!"

"After we swim a while," she said.

"How long is a wile?" he asked.

"I'll let you know," she said.

They passed through the showers, where they were supposed to rinse off before they got in the pool. Claire didn't plan to get her hair or face wet if she could help it, so she kept moving. Outside on the concrete patio that surrounded the pool, people had beach towels and beach chairs set up, and children screamed and laughed.

What was it about a large body of water that made their voices so shrill, Claire wondered.

'And yet you claim to long for your own child,' Laurie said. 'Methinks you like the idea more than the actual practice.'

"Shut up," Claire said.

"Me no shut up," Sammy said. "You's shut up. You's mean, Claire."

"Sorry, Sammy, I wasn't talking to you," Claire said. "Let's get you in the pool."

"Me no like the big pool," Sammy said.

"I know, Sammy," Claire said.

"Me only goes in the big pool with Daddy."

"I know, Sammy, Hannah told me."

As soon as they got within ten feet of the kiddie pool, Sammy pulled his hand free and shouted to the children in the water, "Me's coming! Me's going to shoot you with me's water gun!"

Claire noticed a couple of mothers removing their toddlers from the water while casting not-so-discreet shade toward Sammy as they did so. Claire had learned it was best to ignore those kinds of people, with their bubble-wrapped children, whenever she took Sammy somewhere. Luckily, there were some other children present whose mothers were a bit more relaxed, so he had plenty of playmates.

Claire unhooked the lawn chair from her shoulder and set it down in the grass underneath one of the pool-provided beach umbrellas. She took off her wide-brimmed beach hat, her designer sunglasses, and her rhinestone-studded sandals. She didn't plan to get any more sun than was unavoidable during the hottest part of the day, the better to stave off the inevitable aging process. She kept her eyes fixed on Sammy while she applied sunscreen, and ignored the curious looks of her fellow child-minders. She wasn't there to make friends, and she didn't intend to stay one minute longer than the hour she had promised Sammy.

98

'Returning to the scene of the crime, eh?' Laurie said.

There were no good memories at this pool.

A young woman arrived with four rowdy children and spread out a beach towel in full sunlight. Claire guessed the children's ages were from two to eight. The woman had no beach tote full of the supplies like the other mothers or babysitters, nor the ubiquitous bottle of sunscreen they all slathered on their charges every half hour; just kids, beach towel, and bikini.

Thin, but curvy in all the right places, with long blonde hair and deeply tanned skin, she had an enviable figure for a mother of that many children. Her bikini consisted of a few tiny scraps of fabric held together with string, and there were no tan lines. Claire decided she must be the nanny, not the mom.

'No woman with half a brain would hire someone that hot to mind their children,' Laurie said.

As soon as she was settled, she shooed the children off to "go play," and reclined in the sun, oblivious to the disapproving stares of the assembled.

"She's not even watching that baby," one mother hissed to another. "It can't be more than three."

"She'll leave it for us to do," the other mother said. "She's one of those."

"How their children survive is beyond me," the first said.

"Survival of the fittest," the second said. "Like mongrel dogs."

Claire agreed that the mother was a little too slack for her toddler's best interests, but the term "mongrel" got her back up.

Snobby witches.

The two older children ran off to the big pool, and the next-to-smallest tended to the smallest in the kiddie pool. Claire watched with interest as they encountered

Sammy, who showed them his gun and then let the littlest one play with it.

Claire was pleased to see Sammy playing nicely with these two newcomers. Just then a shadow fell between her and the pool, and she looked up to see her ex-husband, Phillip Deacon, also known as Pip.

"Hey, Claire," he said, and dropped down next to her chair, water streaming off his dreadlocks and the bleached-out orange swim trunks that hung off his beautiful rear end.

'Look at those eyes,' Laurie said. 'He's higher than panties up a flagpole at summer camp.'

Pip was built like the masculine equivalent of a brick shit-house, long, lean, tanned, muscled, and golden-haired, but was completely and utterly "do-less," as they said around these parts. His official trade was construction, but his hobbies of pot-smoking, fornicating, napping, and money-borrowing took up most of his time. If work avoidance had a poster child, it would be Pip Deacon.

Claire watched out of the corner of her eye as the snobby witches put their heads together and whispered. She knew the type. They might look down their noses at Pip in the daylight, but they also might fantasize about him while their pudgy, soft husbands got busy on top of them in their darkened bedrooms later that night. Pip had been known to break up marriages once the bored wives decided to turn fantasy into reality.

'One might be led to think you were still interested,' Laurie said.

"What are you doing here?" Claire asked, still keeping her eye on Sammy.

"Jessie's here with the kids," he said and gestured to the two children Sammy was playing with.

The penny dropped, her mind machinery whirred, and Claire realized who the slacker mom was. She'd never actually met the child-bride, Jessie, but she'd heard a lot about her. Pip met her while doing construction work on her parents' palatial beachfront estate. Jessie's mother was a successful executive in the film business, and her father was a plastic surgeon. Part of what rankled was that Claire had got him that job.

"Are you two back together?"

Pip shrugged.

"Sort of."

"How'd that happen?" she asked. "I thought her parents paid for your bail on condition that she get a divorce."

"They did," he said. "They also paid for her to finish Massage Therapy School. As soon as she graduated, she decided to come here. They're not happy, but there's nothing they can do about it. She's going to work for Gwyneth at the inn."

"Ahh, I see," Claire said. "Where is everyone living?"

"With mom," he said. "I'm in between jobs right now."

"I see," Claire said. "Are the kids enrolled in school here?"

"Not yet," he said. "Jessie wants to homeschool them, so she's trying to work out something with the county. They're being complete buttheads, as usual. We wouldn't have this kind of trouble in California."

"So, why didn't you go out there?" Claire asked.

"It was kind of a surprise when they showed up," Pip said. "I didn't know they were coming."

"Kind of an inconvenience, then," she said. "Girlfriend-wise, I mean."

"Yeah, you could say that," he said with a laugh. "I had a couple close calls that first week."

"Her parents are sending money, I guess."

"Nope," he said. "They cut her off as soon as they found out where she went."

Claire knew what he was going to say before he said it. She was already shaking her head as he started to speak.

'Four, three, two, one,' Laurie said.

"I could use a loan, Claire," he said. "Just a couple hundred until I get started somewhere. I've got an interview for a fracking job in Wetzel County. They pay buttloads of money. I'll be able to pay you back."

"Nope," Claire said. "Not even tempted."

"They're just little kids," he said. "They need shoes and diapers and stuff. My mom's being a real bitch about it, as usual. It's not my fault they showed up here with no money."

Laurie played melodramatic piano music in her head.

"I guess it's also not your fault you have four children and an ex-wife you can't support."

"I didn't want any kids," he said. "She just kept getting pregnant."

"Funny how that happens," Claire said.

"C'mon, Claire," he said. "I know you've got it. You must've got two million for that condo we owned."

"*We* didn't own anything," Claire said. "I paid all the mortgage payments, the insurance, and the taxes."

"We were married in California," he said. "It's a community property state. Mom says I should've gotten half of everything."

"You signed the divorce agreement, I believe, on the same day that first one was born," she said. "You didn't want the condo or spousal support then."

'Oh, snap,' Laurie said.

Pip shrugged.

"She had rich parents," he said. "I didn't think I'd need it."

"Funny how it's turned out, then, isn't it?"

"C'mon, Claire," he said.

Sammy crawled out of the pool and came running toward Claire.

"Me's ready for me's Moonshine Slershy," he said.

"Hey, little buddy," Pip said. "Remember me?"

"Me no like you," Sammy said. "You's mean to Claire."

"God, Claire," Pip said. "I wish you'd quit talking crap about me."

"You hafta gimme a dollar for cussing," Sammy said, and held out his hand.

"Haven't got it," Pip said, and then grinned at Claire.

"C'mon, Sammy," Claire said.

She gathered up their things and slung the lawn chair over her shoulder. She took Sammy by the hand and led him away from Pip, praying he wouldn't follow.

Pip *was* like a stray mongrel. Claire was done falling for those puppy-dog eyes and feeding him on the porch. Pip had a string of porches he liked to visit, and there was a long line of soft-hearted women who had tried to domesticate him.

Claire was determined not to look at his ex-wife as she passed her, but let herself take a quick peripheral look. Jesse's round breasts were falling out of her bikini top, and the bottoms barely covered what her Aunt Bonnie would've called "her business."

'Very nice,' Laurie said. 'Sorry, Claire, but I can see the appeal.'

How dare she look that good after four children?

Claire comforted herself by imagining what the woman's skin would look like in ten years.

'Now, don't be bitter,' Laurie said. 'You were glad enough to be rid of him at the time.'

"Moonshine Slershy!" Sammy insisted.

"Okay," Claire said. "If you tell me the names of those little girls you were playing with."

"Dat baby is Pixie like candy," he said. "Dat big one is Boo Bell."

"Blue Bell?"

"Me sayed that," he said.

'Are you surprised?' Laurie asked.

"Figures," Claire said. "Poor kids."

After Claire dropped Sammy off at Hannah's, she stopped by Maggie's bookstore, Little Bear Books, to pick up an iced cappuccino to go. As she stood in the long line that snaked up to the counter, she observed the college students who took up all the available seats in the café. There were lots of long beards and handlebar mustaches on the young men, and the young women were wearing beach waves in their long, ombre-shaded hair. One current fashion was to have purple, pink, or green stripes in their hair, and one young woman had a virtual rainbow flowing down her back. Claire missed doing hair and idly wondered if she should open a salon in one of the empty storefronts in town.

'You cut my hair once,' Laurie said. 'The night you gave me whiskey and sent me off into the cold, cruel world alone.'

Claire was immediately taken back to that night. Her impulsive offer of a drink had set off a bender that ended with him unconscious in Scott's house while he was supposed to be subbing for him as police chief. It was one of the things she tortured herself about, among many others.

'I know," Claire said. 'I might just as well have put a loaded gun to your head and pulled the trigger.'

'You didn't force me to drink,' he said. 'You just reminded me why I wanted to.'

Claire fled the line for the restroom, which, fortunately, was empty. She locked the door and sank to

104

the floor, crying. When she came out, Maggie was standing there, arms crossed, a fierce look on her face.

"You come with me," she said, as she crooked a finger.

Maggie led her upstairs to her apartment, down the hall to the kitchen.

"Sit," Maggie commanded.

Claire sat down at the kitchen table and rested her head on her arms.

She was so tired, just exhausted down into her bones.

Maggie put the teakettle on the gas ring and placed two mugs on the table. When the kettle whistled, she poured hot water over tea bags in the mugs and sat down.

"Now, you're going to tell me what's going on or I'm going to tell your mother what just happened," Maggie said.

"I'm just tired."

"Nope, there's more," Maggie said. "You've been acting weird, and I want to know why."

"I don't even know how to begin," Claire said.

"Out with it," Maggie said. "There's nothing you can say that will shock me."

Claire took a deep breath. Maggie was very stubborn, and a little psychic like her mother Bonnie, and Claire knew Maggie wouldn't let her leave her apartment until she knew everything.

"You knew Laurie, right?"

"Of course, he was a friend of Scott's."

"While you were on your honeymoon, and he was subbing for Scott, he and I got involved."

"I was only gone a month," Maggie said. "He died before we got back."

"It wasn't long," Claire said. "But it was very fast and intense."

"So, you slept with him, no big deal," Maggie said. "I can see the attraction. He was a smart-ass, and you've always had a weakness for smart alecks."

"I didn't sleep with him, although I wanted to. I know it doesn't seem like long enough to be serious or meaningful, but for me, it was. For him, too, I think."

"I'm sorry, Claire, I didn't know," Maggie said. "Why didn't you tell us?"

"I wanted to keep it a secret," Claire said. "It seemed so crazy to get that attached to someone in such a short time, and also because I didn't want to hurt Ed."

"I'm not a member of Ed's fan club, as I'm sure he'll tell you," Maggie said. "You're the one who matters to me."

"I love Ed," Claire said. "Laurie and I would never have worked out in the long run; too many demons, too many complications."

"You're romanticizing him because he's dead."

"No, not at all," Claire said. "I saw him very clearly, but I still loved him, despite that; even though I also love Ed. It was different with Laurie. I can't explain why."

"No need to," Maggie said. "I loved Gabe and Scott until Gabe almost got Scott killed."

"Do you still think about Gabe?"

"Less and less," Maggie said. "It almost seems like something that happened to someone else."

"I don't want to let go," Claire said, which brought on fresh tears.

"You have to," Maggie said. "You have to get hold of yourself and get on with your life. He's dead, you're alive, and nothing's going to change that."

"I know you're right."

"You're depressed," Maggie said. "That's why you're sleeping so much and don't want to do anything fun."

"I do, too, do fun things with you guys."

"But you're not really there when you do," Maggie said. "We've both noticed."

"I only sleep late because I have trouble going to sleep at night," Claire said. "All these recriminations and regrets just swirl around in my brain, and it hurts, Maggie. It's a physical pain."

"I remember what that's like," Maggie said. "After Gabe disappeared, all I could do was go over and over that last day, and wonder what I did wrong, what happened."

"I don't know what to do with my life. I'm just sort of flailing around, and I can't concentrate on anything long enough to make a plan."

"You need to go see Doc Machalvie," Maggie said. "You need to stop this before it spirals out of control."

"Did you take an antidepressant after Gabe left?"

"Finally," Maggie said. "After Hannah threatened to have me committed."

"I didn't know," Claire said.

"Only Hannah and Scott know," Maggie said, "and I didn't tell Scott until after we were married."

"What did he say?"

"He just wanted to know if I could up the dose until I was nicer."

"What did it feel like?"

"It put an emotional floor underneath me, just like Doc Machalvie said it would. Nothing about my personality changed, sorry to tell you, but my lows weren't bottomless anymore, and I began to see the light where it had only been dark. It wasn't that I couldn't feel pain or have sad thoughts, they just didn't incapacitate me like they had."

"How long did you take it?"

"I never stopped."

"Really?"

"In the Fitzpatrick family, my dear cousin, we come from a long line of devout self-medicators. They were either fat, like Grandma Rose, or alcoholics, like my dear papa. I chose a prescribed medication to keep me from embracing the family's traditional medications: sugar and alcohol."

"Doc offered it after I first came home," Claire said. "Up until Laurie died, I think I was handling everything okay."

"Go see him," Maggie said. "It's the wisest thing I ever did."

"We'll see," Claire said.

"I'm keeping an eye on you," Maggie said. "Don't make me tell Hannah, or you'll get a pirate-themed intervention. She'll dress up Eugene as Mr. Smee."

"Oh, my gosh, Eugene," Claire said. "I was supposed to meet Walter fifteen minutes ago to pick him up."

Hannah walked down Possum Holler to visit Cheat McClanahan. Halfway down the narrow gravel road she crested a hill and could see his house. There, on the front porch, was a young woman who looked as though she was leaving, and parked out front was a brand new red Mustang with a temporary license tag. The woman looked up in her direction as Hannah came into view, and then she stopped, looked at the Mustang, turned around, and started beating on the front door. The language she used was colorful, all words Hannah wished she could still say, but because of her son, Sammy, could not do so without pecuniary repercussions.

Hannah walked up to the end of the broken cement walkway that led to the porch and watched as the young woman took out her very visible frustrations on Cheat's front door. The crux of the situation seemed to be that he owed her money, that she deemed his birth illegitimate, and that she intended to use her foot to inflict upon him bodily harm in an area of his personage where sunlight was unlikely to shine. All of this was delivered very dramatically, and with an excess of emotion, at the top of her voice.

Hannah thought she seemed very young.

When she paused, turned around, and acknowledged Hannah, she pretended to be surprised.

"What are you looking at?"

"Cheat home?" Hannah asked her.

"Yeah, he's in there," the young woman said. "He doesn't go anywhere without that truck; God forbid he should walk somewhere, the lazy son of a bitch."

"He owes you money?"

"I clean houses for him, and the damn check bounced. Bastard owes me twelve hundred dollars."

The young woman was very pretty, with long dark hair and a curvy figure. She wore a very short skirt, a very tight shirt, and very high heels. There was a lot of spangly silver jewelry and dramatic make-up. Hannah thought that without all the trimmings, she probably looked sixteen years old. With it, she could pass for eighteen, which was most likely the point.

She was shaking, either with fear or rage, Hannah hadn't decided. There was definitely something exciting going on.

"Did you go around back and knock?" Hannah asked.

The young woman looked longingly at her car.

"I have to be at my other job soon," she said. "I can't wait around here all day."

"Let's try the back door," Hannah said. "Maybe he's in the shower."

The young woman hesitated, her eyes darting here and there. Finally, she drew herself up and said, "Why not?"

Hannah walked around the side of the house to the back, where it seemed Cheat liked to smoke, based on the number of cigarette butts discarded in a semicircle on the ground just beyond a sagging armchair on the back porch. Hannah peeked through the dirty glass of the door and saw Cheat, sprawled out on the kitchen floor.

"Well, there's your problem," Hannah said to the young woman, who was standing just to the side of the porch. "He's passed out on the floor; must have had a big night last night."

Hannah tried the knob and easily opened the door.

"Cheat," she called out, but Cheat did not move.

It was deathly quiet inside the house, and there was a sour smell.

Hannah froze in the midst of taking a step inside. She looked at the young woman, who looked back at her with naked dread, plus something hard and cold in her eyes.

"Is he dead?" she asked Hannah.

"You tell me," Hannah said quietly.

The young woman took off, and Hannah let her go. She took out her cell phone and punched in the speed dial number for the Rose Hill City Police Station.

Skip answered.

"I've got another dead McClanahan," Hannah said. "It's Cheat this time."

While she waited for the cavalry to arrive, Hannah went around to the front of the house and, using the tail of her T-shirt, turned the knob on the front door. Just as Hannah suspected it would, the door opened. She shut the door and sat down on the front porch steps.

Hannah closed her eyes and mentally retraced her steps to the top of the hill, where she first saw the young woman on Cheat's front porch. What had the woman been doing before she noticed Hannah watching and began her histrionics? Did Hannah actually see her close the door and prepare to leave? She definitely remembered thinking the girl was leaving, not arriving. But did she see her close the door?

She couldn't say for sure.

Claire and attorney Walter Graham were in a private waiting room in the hospital, waiting to speak to Dr. Schweitzer. They were supposed to meet with him before Eugene was released into their care.

"These accommodations you've got lined up at your cousin's farm," Walter said. "Will he be safe there?"

"Hannah's been a good friend to Eugene since we were kids. Her husband, Sam, used to do security work for the government. Now he works with injured vets who need prosthetics and physical therapy. They're good people, they're fond of him, they know the situation, and they won't let anything happen to him."

"If his mother was murdered, he might be safer here."

"If the murderer is who I think it is, he's less safe in here," Claire said.

"I know Jillian is a troubled woman, with poor impulse control ..." he said, "but surely ..."

"Exactly the type of person who might act first and worry about the consequences later," Claire said.

Chip McClanahan knocked on the door frame as he entered the room. Claire hoped he hadn't heard what they were saying about his wife.

Time had been kind to Chip, and instead of the gangly, awkward boy she remembered, he was a handsome, tall man dressed in a professionally tailored suit.

"Claire," he said, as he hugged her in greeting.

He smelled like spearmint gum and musky, sweet cologne that Claire found cloying.

He shook Walter's hand, and they made small talk about the friends they had in common. Claire knew this was a way to establish social standing, and felt like an anthropologist observing their behavior.

"I guess you're in charge of Eugene, now," Chip said to Claire. "I'm not sure why that happened; I assumed Jillian and I would be taking care of things, but I guess Aunt Gigi had her reasons ..."

"I had the privilege of being your uncle and aunt's attorney for over thirty years," Walter said. "Her reasons are, of course, privileged information between client and attorney, but I can tell you she was in complete control of her faculties, and her decision was made after considerable thought using a sound mind."

"I see," Chip said. "Well, I guess the reason will just have to remain a mystery. Who knows why people do what they do? I was afraid Jillian had done something to offend her; which wouldn't be that unusual. Jillian can be very outspoken, and Aunt Gigi could be sensitive. Claire, you've got your work cut out for you; I have to admit I'm a little relieved. Eugene can be a handful, and if what the police are thinking is true ..."

"The police chief I know is keeping an open mind," Claire said. "I don't think Eugene has anything to worry about."

Chip gave Claire an irritated look, which he quickly covered with a concerned frown.

"It's certainly a sad situation," he said. "I hear Eugene's made good progress here, but he's still very angry. He didn't want to see me, and I honored his wishes. I'm not sure my being here today is a good idea, but he's my cousin, and I feel responsible for him. He's welcome to live with us, of course, though I doubt he'll want to."

"You weren't close growing up?" Walter asked.

Claire was surprised. She was certain Walter knew all the family business, financial and personal. She realized then, with amusement, that Walter was doing some investigating.

"I was close with my aunt and uncle, of course, because they raised me," Chip said. "I wouldn't have anything if it weren't for them. Uncle Eugene was like a father to me, and Aunt Gigi was very supportive. Now, with both of them gone, I feel like an orphan."

"I take it you're not close with your own father," Walter said.

"No," Chip said. "We haven't been on speaking terms for a long time. My father's what they call a colorful character. He was never interested in being a parent."

"And Eugene Junior?" Walter asked. "Was he like a brother to you?"

"Sure, sure," Chip said. "It was just hard to communicate with him because of his mental and physical problems. He didn't like me, he resented his parents' affection for me, and frankly, I think he was so jealous he couldn't see beyond that."

"I see," Walter said. "Well, if that's the case, maybe you shouldn't be here, Chip. I appreciate the effort, I recognize that you feel a certain responsibility, and I'll be sure to let Eugene know that you stopped by."

"Oh," Chip said. "You don't think I should stay?"

"No," Walter said. "In fact, I think it would be detrimental if you did. I know you want what's best for him, so let's make this transition as stress-free as possible."

"Oh, okay," Chip said with a shrug. "Well, then, I'll just go, I guess. It was good to see both of you."

He shook hands with Walter and gave Claire another quick hug.

"Tell your mom I said hi," he told her. "I miss seeing her at church."

After he left the room and closed the door, Claire looked at Walter.

"What was that all about?"

"I'm going to read the will tomorrow after the funeral, and he's not going to be happy about what it says,"

Walter said. "He thinks he's getting everything, or close to everything when in reality he's not getting one thin dime."

"Really?"

"The day you signed the papers making you a guardian to Eugene Junior, you also witnessed her signature on a new will that cut him and Jillian completely out," he said. "Everything goes into a trust for Eugene Junior."

"Was it Jillian she was mad at?"

"Jillian irritated Gigi, that's all," Walter said. "She once said Jillian reminded her of a younger version of herself. The social striving, the ambition ... Gigi came from a very underprivileged background; she worked her way up from nothing to something, and she recognized that hunger in Jillian. She didn't resent that, she just didn't like the way Jillian treated Chip like he was her servant.

"Gigi waited on her husband hand and foot. She saw that as his reward for rescuing her, for marrying her. She never made him regret it. I think Chip probably regrets marrying Jillian. Gigi said she embarrasses him, even emasculates him, quite publicly and frequently. They both make good salaries here, but their lifestyle is still way beyond their means. He may anticipate an inheritance will enable him to escape the marriage."

"You don't think he would have killed Gigi to get the money?"

"Money is often a motive," Walter said. "And the previous will would have made him a rich man. He has just as much motive as his wife, maybe more."

"If Eugene inherits everything, he would have to be eliminated for Chip to inherit."

"I've been thinking about that," Walter said. "I'm working on a will for Eugene that would remove that possibility."

"Let's get him to sign that straight away."

"Easy, now," Walter said. "Let's get him somewhere safe and settled first. Once the will is read, I'll meet with him to talk about his own estate plans."

"Did Gigi tell you what she was so mad at Chip about?"

"She did," he said.

"Doesn't privilege end at death?"

"It does."

"So, spill it," Claire said, and Walter laughed.

"I'm going to enjoy being on Eugene's team with you," he said. "Privilege may have expired, but discretion is still the better part of valor. I can't have my living clients thinking I'll gossip about them after they're gone."

"Nonsense," Claire said. "The other day at lunch you told me story after story about your dead clients."

"You're a bad influence on me," he said.

"Just give me a hint," she said. "I'm swearing before you and God that I will not tell who told me."

Walter smiled, looking greatly amused. He lowered his voice and leaned in.

"Just over the county line, out by the highway, there is an establishment that goes by the provocative name Tiger Tails."

"Yes, and ..."

"That's it, really," he said. "You drive by there some night and see if you don't find Chip's newest BMW parked behind the building, where he thinks no one can see it."

"Oooooh, does Jillian know?"

"I can't imagine he'd still be married to her if she did."

The door opened, and Dr. Schweitzer came in. He shook Walter's hand and then Claire's, and he blushed when he did so. Making a psychiatrist blush was no mean feat, and Claire wondered what Hannah had been saying to him. Her diminutive cousin was an unrepentant matchmaker, and Claire had often found herself in awkward situations due to her romantic meddling.

"So," Dr. Schweitzer said. "Let's talk about Eugene. Shall we sit?"

Later that evening, Claire was sitting at Hannah's kitchen table while Sam was giving Sammy a bath in the upstairs bathroom. Everyone else had dispersed after attempting to make Eugene feel welcome. It had just been the three cousins, their significant others, Sammy, and Eugene at dinner, but their good intentions seemed to have had the opposite effect, unfortunately, making him withdraw into himself, uncomfortable with all the attention. Eugene was now tucked up in his barn studio apartment, where they were giving him some space, some time alone.

"You were supposed to wait for me to go see Cheat," Claire said.

"I got tired of waiting," Hannah said.

"When we were down at the hospital talking to Chip," Claire said, "I don't think he knew Cheat was dead."

"I found Cheat about the time you picked up Eugene."

"At least he has an alibi," Claire said. "And so does Chip, for that matter."

"Depending on how long Cheat had been dead and what killed him," Hannah said. "The ambulance driver said the body was still warm."

"What do you think killed him?"

Hannah shrugged.

"Death by teenage floozy, I guess," she said.

"Could have been a heart attack or a stroke."

"Or poison."

"And the girl?"

"She looked familiar to me, but I can't think where I've seen her."

"You think she killed him?"

"She was acting so weird, I think if she didn't kill him she found him dead and wanted me to think she hadn't been in the house."

"Did you get her tag number?"

"Of course I did. What do you think I am, an amateur?"

"She said she cleaned houses for him?"

"He managed all those rentals."

"It was someone who still thinks Chip will inherit, and wants all other potential heirs out of the way."

"Or someone Cheat saw up at the house that day. Someone who didn't want him to tell."

"Someone he was blackmailing, maybe?"

"Wouldn't put it past him."

"Jillian."

"Maybe Cheat saw Jillian up at Gigi's earlier in the day when she put something Gigi was allergic to in her food or drink ..."

"Or injected her with something; she was a nurse."

"But why would Gigi let her inject something, anything?" Claire asked. "Was she a diabetic? Did she regularly inject something?"

"Gail Goodwin cleans the house and has known Gigi since they were girls in grade school," Hannah said. "She says Gigi was as healthy as a horse and was only allergic to penicillin."

"What did Gail say about the cup?"

"All present and accounted for. They let her back in this morning."

"How many ways could you get penicillin into someone? Food, drink, injection?"

"There are antibiotics in some meat," Hannah said. "Maybe one bite of hamburger and, boom, she's dead."

"I don't know if that's enough to kill someone."

"I'll call Elvis and get him to look into it for me," Hannah said. "He'll report back, and I'll let you know."

"Elvis, as in the twelve-year-old who's going to college at Stanford?"

"He's a genius," Hannah said. "He told me that if you can smell poop, you're actually inhaling poop particles."

"That's disgusting."

"Makes you think, though, doesn't it, about public restrooms?"

"Gross, Hannah."

"He's one of my best resources. He doesn't care what time I call, and he loves to do research."

"Someone who knew she had a penicillin allergy makes sure she gets enough to kill her," Claire said. "That would explain the swelling and the hives."

"Jillian would know."

"So would Chip," Claire said. "Even if she didn't tell him, he has access to all the medical records at the hospital."

"Are you going to the funeral?"

"Wouldn't miss it."

They walked outside and looked up toward the barn.

"Is it weird I kind of want to sit out here all night to make sure nobody messes with him?" Claire asked.

"Sam has motion detectors set up everywhere. Nobody is going to get anywhere near him."

"I'm so glad," Claire said. "I need Sam to put a GPS on my dad."

"He could do it," Hannah said. "In his watch or on his belt. Just say the word."

"We're lucky if he remembers to wear pants," Claire said. "I'll meet you at the funeral home tomorrow, say about fifteen minutes before?"

"No way," Hannah said. "We get there at least an hour beforehand and stake out the best seats. We have to observe everyone as they arrive and see who acts the guiltiest; or who acts the fakest, anyhow."

"Sorry, rookie mistake."

"Stick with me, kid, I'll turn you into a junior detective in no time."

"What are the scanner grannies saying?"

The scanner grannies were a group of Rose Hill senior citizens who used illegal scanners to listen in on cordless and cell phone calls.

"Nine out of ten scanner grannies think Jillian did it," Hannah said. "The tenth one thinks it was aliens."

"Are they often correct?"

"Nine times out of ten," Hannah said. "These crimes have a distinctly Jillian sneakiness to them. Whoever did this is resourceful, cunning, and has a pathological talent for acting."

"A sociopath, in other words."

"If he's hanging out in strip clubs and doesn't think Jillian will find out, Chip certainly isn't bright enough to have pulled this off."

"I could swear he didn't know Cheat was dead," Claire said. "If he knew, he's a scary psychopath."

"Watch your back," Hannah said. "You're an obstacle now, too, you know."

Claire stopped by the newspaper office and found Ed there, talking to a couple of very attractive young women. Very young and dressed in the latest body-baring fashions, they were flirting with him, she could tell, all soft girlishness and big round eyes, laughing at his bad jokes, no doubt.

When Claire walked in, they looked her up and down and exchanged amused glances. Claire walked up to

Ed, who was gratifyingly glad to see her and kissed him on the cheek.

"Hi, Honey," she said. "You about ready to quit working?"

"Sure," he said. "Hilly and Posy just happened to be passing and saw me working. They're in one of my classes. Girls, this is Claire."

They smirked at Claire and smiled brightly at Ed.

"We better be going," Hilly said.

"See you tomorrow, Professor Harrison," Posy said.

As soon as the door shut behind them, Claire bent him back over the work table and laid one on him, just in case they were still looking.

"Whoa," he said, as soon as she let him up. "What was that about?"

"Just marking my territory," she said. "I may pee a circle around your house later."

"Mark me anytime," he said. "I thought maybe it was the new beard."

"Oh, it is," Claire said.

"Did Eugene get settled?" Ed asked her. "I felt so sorry for him this evening. It was way too much. I warned Hannah about that, but she said it would mean more to him later, when he looked back, and that was what was important. She said his first instinct is to freeze. It takes him a while to process things, and then he decides how he feels about them."

"I was just relieved he didn't vomit and faint."

"The medication seems to be working," Ed said. "I couldn't believe how much better he can speak."

"Dr. Schweitzer said chronic stuttering can be related to too much dopamine in the system, kind of like Tourette syndrome. I didn't understand everything he said, but he's got Eugene on a dopamine-blocking antipsychotic medication, and it's smoothed things out somewhat. Eugene's also going to keep visiting a psychologist and a speech therapist, and the doctor's hoping things will improve even further."

"He still stuttered, but it wasn't the paralyzing kind of lockup he used to have. Now he stutters but keeps going."

"He will still stutter, especially when stressed," Claire said. "At least now there's some hope for him. That may help his self-esteem."

"What about side effects?"

"It's a list as long as your arm. Basically, if it doesn't kill him, he'll do fine."

"Did Dr. Schweitzer say if he thought Eugene could harm someone?"

"He said Eugene gave no indication he had harmed his mother. On the contrary, he's grieving very deeply. He's confused as to why someone would kill her, and he's having a hard time accepting she's gone."

"It will take a while," Ed said. "I hope that he's strong enough to get through it."

Claire was feeling Laurie's presence and was telling him to go away.

"Are you okay?" Ed asked her. "You seem preoccupied and down lately. Is everything all right?"

"I'm okay," Claire said and embraced him. "I'm just kind of lost, and looking for the path out of whatever this funk is."

"Let me show you the way," Ed said, as he switched off the lights in the office, and locked the door.

"Professor Harrison," Claire said. "I didn't see this on the syllabus."

"It's for extra credit," he said. "And only for you."

Ed's son, Tommy, was home when they got there, watching TV on the couch. He greeted them with the usual, "'Sup?"

Claire asked him about Jillian and Chip's son.

"He's an ass-hat," Tommy said.

"Language," Ed said.

"He's the head covering for a human posterior," Tommy said.

"Much better," Ed said.

"How so?" Claire asked him.

"One of those spoiled rich kids," Tommy said. "Has a convertible sports car, pops his collars, you know the type."

"Ew," Claire said. "I do."

"He's always bragging about their vacations and all the stuff they buy for him," Tommy said. "He's obnoxious, but he's, like, boy-band-pretty, so all the girls swoon when he walks down the hall."

"Like?" Ed said.

"Sorry," Tommy said. "I'm working on it."

"Does he have a steady girlfriend?"

"Nah," Tommy said. "Apparently, nobody's good enough for him. He says he's going to be a sports agent and only date models."

"Is he good at sports?" Ed asked him.

"He's good at looking in every mirror he passes," Tommy said.

"Does he get in fights, or get in trouble at school?" Claire asked him.

"Not that I know of," Tommy said. "Why?"

Claire told Tommy about the case.

"Wow!" Tommy said. "You think Chip's dad might have done it?"

"No," Ed said. "Claire's just nosy."

"You, Hannah, and Maggie should open a detective agency," Tommy said. "You're good at it."

"The Three Cousins Detective Agency," Claire said.

"The Nosy Neighbor Detective Agency," Ed said.

"No, I've got it," Tommy said. "The Curious Cousins Detective Agency."

"Perfect," Claire said.

"I'm gonna go design your logo," Tommy said.

He jumped up and hurried down the hall.

"Have you given any more thought to my business idea?" Ed asked her.

"It's a good idea, and somebody should definitely do it, but it's just not me."

"But, it's brilliant," he said. "We get you a van, and turn the inside into a state-of-the-art salon, and you can take your salon to your customers' homes. We can get the van wrapped in your advertisement, so when you drive around it's like a traveling billboard."

"I understand the concept, I just don't want to do it."

"You're too cool for that, aren't you?"

Claire popped her collar and looked down her nose at him.

"Like, for real," she said.

'He looks like the son of Larry and Curly from The Three Stooges,' Laurie said in her head. 'Bald and ginger.'

Claire closed her eyes and willed him to shut up.

"What happened?" Ed asked her. "You just shut down."

He took her in his arms as she felt her eyes fill with tears.

"I'm sorry," she said. "I just have these spells."

"You need to talk to somebody," Ed said.

"I need to figure out a job," Claire said. "I need to figure out my life."

'At least you have one,' Laurie said.

"I'm going to go," Claire said, gently pushing Ed away.

"I thought you were going to claim your territory," he said. "I feel like everything below my waist is in danger from those insatiable college girls."

Claire pinched him, and he cringed.

"Very funny," Claire said. "I really need to touch base with my mom and dad."

"All right," he said. "But tomorrow night we'll have a sleepover, okay? I've been missing you."

"Rain check," Claire said.

She kissed him and scooped up her handbag.

"Hey, Claire," he said.

Claire turned.

"Everything's going to be all right, you know," he said, "eventually."

"I know," Claire said. "I just wish it were then already."

At home, she was surprised to see Ava sitting at the kitchen table with her mother. The atmosphere was strained, and Claire looked at her mother with concern.

"Ava's been waiting for you to come home," Delia said.

"I was just about to give up on you," Ava said and rose to give Claire a hug.

The thing about her cousin-in-law, Ava, was this: she was beautiful. Not pretty, not cute, not just lovely; she was stunning. Men lost their minds when she walked into a room. She had dark hair and eyes, a dancer's form and grace of movement, and a smile that lit up the tri-county area.

None of her features were that remarkable on their own, but there was something about how they were put together, the symmetry or something, that had a strong effect on everyone who encountered her. It was star quality, and Claire was an expert at recognizing it when she saw it.

Ava knew it, of course, Claire was certain of that.

Maggie hated her for leading Scott on while they were estranged. Hannah hated her because Sam had once confessed to having a crush on her in grade school. Claire didn't have anything against Ava, not really; but then the woman never had so much as looked at Ed with anything but kind tolerance. The thing that bothered her about Ava was that she didn't feel like she ever saw the real person beneath all that beauty and graciousness. She would've liked to see Ava get mad, or drunk, or go off on someone. She seemed too good to be true.

Delia left the room, and Ava helped herself to more coffee.

"I'll regret this later when I can't sleep," she said.

"What's going on?" Claire asked as she sat down.

"Probably nothing," Ava said. "I saw something the other day at Gigi's, and I can't quit thinking about it."

"Why tell me?"

"I want somebody to tell Scott, and it's no secret how Maggie feels about me," she said. "I thought you might tell him for me."

"I'll be glad to," Claire said.

"After Jillian found Gigi, Hannah told us to go downstairs and wait for the police. Gwyneth had another appointment or something, so she left. Jillian and Candace went into the dining room, and Jillian gave something to Candace. They had a heated discussion over whatever it was, and then Candace put it in her handbag."

"What was it?"

"I didn't get a good look at it, but my first impression was that it was a note."

"Like a suicide note?"

Ava shrugged.

"I don't know, I just thought it looked very suspicious, and I wanted to tell someone."

"I'll let Scott know," Claire said. "Hey, Ava, has Charlotte ever mentioned Chippie's son? They're probably in the same grade at school."

"I've met him," Ava said. "He's part of the group of kids she runs with. He seems like a nice boy, has good manners. Why do you ask?"

"No reason," Claire said. "I just wondered what Chippie's son was like."

Ava stood up and smiled at Claire.

"It's so good to have you back home," Ava said. "I know your parents are thrilled about it."

"I'm glad I can help," Claire said.

"Well, if you're ever bored and want someone to hang out with, I'm always around."

"Thanks, Ava," Claire said.

"You probably won't, I know," Ava said. "But I would love it, really. I don't have many friends, and it gets lonely sometimes."

"We'll definitely do something," she said and hugged Ava.

After Ava left, Claire made some hot tea and wondered what was in the note Jillian had given Candace.

'Now that is one good-lookin' dame,' Laurie said.

'Why have you turned into a Damon Runyon character all of a sudden?' Claire asked.

'I knew she was trouble when she walked in the joint,' he said.

'I knew you were trouble when I danced with you in my dad's bar,' she said.

'There are all kinds of trouble, sister, and I'm the kind you run to, not away from.'

'You're ruining my life.'

'It was ruined when I met you,' he said.

"Claire," her mother said from the doorway. "Who are you talking to?"

"Myself," Claire said. "Sorry."

Claire woke up in a sweat, her heart pounding. It took her a moment to figure out where she was, and what had happened.

She had been dreaming about Laurie. He was trapped in a car, and she was trying to rescue him. She had smashed the window with a rock, unlocked the door, and tried to pull him out, but he was heavy and unconscious. His ex-wife was there along with his dead wife, standing behind her on a hill. Claire begged them to help her, but they were too busy arguing about whom he'd loved the most.

A fire started under the hood of the car, and Claire knew it was going to explode within seconds.

"Help me!" she screamed, but her voice made no sound.

Laurie opened his eyes and smiled at her.

"Fancy meeting you here," he said.

Then she woke up.

There had been an earlier dream, she now remembered, something about Jillian and Candace, and a note they were passing in class. The teacher took it away from them and read it silently in front of the class.

"Shame on you," the teacher said to them. "You ought to be ashamed."

Claire was wide awake now. The clock read 3:14 a.m. She pulled her tablet out of her handbag, turned it on, and went to the list-making app she used when she was a personal assistant.

She wrote:

1. Tell Maggie and Hannah about the note
2. Ask Candace about the note

3. Ask Jillian about the note
4. Tell Scott about the note
5. Ask Laurie if his first wife is with him wherever it is he is
6. Call Doc Machalvie

CHAPTER SIX

I know I can't stop you from nosing around in this case," Scott said. "But ..."

"That was in our prenup," Maggie said.

"We don't have a prenup."

"Post-nup, then. We had this discussion in the car on the way to Myrtle Beach after the wedding," Maggie said. "About all the things we didn't say in our vows but are still part of this marriage deal."

"I promised not to try to change you," Scott said. "That doesn't mean standing idly by while you risk your life."

"My investigations with Hannah are part of who I am," Maggie said. "We aren't pretending to be cops, we're just efficiently nosy."

"If you break the law, I can't protect you," he said. "Sarah would enjoy nothing more than to arrest you for interfering with her investigation."

"I can handle her," Maggie said. "Just let Hannah and me be us."

"Please be careful," he said. "I say that all the time but I wonder if you even hear the words."

"I hear you," Maggie said. "I don't want to get hurt. I'm a pretty smart person. Have some faith in me."

"I just don't want you to end up getting shot at in the state park."

"That was Claire. She's such an amateur."

"Well, watch out for her. She wants to be close to you and Hannah, so she's likely to do something stupid just to fit in with you guys,"

"You make us sound like twelve-year-olds."

"Well ..."

"Don't say it," she said. "Kiss me instead."

"You're always distracting me with your womanly wiles," he said. "Please don't ever stop."

"Where have you been?" Hannah asked Maggie when she arrived at the farm an hour after she said she'd be there.

"I got waylaid," Maggie said.

"I can tell," Hannah said. "You've got bed-head."

"Will you braid it for me?"

"Come here," Hannah said.

Maggie took a root beer out of the refrigerator and sat down at Hannah's kitchen table while Hannah went looking for her wide-tooth comb. She found it in Wally's dog bed, with tooth marks all over it. She started at the bottom of Maggie's long, curly red hair and gently tugged the knots out until it was sorted out enough to braid.

"Not too tight," Maggie said. "It gives me a headache."

"*Not too tight*," Hannah mimicked. "Yes, your majesty."

"How's Eugene?"

"Not good," Hannah said. "He's still talking great, but he had a bad headache this morning, so bad that he threw up. I called Dr. Schweitzer, and we're going to see him tomorrow."

"I feel so sorry for him," Maggie said. "He must feel so helpless and alone."

"He's got us," Hannah said. "He'll be okay."

"How's Sam taking this addition to the family?"

"It was his idea," Hannah said.

"No way."

"It was," Hannah said. "I was as surprised as you."

"Has that girl still been calling him?"

130

"Yes," Hannah said. "I decided not to worry about it, but then I still am."

"We'd kill him; he has to know that."

"I think he has good intentions, but she's got a huge crush on him. It's happened before. His buddy David says it's called transference; something patients do with their doctors."

"As long as Sam behaves himself."

"You know, I never worry about him cheating on me. He can barely stand being in a relationship with me, let alone with some high-maintenance, clingy young thing," she said. "Can you picture it?"

"No," Maggie said.

"I keep reminding myself of that," she said. "If she just wasn't so pretty."

"And so needy."

"Exactly," Hannah said. "Sam loves to rescue people like I love to rescue animals. The only difference is he doesn't want anything to do with them once they're out of danger."

"This, too, shall pass."

"Let's hope."

"What's our game plan today?"

"Follow everybody and find out stuff."

"That's about as well-thought-out as anything else we do."

"Oh, I have a scanner granny update," Hannah said. "Did you ever wonder how Candy and Jillian got to be friends?"

"Should I care?"

"Yes, shut up," Hannah said. "There was a brief period when Candy and Bill were broken up, and Candy used that time to sow some wild oats."

"Was this at college?"

"Yes," Hannah said. "Jillian was in nursing school at WVU and Candy started running around with Jillian and her friends."

"Setting fire to couches up on Sunnyside, that sort of thing?"

"Absolutely, guaranteed," Hannah said. "Then Candy and Bill got back together and got engaged."

"Jillian has sort of a rough background, doesn't she?"

"Oh, yeah," Hannah said. "She was a wild child at Pendleton High School, back when there was one. No football player left behind, that sort of thing."

"So, Miss Perfect walked on the wild side for a while," Maggie said. "That's pretty common for girls like Candy. I'm just surprised they stayed friends."

"That's just it," Hannah said. "Candy was glad to leave Jillian behind, but Jillian wasn't happy to be left."

"Blackmail."

"Mm-hm," Hannah said. "Candy must have done something pretty wild during that time, and Jillian has proof."

"All this time has passed," Maggie said. "You would think things would change, that people could change, but evidently, we are all still the same idiots we were in high school."

"I saw Hatch yesterday," Hannah said.

"I see Hatch every day," Maggie said. "He works at your dad's gas station."

"I mean he came out to the farm to see me."

"That's interesting," Maggie said. "Was Sam here?"

"Sam's not jealous of Hatch," Hannah said. "It's insulting how not jealous that man is of anybody."

"When you're a narcissist, you can't imagine anyone can compete."

"Sam is not a narcissist," Hannah said. "He's just infuriatingly confident."

"Same thing."

"Shut up," Hannah said. "I'm trying to tell you something."

"What did Hatch say?"

"He said Claire's dad is getting worse," Hannah said. "Evidently, he's been picking fights with the old coots who hang out at the gas station, and no one wants to tell Delia."

"Well, crap," Maggie said. "We need to tell Claire."

"I don't want to do it," Hannah said. "She's been so weird lately. I feel like we have to tip-toe around her. What's her deal?"

Maggie hesitated.

"What do you know?" Hannah asked. "I know you know something."

"I don't know anything," Maggie said.

"I love her, don't get me wrong," Hannah said. "But sometimes she irritates the hell out of me. All that fussy hair and makeup, dressing up like it's a fashion show every day, and worrying about celebrities like she knows them. How could we three grow up so close together and turn out so differently?"

"She's just a girly girl," Maggie said. "There's nothing wrong with that."

"All that worrying about your appearance must be exhausting," Hannah said. "It's no wonder she sleeps all the time."

"We have to tell her about her dad."

"You go ahead," Hannah said. "I've got my hands full."

"Let me think about it," Maggie said.

"Okay, Rapunzel," Hannah said. "I've tamed the wild beast that is your hair. Now you have to help me round up the dogs and get ready for the funeral."

Claire and her mother, Delia, dropped her father off at the family service station where his brother, Hannah's father, Curtis, would watch him. As soon as they got out of the car in the parking lot of Machalvie's Funeral Home, Claire's mother walked up the hill to the Rose Hill Community Center, where the reception was to be, in order to help prepare. Claire met Hannah and Maggie in the funeral home parking lot.

"Okay, here's the game plan," Hannah said. "Maggie, you watch Jillian, go everywhere she goes. Claire, you've got Chip. When he leaves, you follow him in your car. If he and Jillian leave together, take both cars in case they split up later. You're both also on suspicious character watch. Anybody does anything weird, you take note."

"Who are you watching?"

"Sam and I are all about Eugene today. Sam's his bodyguard, and I'm running social interference. Anybody upsets Eugene, and I'm in there like a flash, removing them from his proximity using my expert charm and social dexterity."

"This I have to see," Maggie said.

"I know how to do it," Hannah said. "I just mostly choose not to."

"They're going to read the will here at the funeral home," Claire said. "I'm supposed to be there."

"Great," Hannah said. "Now I don't have to figure out how to get one of us in there."

"What did you find out about the son?" Maggie asked.

"Tommy says Chippie Junior's the high school equivalent of a boy bander," Claire said. "He's a huge, spoiled brat with more money than sense."

"Figures," Maggie said.

"On the other hand, Ava says he's a well-mannered young gentleman."

Hannah snorted.

"He's probably in love with her," Maggie said.

"Okay," Hannah said, as cars began to arrive. "Let's go."

Maggie was sitting over near the side exit, where she would have a clear view of the bereaved family members. Hannah was hanging out in the foyer, trying to avoid the funeral home owner, AKA Queen of Darkness, Peg Machalvie, and her sons, AKA Creepy Minions, Hugo and Lucas, while she scoped out everyone who entered. Claire was twitchy and bored on the back row, feeling awkward and obvious. She was hoping Walter would arrive soon so she could corral him into sitting with her.

'He's too old for you,' Laurie said.

'I'm ignoring you,' Claire replied.

'No, you're not. If you were ignoring me, you wouldn't even acknowledge my presence.'

'La, la, la.'

'You're going about this investigation all wrong, by the way."

'What do you mean?'

'The question you should be asking is with whom did Gigi meet on the morning of the day she died. Notice how much my grammar has improved upon my death.'

'We think she met with Jillian.'

'But you don't know that for a fact,' Laurie said. 'Find out with whom she met and you'll know why she died. Or is it with whom she did meet? I'll have to ask Aelius. That man cannot carry a tune, but he sure does love to talk about words.'

'How do I find out who it was?'

'By detecting, my dear.'

'Do you know?'

'I only know what you know,' Laurie said. 'I only have access to your thoughts and what you see and hear.'

135

'I think Jillian did it.'

'You need more than an opinion, doll face; you need facts.'

'Where do I begin?'

'At the beginning, of course.'

"Excuse me," Walter said, looking down at her with affection. "Is this seat taken?"

Claire gladly welcomed Walter to her row. The other rows were beginning to fill up now, and pre-recorded organ music was playing over the sound system. Gigi's casket was closed, thank goodness. Claire could barely stand to be in a room with a casket, let alone with a dead body on display like hamburger in a grocery store, under a red spotlight to make it seem more lifelike.

Eugene came in with Sam, who looked every bit like a bodyguard. No one who saw him, with his scanning eyes and menacing scowl, could think otherwise. Eugene stopped at the casket, patted it awkwardly, and then he and Sam sat down in the front row.

"Everything all right with Eugene?" Walter asked.

"Physically, he's safe," Claire said. "Emotionally, he's struggling. Hannah turned out to be the perfect person to take care of him, though. She understands him, and he trusts her. It's all good."

"I'm glad," he said. "I'm dreading this will business. I hate this part of my job."

"Greedy relatives waiting to hear what they won, and then threatening to contest the will if they don't like what they hear?"

"They can't break this one," he said. "This is not my first rodeo, as they say."

"I like you, Walter," Claire said. "You're not like any attorney I've ever met."

"That's high praise, indeed," he said. "Thank you."

"What should I do during the will reading? Where should I sit?"

"Say absolutely nothing, no matter how much you're provoked. You're there on behalf of Eugene, so you sit with him, as his advocate, to hear the wishes of the deceased."

"Chip and Jillian are going to flip out."

"Well, if they do, it will be in front of a room full of witnesses, and it won't make the slightest bit of difference."

The family arrived, and although she was assigned to Chip, Claire couldn't help but notice that Jillian's face was so flushed she looked ill. Chip was dressed in a black suit, but he was chewing gum, which struck Claire as inappropriate. Everyone he spoke to or shook hands with, there he went, chomp, chomp, chomp, on that gum. If his aunt had been alive, she would have insisted he spit it out immediately.

Claire finally got a good look at Chippie Junior. He was beauty and grace where his father had been gawky and gangly, and movie star handsome where his father had been cute, but he kept flipping his forward-brushed hair across his forehead in a way that betrayed his youth.

Claire caught one exchange between father and son where Chip gripped his son's arm so tightly that the boy winced and whispered something into his ear that made his son flush with anger. It ended almost as soon as it began, as Jillian moved in to separate the two, a big fake smile plastered on her face. Chippie Junior sat on the other side of his mother, away from his father. Chip sat next to Sam, and Hannah sat on the other side of Eugene.

The music swelled and then stopped. To Claire's surprise, the clergyman who walked up to the podium was Ben Taylor, whom she had met in the hospice house garden. Suddenly, all her mother's talk of the new minister, Reverend Taylor, came back to her. Half listening, she had pictured an old man, not this young, vibrant sweetheart of a guy whom she had poured her heart out to in the garden. She also remembered Chip saying he missed seeing her mother at church. They all must go to the Rose Hill United Methodist Church, Ben's church.

Claire caught Ben's eye, and he smiled at her. It made her instantly teary-eyed. Walter handed her a handkerchief.

"Are you okay?" he asked.

"Funerals do this to me," Claire whispered.

She wished fervently that Ben had officiated at Laurie's funeral, instead of the dour-faced old man who said three words about Laurie and then spent an hour castigating the congregation for not taking the Bible seriously enough.

"You ignore the word of God at your own peril!" he had shouted.

Laurie's ex-wife and a former girlfriend had made the graveside service a ludicrous drama-fest, what with the fist-fighting and hair-pulling. That had been the first time she heard Laurie in her head, after a day of near-constant piano playing in there instead.

'I don't know what piece would best accompany a girl fight at a funeral,' he'd said after the women were physically separated but still cursing each other. 'Maybe something by Chopin.'

Whereupon, Claire's head was filled with classical music.

"If we think of the world as our church, our mosque, our synagogue, our temple, our shrine," Ben said, "then all of us are fellow congregants, and our actions should be the same outside in the world as they currently are inside our separate houses of worship."

"He's very progressive," Walter said.

"He's the best," Claire said.

"If the Earth is our spiritual school, then everyone is your friend, your brother, your sister, your classmate, your teacher. To practice our religion is to tolerate each other, teach each other, help each other, forgive each other, and love each other. It's acting with kindness, it's feeling compassion. The more we do that, the more we fulfill our purpose here on Earth."

'He's not so bad,' Laurie said in her head. 'He needs to stop soon, though, or he'll lose them. They're hungry, their clothes are hot, itchy, and too tight, and they have to pee. Oh, wait, that's just you.'

Claire ignored him. He was starting to get on her nerves.

"Gigi had a larger-than-life personality and a great big heart," Ben was saying. "She will be remembered by the people she loved for the many ways in which she left our Earth school better for having attended."

'Your friend Tuppy says hi, by the way,' Laurie said. 'Nice chap, your Tuppy. Terrible at chess, but a gifted tennis player.'

"Stop it," Claire said, immediately aghast to realize she had said it out loud. Several people turned to look, and she flushed with shame.

Walter took her hand, patted it, and looked straight ahead. He nodded to Ben to continue. Tears filled Claire's eyes until she could not see. She spent the rest of the service with her face buried in Walter's handkerchief, trying not to sob out loud.

When everyone stood to leave, Claire hurried out and hid in the farthest stall in the women's restroom. There she took out her make-up kit, repaired her face, put drops in her eyes, and talked to Laurie.

'I'm done,' she told him. 'You can't talk to me anymore. You're interfering with my ability to get on with my life; to be here, to be present, with the people I care about. I love you, I miss you, but I can't have you here anymore. I'm letting you go. I'm sorry, Laurie, but please, please, please, leave me alone now.'

She didn't wait to hear what he had to say, or what he would play on the piano. She checked her face in the mirror, decided to feign amnesia about what happened during the funeral, and left to find Chip, whom she was supposed to be watching.

She found him with the other family members and Walter, gathered in a small room furnished with sofas and coffee tables, a faux living room for the bereaved. Sam had stationed himself outside the only door to the room and merely nodded to her as she passed him.

"Good, Claire's here, so we can start," Walter said.

He smiled at Claire, and she felt bathed in his warm regard. She sat down on the only unoccupied chair, which coincidently gave her an unencumbered view of the whole family.

Walter wasted no time with a preamble. He read the will, and as anticipated, Jillian had the most visceral reaction. As soon as she understood what was being said, she gasped and almost stood, but Chip grabbed her arm and forcibly pulled her back into her seat. Chip seemed to be working out his emotions on his gum. He blinked a little more frequently, and his face was flushed, but he held it together.

Chomp, chomp, chomp.

Eugene didn't seem to be paying attention. He had his hands clasped in his lap and was staring at them. He didn't seem to hear or care what was being said.

After Walter finished, he said if anyone had questions he would stay as long as they needed. Jillian and Chip were the first to approach him, and there followed a heated exchange.

Finally, Chip said, "That's it then," and left the room.

"You haven't heard the last of this," Jillian told Walter and followed her husband.

Claire was torn. She was Eugene's advocate and Walter's teammate, but she was supposed to be following Chip.

Eugene was still looking at his hands. Claire went over and sat down next to him.

"Hey," she said. "We're all done here. We can go up to the reception or back to Hannah's if you've had enough."

His mother's wishes were to be cremated so there would be no graveside service.

Eugene looked up at Claire, sadness in his eyes.

"Wh, wh, what would Mother have wanted me t, t, to do?" he asked her.

"What do you want to do, Eugene?" she asked him. "You're in charge now."

"Then why do you and Walter c, c, control everything?" he asked, not without a little resentment.

"I don't know why your mother made it that way," Claire said. "Honestly, I thought I was witnessing her signature, not signing on as your guardian."

He snorted a short laugh.

"She duped you," he said. "That'th a g, g, good one."

"I'm glad to be the one helping you," she said. "And Walter is a lovely man. We both want whatever's best for you, Eugene, and we both agree it should be what you want, not what anybody else wants."

"If that'th true," he said. "If that'th really t, t, true, then I want to g, g, go home."

"To Hannah's?"

"No," he said. "My home."

"You can't right now, Eugene, because they don't know what killed your mother."

"Or who k, k, killed my mother," he said, clenching his fists.

"Or who killed your mother," Claire said. "Sam's outside, and he'll take you wherever you want to go."

"Well, I gueth if there are p, p, people who loved my m, m, mother, and they are at the retheption, I sh, sh, should shake handth with them and th, th, thank them for coming. She'd like that, wouldn't she?"

"She would."

"Then I guess I'll do that," he said. "It's the leatht I c, c, can do."

Walter spoke to Eugene briefly, said he would be in touch, and if he had any questions he should call. Eugene shook his hand and in a very formal way, thanked him for coming. Walter and Claire exchanged a meaningful look, and he winked at her.

Claire delivered Eugene to Sam and walked rapidly to the parking lot, looking for Chip. She found him in an altercation with his son. His son's lip was bloody, and Jillian was standing between them.

"You're a freakin' idiot," Chippie Junior said.

Chip lunged, but Jillian pushed him away.

"Haven't you done enough?" she hissed at him.

Chip threw up his hands and turned away. He then hurried to his car and spun his tires leaving the parking lot. Claire went to her car, and as she did so, overheard Jillian saying, "Come on, sweetie-pie, let's get you cleaned up," to Chippie as if he were six instead of sixteen.

Claire saw Maggie hanging back at the edge of the crowd that had gathered to watch. She stuck out her tongue at Claire and held up her phone. Claire held up hers and nodded. She had to drive slowly to avoid running over people as she left the parking lot and headed north. She hoped she could catch up to him without breaking too many laws.

By the time she reached the interstate she had realized he must have been flying because she'd been driving way too fast and never caught up to him. She pulled over into a gas station and called Maggie.

"I lost him," she said. "I'm next to the interstate, and I don't know which way he went."

"Way to go," Maggie said. "I, on the other hand, am right behind Jillian. Her son had his own car, and I don't know where he went. We're headed your way."

"I'm going to cruise past the strip club and see if he's there," Claire said.

"Good luck," Maggie said.

Evidently, it was way too early for anyone to be working at the strip club. She circled the parking lot, but there were no cars parked there. Dejected, she drove around aimlessly, scouring the parking lots of the businesses on the same frontage road as the club. As she passed a motel, she noticed a bright red Mustang with temporary tags parked in front of one of the rooms. When she drove around to the back side of the building, there was Chip's BMW.

"Bingo," Claire said. "Who's the good detective now?"

No one answered, and no one played a single note on the piano in her head.

She called Hannah.

"I'll get there as soon as I can," Hannah said. "We need someone to follow each of them when they leave."

"We don't even know that they're together," Claire said. "It could be a huge coincidence."

"They're together," Hannah said. "They're connected by his father. I'll be there in ten minutes. Hey, Aunt Delia! Can you take my kid for an hour or so?"

The call ended.

'Which room should I watch?' Claire wondered, 'the Mustang room or the BMW?'

Again there was no answer from Laurie.

'I'm going with the Mustang,' she thought. 'I bet she doesn't care who knows they're here together.'

Claire circled back around the parking lot to the front of the motel and backed into a space that gave her a good view of the room. A young woman came out of the room with an ice bucket and eventually returned with ice. With no make-up on, dressed in yoga pants and a T-shirt, she looked too young to be in a room with a man Chip's age.

Hannah arrived, backed in next to Claire, and jumped in the passenger side of her car.

"How'd you get here so fast?"

"I know a shortcut," she said. "Plus I drove like a bat out of hell."

"What do you think?" Claire asked.

"The tags match."

"Did the cops bring her in for questioning?" Claire asked.

"They might have; no one's telling me anything," Hannah said. "I can't even get Skip to drink a beer with me, let alone ply him with chips. Scott's got those boys on a short leash."

"She looks so young," Claire said. "It makes me want to smack him."

"Well, she's at least sixteen 'cause she's driving," Hannah said. "So, it's legal."

"Sixteen is way too young to be making those kinds of decisions," Claire said.

"You'd know," Hannah said.

"Thanks."

"Oooh, look," Hannah said excitedly, as she scrunched down in her seat, "Here comes Jillian."

Sure enough, Jillian's Lexus came rolling through the parking lot toward them. Claire stuck a ball cap on her head and flipped the car visor down. Jillian was too busy scouring the motel to notice them.

"It's sad to me that there was a reception after Gigi's funeral and not one of these people bothered to attend," Claire said. "She was so good to all of them."

"As soon as Jillian sees his car, the stinky stuff is going to hit the whirly thing," Hannah said.

Maggie's Jeep crept into the parking lot. She backed in on the other side of Claire.

"Where'd she go?" she asked.

"Around back," Hannah said.

Maggie pulled out and drove around the backside of the motel.

Hannah's phone rang, and she answered it on speaker.

"She's banging on the door of the room he's parked in front of, but no one's answering," Maggie said.

"Is she armed?" Hannah asked.

"I don't think so," Maggie said. "But by her mood, I'd say she's still dangerous."

"Her mighty anger doth power her fists," Hannah said. "For hell hath no fury like a woman scorned."

The door to the Mustang room opened, and Chip and the young girl came out, but not in any hurry. They got into her car and backed out.

"Follow them!" Hannah yelled.

Claire started the car and put it in gear. Hannah called Maggie to tell her what they were doing.

Maggie gave them an update.

"She got a crowbar out of her trunk and is breaking his car windows. There's a crowd gathering."

"What should we do?" Claire asked.

"Follow the Mustang," Hannah said.

The Mustang was flying down the frontage road.

"I can't drive this fast," Claire said as the speedometer hit 90 MPH.

"Don't be such a testicle," Hannah said. "I should be driving."

"It's dangerous, and I don't want to be responsible for killing someone," Claire said and took her foot off the gas.

Claire was relieved when the Mustang did not get on the interstate. Instead, it kept going west and turned left into the parking lot of the strip club.

On the marquis several names were touted, one of which was "Mustang Sally."

"It's all coming together now," Hannah said.

"How so?"

"Her second job must be here," Hannah said. "Although I could swear I've seen her somewhere before, and I've never been here. I wish I could remember."

The main parking lot was still empty, but there were several cars parked behind the club, near the back entrance. They watched the young woman and Chip get out of the Mustang and go in the back door; Chip used a key.

"Why would he have a key?" Claire asked.

Hannah shrugged.

"Maybe it's hers."

"This scandal will derail Jillian's social campaign," Claire said.

"I don't think he cares about that," Hannah said. "Otherwise, why would he be so blatant about it?"

"Maybe he's one of those guys who wants to end his marriage but doesn't want to be the bad guy."

"So, he does everything he can to drive his wife away and then blames her when she files for divorce."

"I like him less and less," Claire said. "What do we do now?"

"Well, I'm going to wait to hear from Maggie while you go in there and talk to Chip."

"Why me?"

"You're the one with all the strip club experience."

"I did hair and make-up," Claire said.

"So, get in there and offer your services or something," Hannah said. "We need to know what this chick's deal is and if she's been killing everyone in between Chip and his inheritance."

"He didn't get a penny," Claire said.

"No way!"

"So, if she has been killing people, it was all for nothing."

"I still think Jillian's the maniac," Hannah said. "She's got crazy eyes."

"She just needs to lighten up on the black eyeliner and frosted blue eyeshadow," Claire said.

Hannah's phone buzzed, and she answered it on speaker.

"Jillian's in state police custody," Maggie said. "Where are you guys?"

"Strip club," Hannah said. "Chip's got a key to the back door."

"Interesting," Maggie said. "Be there in a sec."

Claire approached the back door of the strip club and knocked on the gray steel door. There was a buzzer, but she didn't want to alert the whole club, just whoever was nearest to the door. It was opened by a very pretty woman in a big blonde wig, heavy make-up, platform heels, a skimpy red one-piece bathing suit, and a lifeguard float.

"Hi," Claire said. "I'm supposed to meet Chip, but I wasn't sure which door to use."

The woman looked Claire up and down and raised an eyebrow.

"You're kind of old for this, aren't you?"

"I do hair and make-up," Claire said. "You look just like a Baywatch girl."

"So I've been told," the woman said, 'if you ask me, she's past it, but the geezers with all the money just love her. Okay, come on in. Chip's up front at the bar."

"I'm Claire," Claire said and stuck out her hand.

The woman looked at it as if it were a snake.

"I'm Carolina Dawn," she said. "I have kind of, like, a germ issue? So, if you don't mind, I'll just pass on the human contact."

Claire shrugged, wondering if Carolina paid someone to swab the pole before she swung on it.

Claire thought to herself as she made her way up to the front of the house that all strip clubs must smell the same. It was a unique combination of hairspray, perfume, pine cleaner, urine, and hard liquor vomit. She walked down the stairs next to the stage and made her way through a large room crowded with small round tables and chairs. Chip was sitting at the end of the bar, a laptop open with a spreadsheet on the screen. Next to his beer on the bar was a stack of register tapes.

"Chip," Claire said.

He glanced at her as he said, "Yes ma'am," and then as it registered whom he was addressing he looked up in surprise. "Claire?"

Claire slid onto the barstool next to him, and when the bartender approached, she ordered a club soda with lime.

"What are you doing here?" he asked her, with real concern. "You're not looking for a job, are you?"

"Don't worry," Claire said. "I know I'm too old for this work. If you need a hair and make-up person, though, I might be interested."

"The girls do their own make-up," he said. "Why are you really here?"

"Jillian just beat the crap out of your car at the motel up the road," Claire said. "The state police have arrested her. I thought you might like to know."

148

"Aw, geesh," he said and rubbed his face. "Damn it, Jillian. That's just great. I paid off that car not two months ago."

"I'm not sure insurance covers your wife demolishing it."

"Wait a minute," he said. "How did you know I'd be here?"

"A little birdie told me," Claire said. "Are you an investor in this place?"

"I own it," Chip said. "It's an LLC Corp, but I'm the president and CEO."

"How did that happen?"

"Did a little birdie also tell you about someone named Amber?"

"Mustang Sally?"

"That's her stage name," he said. "She's Amber off the stage."

"It doesn't seem like you're trying very hard to hide your relationship," Claire said. "You can't be surprised Jillian found out."

"Well, it was only a matter of time, I guess, and really, Claire, I couldn't care less who knows. I'm giving my notice at the hospital on Monday, and starting here full time in thirty days."

"Business is that good, huh?"

"It's a gold mine," Chip said. "All it needed was someone with some brains and business experience to run the place. The last guy snorted up all the profits and treated the girls like crap. He'd let anybody in, they were selling drugs behind the bar, and nobody but the most desperate, drug-addicted girls would work here. It had a really bad reputation. I'm changing all that."

Claire was remembering things she'd worked hard to forget.

"No one is ever totally safe," she said. "Not when hormones and alcohol mix."

149

"I've got two ex-Pittsburgh Steeler linebackers working as bouncers," he said. "I've got a state-of-the-art security system and a full-time security staff remotely monitoring every inch of this place. Everyone who works here has a background check and monthly drug test."

"Sounds like a prison," Claire said. "How are you paying for all that?"

"It's a fifty dollar cover to get in," he said. "Beers are ten dollars, shots are fifteen, and mixed drinks are twenty."

"I better slow down, then."

"Private shows start at two hundred."

"Wow, you really are raking it in."

"We don't let anyone drive drunk," he said. "We keep the criminals out of the parking lot, and we don't let anyone hassle the girls."

"Are they making anything?"

"They keep all their tips."

"Same as the wait staff?"

"They are the wait staff," he said. "They can sell more drinks than anyone."

"If it weren't for the soul-sucking work, I'd almost say it sounds like an ideal business to be in."

"I'm not forcing anyone to do this," he said. "I've got girls begging me to work here. We hit full capacity every night at midnight, and after that, I'm turning people away. I'm planning on opening two more next year."

"So, this is why Gigi cut you out of the will."

"She asked me, and I told her the truth," he said. "I don't need their money; I'm making my own."

"After all they did for you."

"I didn't ask for any of that," he said. "They bought me, plain and simple. They didn't like the son they had, and I needed a family. I never knew what they paid for me, but my dad dropped me off there and never looked back. He barely stopped long enough for me to get out of the car."

"What about Jillian?" Claire asked.

"You know, Claire, I finally don't care what Jillian thinks. She only married me for my money and Eugene and Gigi's connections. I'll make more than enough to keep her in that big house and send my son to a good college. That's all I'm willing to do for her, and it's more than she deserves."

"And Amber's not after the same thing?"

"No, Claire, not at all," he said. "She refused to go out with me for the longest time; I had to beg her to take my phone calls. She's a very strong, independent woman. She's determined to make her own way. She has lots of great ideas for other clubs, like one for straight women and gay guys, called 'Cocky Locky's.' Isn't that brilliant?"

"She's certainly no dummy."

"It was her idea to offer health benefits and dental," he said. "Next year we're going to build a day care facility across the road for the moms."

"More like night care, though, right?"

"Amber's really into lighting and music. We're going to Vegas next month to do research. This is going to be a real classy establishment, not just your average dive."

"Does Jillian know your plans?"

"We don't see each other very often," he said. "I've been living up at the motel since April."

"Are you planning to go bail her out?"

He sighed.

"I guess I better," he said.

"In the past week you've lost your aunt and your father," Claire said. "You seem to be doing okay, though."

"My biological contributor lost the right to be called my father the year I was ten, when he stole my baseball card collection so he could sell it to fund his gambling problem," Chip said. "He was a mean bully and a drug addict. If it weren't for my Uncle Eugene, I probably would have killed him myself by the time I was sixteen."

"Who do you think killed him?"

"Someone he owed money to," Chip said. "Or someone he stole from. That doesn't narrow it down much."

"What about your aunt?"

"I think that was an accident," he said. "She must've somehow gotten ahold of something she was allergic to and died of anaphylactic shock. Happens all the time, unfortunately."

"What was she allergic to?"

"I have no idea."

"Do you think Jillian was capable of killing her thinking you would inherit?"

"What? No. No way," he said. "Jillian's a little too ambitious, but she wouldn't kill anybody."

"I've talked to some people who worked with her at the hospital around the time you broke up with Sophie."

"That was a crazy time, and you know, Claire, you get two women with a flair for the dramatic, and they both want the same man ..."

He enjoyed this version of events, she could tell. He seemed proud to have provoked such crazy behavior.

"I think you must have some flair, yourself," Claire said.

"Why do you say that?"

"Oh, I don't know, maybe it's the cheating on your wife in a way you know she'll find out about, even though you also know she's likely to try the same stuff on Amber she did on Sophie."

"Not if she wants my money," he said, as he snapped the laptop shut. "This time she's going to have to play for pay and play nice."

After Chip left, Claire flirted with a bartender a bit, but couldn't get anything out of him about his employer.

"Chip's the best boss I ever had," he said.

"What about Amber?" she asked.

"What about me?" someone said, and Claire turned to see who was speaking.

Not only was she skilled with lighting and music, but Amber was as good as any professional when it came to hair and make-up. The merely pretty teen had turned into a stunning pop music queen, done up in ponytails and a fantasy schoolgirl costume, complete with plaid mini skirt and knee socks.

She may have dressed like an innocent teenage tease, but her eyes were sharp and canny. Claire introduced herself, saying she had gone to school with Chip.

"Why are you here?" Amber asked.

"His wife just got arrested for beating the hell out of his car up at the motel," Claire said. "I thought he might want to know."

Amber smirked but didn't comment.

"I heard you worked for Chip's father," Claire said. "Is that how you met?"

"No," Amber said.

"I heard you were there the day he died."

"Yes."

"What happened?"

Amber turned and walked away.

"You've pissed her off," the bartender said. "I'd leave now if I were you."

"Why?" Claire asked. "What's she gonna do to me?"

He just shook his head and backed away.

About that time something zinged past Claire's head, and the glass mirror behind the bar shattered. Claire dropped to the floor and scooted around behind the bar where the bartender was cowering, a metal tray held over his head.

"How do I get out of here?" Claire asked.

He pointed toward the front foyer.

"If you hit the emergency exit bar, you can get out," he said. "The alarm will sound, but keep going."

Another shot hit the bottles on the top shelf. Glass exploded, and liquor drenched Claire. She crawled around the bar to the entry foyer and got up as soon as she was behind the wall. She spied the emergency exit and hit it at a full run.

Outside, Hannah had the car pulled up out front, with the motor running. Claire opened the back door and leaped in, screaming, "Drive!"

They peeled out of the parking lot with Maggie right behind them, but Amber did not follow her outside into the parking lot.

"What the hell happened?" Hannah said. "I heard gunshots."

"Mustang Sally just tried to kill me," Claire said, as she shook glass shards from her hair.

"Should we call the police?"

"Let me think about that," Claire said. "What would we gain?"

"Justice? Revenge?"

"I think I can do better than that on my own," Claire said.

Back at Hannah's, Scott and Ed were sitting in the kitchen, eating pizza with Sam and Eugene. The two little dogs, Bunny and Chicken, were curled up at Eugene's feet. The two big dogs were curled up at Sam's feet.

"Where've you girls been?" Scott wanted to know.

"Oh, you know, just out doing lady stuff," Hannah said. "Manicures, pedicures, ripping the hair out of our tender skin so we can be more attractive to men ..."

"Shopping for cute tops," Maggie said, "and pretty shoes."

"Wait a minute," Claire said. "Are you making fun of me?"

Ed laughed out loud, and Eugene looked at him, perplexed.

"With these three," Ed explained, "you can bet they were doing quite the opposite."

"Doing men stuff?" Eugene wanted to know.

Ed looked at Scott in horror.

"I'm in trouble, aren't I?" he asked.

"You're on your own," Scott said.

"We'll talk about it later," Claire said sweetly, as she pulled Ed's beard.

"You smell like whiskey," he said.

"It's a long story," she said.

"This is not nearly enough pizza," Hannah said. "I'm calling for more."

"Let's go swimming, instead," Maggie said.

"Oh, no, thank you," Eugene said. "I don't have a bathing suit."

"We float more than we swim," Maggie said, "and you can wear shorts. We sometimes have to bribe Hannah to wear anything."

"Hey," Hannah said. "I only did that once, and I was very, very drunk at the time."

"I don't know," Eugene said.

"I'm the captain of the dread pirate ship The Black Frog," Hannah told him. "Nobody says no to the merciless Hannah of the High Seas and lives to tell about it."

"I'm not the best swimmer," he said.

"Come on, Euge, it's fun. You can wear Sammy's swimmy wings if you're scared. Where is my son, by the way?" Hannah asked Sam.

"Delia's keeping him overnight," Sam said.

"God bless her," Hannah said.

Once ensconced in his own inner tube, and armed with a squirt gun, Eugene had the time of his life. Claire realized it was probably the first time he'd ever played with anyone and enjoyed it. The no vomiting or fainting probably contributed to that. He laughed so hard he choked, and nobody panicked. Sam just whacked him on the back and said, "Okay, partner?"

"Okay," Eugene replied, and he did not stutter.

Later on, after the sun had gone down and the air had grown chilly, the three cousins sat around the fire and compared notes.

"Jillian is just a younger Gigi," Maggie said.

"But Gigi had way more class and finesse," Claire said.

"Amber's just a younger Jillian," Hannah said.

"Except way more psycho," Claire said. "She's got Chip completely vagi-matized."

"He certainly has a type," Hannah said. "Now that we know Sophie's a little psycho, too, it all makes sense."

"There's wacky psycho, and then there's murderous psycho," Claire said. "Big difference."

"We should have called the cops," Maggie said.

"I didn't actually see her shoot," Claire said. "I was too busy fleeing for my life."

"What are you going to do to her?"

"I don't know yet," Claire said. "I need to think about it some more."

"Stay classy," Maggie said. "Remember to use your finesse."

"Don't worry," Claire said. "I'm going to finesse the hell out of that pop tart."

"Top suspects," Maggie said. "Claire, go."

"I think Jillian must have killed Gigi," Claire said. "She had to be the person Gigi was meeting with that morning, to talk about Chip and the will."

"*You're not getting a penny of my money!*" Hannah imitated Gigi's voice. "What then? Jillian runs out and gets a prescription for penicillin filled and puts it in her tea? Nope. That would take too long. This was premeditated."

"So, maybe the meeting happened a few days before, and this was the follow-up," Maggie said. "Jillian's come to beg for another chance, hoping the will hasn't been changed yet. She brings the penicillin in case things don't go her way."

"Okay, how does she get the penicillin into Gigi?" Claire asked.

"Her coffee," Hannah says. "The food. Anything she ate or drank."

"Or rubbed on her skin," Maggie said. "Lotion, maybe?"

"Oh my goodness, I know how she did it," Claire said. "It was the perfume! I watched Gigi put it on."

"That would do it," Maggie said. "We need to tell Scott to get the perfume tested."

"Okay, what about Cheat?" Claire asked.

"Amber did that, fo sho," Hannah said. "I saw her leaving the house, she admitted he owed her money, and she took off like a bat out of hell."

"I think there's even more to the story there," Maggie said. "Maybe Amber was in cahoots with Cheat. He told her, 'My son has all this money coming to him, and you're young and promiscuous, do the math.' And then he demands a cut, or he'll tell Chip what Amber did."

"I believe it all except the last bit. Chip wouldn't believe anything Cheat said."

"Maybe he had photos," Hannah said.

"Ew," Claire said.

"So, Amber killed Cheat for money and to keep him quiet," Maggie said.

"Or just for kicks," Claire said.

"How do we prove it?" Maggie asked.

157

They were silent, seemingly stumped.

"She's not likely to get drunk and brag about it," Claire said. "She's too tough and smart for that."

"We can't force her to confess," Hannah said. "Can we?"

"What would threaten her?" Maggie asked. "What's she afraid of?"

"Being out of control," Claire said. "Being made a fool."

"Can you arrange that?" Hannah asked.

"I'll do my best," Claire said.

CHAPTER SEVEN

T he next morning, Maggie came out to Hannah's for breakfast. She had promised Maggie bacon, eggs, and pancakes, but when Maggie got there, there was nothing cooking.

"Where's my breakfast?" Maggie asked.

"Sorry," Hannah said. "My cupboard is bare. I have instant oatmeal or toast."

"Never mind," Maggie said. "We'll just go down to the bakery later. I've texted Claire several times, but she hasn't answered yet."

"What in the hell is wrong with her?" Hannah asked. "I invited her to go with us to the Kelly Clarkson & Pink show in Pittsburgh next weekend, and she passed."

"Leave her be," Maggie said. "She's going through something."

"I knew you knew something," Hannah said. "What is it? Did she break a nail? Did a celebrity couple break up? How will she cope?"

"She's in a dark pit of recrimination and regret."

"What are you talking about?" Hannah asked. "She's been kinda spacy but not suicidal."

"She's seriously depressed," Maggie said. "She can't sleep at night for thinking about every mistake she ever made and every humiliating thing that ever happened to her. That's what depressed people do. They go over and over all the ways they think they've failed, like an endless loop of self-torture."

"That sounds horrible," Hannah said. "I knew something was up, but not anything that bad."

"She only told me because I heard her sobbing in the bookstore bathroom," Maggie said.

"Well, we gotta fix this," Hannah said. "What do we do?"

"We can't fix it, only Claire can," Maggie said. "I told her she needs to get some help, but I can tell she thinks it's just something she's going through and it will pass."

"What do you think brought it on?"

"She was more involved with Laurie than we knew."

"What?" Hannah said. "Laurie Purcell? I didn't even know she knew who he was. The scanner grannies didn't know about this, how is that possible?"

"Evidently they met in the Thorn while we were at the beach and got close just before he died."

"Does Ed know about this?"

Maggie shrugged.

"Laurie Purcell," Hannah said. "I had no idea. Poor bastard. Blown up by a mobile meth lab. I wouldn't be a policeman if you paid me a million dollars. I'd much rather be a nosy parker."

"I think maybe hospice isn't the best place for her to volunteer right now, feeling like she does, but she says she needs to keep busy. It's the only thing that helps."

"Oh, crap," Hannah said. "I was giving her a hard time the other day for sleeping all the time now that she's unemployed. I thought she was lazy. I didn't know she was sad."

"It's more than sad," Maggie said.

"We gotta do something."

"Her fortieth birthday is this weekend," Maggie said.

"I guess I better not make it a cemetery theme."

"And no walkers and canes."

"We'll make it fun," Hannah said. "That will cheer her up."

160

"Better keep it low key," Maggie said. "Just family and friends."

"But not my mom," Hannah said. "Alice is not someone you want around if you're feeling fragile."

"Tell Alice there will be loud music," Maggie said. "She hates that."

"I'll tell her there will be loud *bluegrass* music," Hannah said. "She'll leave town."

"What's your plan today?"

"I'm taking Eugene to three doctor appointments," Hannah said, and then ticked them off her fingers. "Allergy doctor at ten, MRI at one, and then Dr. Schweitzer at three."

"How's he doing?"

"He still has a headache," Hannah said. "It's probably just a side effect of his medication, and they can adjust the dose."

"You should invite that cute shrink to Claire's party," Maggie said.

"Like an intervention?"

"Heavens no," Maggie said. "But if you let him know what's going on and he just happens to talk to her ..."

"I'm on it," Hannah said. "Maybe he can examine my husband's head while he's at it."

"Has that girl called again?"

"Not since the last time I told you about," Hannah said. "He's just such a prick sometimes."

"He was like that when you married him."

"You're right," Hannah said. "I know he loves us, but we don't ever feel like a family; at least not how I thought a family would feel like. It's more like we're two single parents raising one child. That doesn't make any sense, I know. Don't pay any attention to me. I don't know what I'm talking about."

"Sam's been closed off since he came back from overseas."

"It's PTSD," Hannah said, "and it's not going to go away. I know that."

"I think it would be hard for anyone to be married to Sam."

"If he weren't so damn handsome," Hannah said. "And he's not mean to us. I know he would lay down his life for us."

"That's true."

"Ahhhh, forget about it," Hannah said. "He's a good-enough husband, and I could have done much worse."

"That's the spirit!"

"Shut up. What's your plan today?"

"I'm going to talk to the caterer who was at Gigi's house the day she died," Maggie said. "I want to find out if anybody saw or overheard anything useful."

"You guys should come out this evening; we'll barbecue something."

"Sorry," Maggie said. "My husband has requested a date night, whatever the hell that is."

"I think you should have married Sam and I should have married Scott," Hannah said. "I'd love to go on a date night."

"I love Sam," Maggie said. "But one of us would kill the other one before a week was out. Two cranky people cannot live together."

"Tell Scott if he needs a sub for date night I'm in," Hannah said. "Sam won't care. He'll be relieved."

"I'll tell him."

The catering company that had worked Gigi's event was located in a metal building on the highway frontage road near the motel where Chip and Amber met. There was a small sign on the door that read, "Johansen Event Company."

"Hello," Maggie called out as she went inside.

Stacks of chairs and tables filled the cavernous central room, with only a narrow passageway between them. Overhead, what looked like huge rolled up tents were hoisted up just below the steel ceiling joists.

Maggie could hear voices coming from a back room, where the delicious smell of frying onions was emanating. Maggie walked to the doorway and listened.

"I really wish you'd given me more notice," a woman said.

"Sorry," another woman said. "But I'm making way more money over there, and I need to focus on building my own business."

"You know how I feel about it. You're smart and a hard worker, and in a few years you could be a partner in this business."

"But I don't want to do this. It's too much work for the money."

"Well, if you ever want to come back, I'll make a place for you."

"Thanks, Ing. See you around."

Maggie pushed the door just as a young woman was pushing the other side of it.

"Sorry," Maggie said, but the young woman just scowled at her and pushed by.

"Nice manners," Maggie said to her retreating back.

The young woman held up her middle finger but did not turn around.

Maggie felt her whole body flush with rage, but she took a deep breath and shook her hands out.

'Let it go,' she told herself. 'A snotty little twerp is not worth it.'

After a few deep breaths, still hot but somewhat calmer, she entered what turned out to be a large professional kitchen, where a woman sat on a high stool at a stainless steel island, looking over a huge calendar with

163

something scribbled on each day. She looked over her half-moon reading glasses at Maggie.

"May I help you?" she asked as she stood up.

The tall, statuesque woman had a great mass of blonde curly hair twisted up on the back of her head, with tendrils escaping just as Maggie's wild red hair was known to do. She wore a chef's smock, black leggings, and bright red clogs.

"I'm looking for the owner," Maggie said and introduced herself.

"Ingrid Johanson," she said as she gripped Maggie's hand and gave it a firm shake. "I'm the owner. You aren't related to the Fitzpatrick Bakery family in Rose Hill, are you?"

"That's us," Maggie said. "I started working there before I could talk, so they say."

"Any chance you'd share some of your family recipes?"

"Not if I value my life," Maggie said.

"It was worth a try," Ingrid said. "Your cinnamon rolls are amazing. I've tried to duplicate the taste but I can't. I'm usually pretty good at identifying the smallest ingredient. There's something in those rolls that tastes wonderful, but I can't tell what it is."

"Ah, yes," Maggie said. "They're very popular."

"The croissants are the best I've ever eaten," Ingrid said. "I stole your lemon blueberry muffin idea, and everyone loves them, but they're still not as good as yours."

"I hear you're very good," Maggie said, "and from the looks of that calendar, very busy."

"I've finally been discovered, after only ten years of doing this," Ingrid said. "Now I'm so busy I can't remember the last day off I had. But the money's so good I can't say no."

"I love hearing a small business success story," Maggie said. "I own Little Bear Books in Rose Hill."

"Your cookbook section is killer," Ingrid said.

"That's due to Jeanette, my manager," Maggie said. "She reads cookbooks like I read fiction."

"Me, too," Ingrid said and gestured to a glass-fronted bookcase filled with cookbooks.

She went to the stove and used a long metal spoon to stir a mass of onions cooking in the largest sauté pan Maggie had ever seen. She poured some water on them, and it sizzled as she stirred.

"I'm caramelizing onions," she said. "It's a lengthy process, but I find if I add some water occasionally and then cook them until it evaporates, they benefit from the extra time. Not my idea, by the way, just something I read and tried."

"I don't cook," Maggie said. "But I love to eat. That smells amazing."

"I'm flattered you'd hire me to cater something," she said, "considering what your family does."

Maggie couldn't fault Ingrid for making that assumption, and since things were going so well, she decided to play along.

"My cousin's fortieth birthday is on Saturday," she said. "She's having a hard time right now, and I want to give her a nice party, nothing huge and noisy, but fun and cheerful."

"Where will the event be held?"

Ingrid grabbed a legal pad and took down Hannah's address.

"I know that farm," Ingrid said. "What a great venue for an event. Tell me about your cousin. What's her name?"

"Claire Fitzpatrick," Maggie said. "Her dad was chief of police for a long time, and her parents own the Rose and Thorn. Claire left Rose Hill right after high school and just recently moved back. She worked for a famous actress for twenty years, so she's traveled all over the world, and eaten at five-star restaurants. She's pretty; a girly girl, you know what I mean? High heels, ginormous designer purses, and lots of make-up; but she's not shallow or snobby. She's actually one of the nicest people I know."

"What does she like to eat?"

"I don't really know," Maggie said.

"You two aren't close?"

"I'd say we are," Maggie said. "She just doesn't eat very much."

"Big salads, hold the dressing, that kind of thing?"

"Oh, yes," Maggie said. "Not like me."

"Or me," Ingrid said. "To me, a salad's not worth eating unless it's covered in cheese, meat, bacon, and way too much chunky blue cheese dressing."

"That sounds wonderful."

"Stick around, and I'll feed you lunch," Ingrid said. "You can preview what I do."

"I'm not even sure I can afford you," Maggie said. "Maybe we better talk price."

They discussed how many people and what kind of event it would be.

"What are her hobbies?" Ingrid asked. "What does she like?"

"Claire loves old movies," Maggie said, "and bluegrass music."

"Great!" Ingrid said. "I did this great kid's party once where I put up a white sheet on the side of the house, and we projected old cartoons on it. The parents loved it even more than the kids. What's her favorite old movie?"

"That's easy," Maggie said. "Anything with Cary Grant in it."

"Super!" Ingrid said. "I see a bluegrass trio playing until dark, and then we'll show *His Girl Friday* or *Bringing Up Baby* on the side of the barn. I picture hay bales covered in old quilts for seating, barbecue sliders, a crab, shrimp, new potato, and corn boil, lemonade for the kids, small-batch-brewed beer and champagne punch for the grownups, miniature cupcakes, and fruit tarts."

"That sounds expensive."

"I'll give you a professional discount," Ingrid said.

She punched some numbers into her calculator and named a figure per person that made Maggie's eyes water.

"Maybe not champagne," Maggie said. "And just crab or shrimp, but not both."

"Okay," Ingrid said and punched some more numbers. "How about this?"

She showed Maggie a much more reasonable number.

"Perfect," Maggie said. "I can't believe you're even available that night."

"I've got two other events," Ingrid said with a smile. "I'm good at multi-tasking, and I have a great crew."

"The one that just left wasn't so friendly."

"Amber," Ingrid said with a sigh. "She's had a hard life."

"Amber, who works at the strip club, Amber?" Maggie asked. "I only know that from gossip I've heard, sorry."

"Unfortunately, yes," Ingrid said. "She started working for me a couple years ago, said she was sixteen, but I knew she was younger. She ran away from home. I guess her mother and she couldn't get along. I've met the mother. She seems kind of flaky, but I don't know what really happened. Amber was living in a tent in the state park. I let her move the tent to my backyard, and I put her to work. Terrible manners, and horrible with people, but there was just something about her. She was like a suspicious, abused stray, and I couldn't turn my back on her. I offered for her to live in my house but she refused. She used to steal food from my kitchen and sneak in when I wasn't home to use the bathroom and shower. I would have given her the run of the house, but she seemed to prefer sneaking."

"Why stripping?"

"She was cleaning rental houses for some dirty old man in Rose Hill. He told her how much money she could make stripping, and offered to buy her the clothes and make-up she would need if she gave him a cut of her tips. I'd like to kill that man."

"Someone did, a couple days ago."

"Good riddance to bad rubbish," Ingrid said. "I tried to talk her out of it, even promised to let her work up into a partnership here, but all she could see were dollar signs. She still worked for me occasionally, but now she's got some rich boyfriend, and she's quit for good."

"Maybe she'll come back," Maggie said. "She's young; she doesn't know what she's doing."

"She does know," Ingrid said. "That's just it. I'm fond of her, she's smart and a hard worker, but I'd never put her in charge of the petty cash if you know what I mean. Life has made her hard, and I don't think me being kind to her has changed that at all. She just thinks I'm a fool for being so soft-hearted. She can't imagine anyone would be kind to her without an agenda."

"Yet you still helped her."

Ingrid shrugged.

"She says if she can get money out of old men by selling them booze and shaking her behind, she's going to do it while she's got a good behind to shake. She only has contempt for the customers, but she loves that money. She thinks being rich will solve all her problems."

"I wish I could find out if that's true," Maggie said. "It seems to me that money might solve many of my problems."

"I guess there's some truth to that," Ingrid said. "I just hate to think what it's doing to her soul."

They were silent for a few moments, lost in their own thoughts.

"Anyway," Ingrid said, as she turned off the heat under the now perfectly caramelized onions. "I hate to lose her. She's not good with clients, but she's an awesome event manager. The other kids are scared to death of her, so there are no shenanigans."

"Speaking of events," Maggie said. "I understand you catered the luncheon at Gigi O'Hare's the day she died."

"Nothing I served, I promise," Ingrid said. "She was dead before the food got there."

"Did Amber work that event?"

"She was in charge, yes. Why?"

"I just wondered if she saw anything unusual that day," Maggie said. "Gigi was a good friend of Claire's, and she's really down about her death."

"Amber and Chloe were in the house earlier, doing prep work," Ingrid said. "Amber didn't want to talk about it, but Chloe's a big talker. I could give her your number. She'd probably love to tell it all again to someone. I warn you, you probably won't be able to get her to shut up about it."

"It might help Claire get past it," Maggie said and gave Ingrid her business card.

"All the more reason we should make her party the best one she's ever had," Ingrid said. "Let's start with the guest list."

Chloe called Maggie later that afternoon and agreed to come to the bookstore to meet her. She was a very young girl, Maggie thought probably sixteen or seventeen, with big, pale blue eyes, long blonde hair, and fair skin. She wore a tight white T-shirt and low-rise, midriff-baring jeans with platform sandals. The bookstore customers couldn't seem to take their eyes off of her, but she seemed oblivious to the attention.

Maggie offered her anything she wanted from the café side, gratis, and with wide, excited eyes, Chloe chose a chocolate croissant and a mocha iced latte.

"I'll have to work this off in the gym tomorrow," she said as she bit into the croissant. "O.M.G., this is, like, so good!"

Maggie sipped her tea and wondered if she could recruit Chloe to work in the bookstore. She would certainly attract the college students, who were her bread-and-butter customers nine months of the year, as well as the seasonal tourists. Chloe had that bright, young enthusiasm that was irritating as hell but good for business.

Maggie liked Ingrid, but business was business.

"Ing said you wanted to know about the event when the lady died," Chloe said.

"I understand you and Amber were there earlier?"

"Are you, like, investigating her death?"

"Sort of," Maggie said. "She was a good friend of my family."

"Nobody from the police, like, even called me," Chloe said. "I was dying to tell them what happened, but Amber said we'd better stay out of it."

"What's Amber like?"

"Um, not very nice, like, kind of a bitch," Chloe said. "I don't mind, like, working with her on events but we could never be friends. She tried to get me to do stripping, but I could never! My mom and dad would kill me! She showed me this roll of hundred dollar bills she had? It was amazing. But I'd be too embarrassed. She showed me some moves, though, and my boyfriend really enjoyed me showing them to him."

She didn't even blush, as fair as she was. Maggie marveled at the shamelessness of the young people she met these days. It made her feel like an old, cranky prude. Worse, it made her feel like her mother.

"What happened that morning?"

Chloe leaned across the table and spoke in a low, excited whisper.

"We got there at eleven, and like, the front door was open, so when nobody answered the bell, we went in. We carried in the equipment and set it up in the kitchen. We could hear people arguing in the backyard, and I, like, opened the back door a little bit so I could hear what they were saying? Amber listened, too."

"Men or women?"

"The old lady, I mean, Mrs. O'Hare, and she was giving this guy hell. She kept saying how disappointed she was?"

"Young man or old man?"

"An old guy? Like forty?"

Maggie, who was turning forty in the fall, let that pass without so much as an eye roll.

"What did they say?"

"Mrs. O'Hare was like, 'I'm cutting you out of the will,' and he was like, 'I don't need your money,' and she goes, 'Your uncle would be so disappointed in you,' and he goes, 'I didn't ask you for anything.' She was just really, like, mad at him? And he was all, like, 'I don't care.' She even cried? It was just, like, something on a reality show, you know?"

"Was anything else said that you can remember?"

"Just more fighting, and, like, mean stuff. He seemed like kind of a brat, like those spoiled rich kids at school. Their parents give them everything, and they don't respect them for it. They just feel like they deserve it, you know?"

"Not like your parents?"

"No way! If I want to go to college, I have to save up half, you know? Then my parents will match that. That's

171

why I'm working so much? I hardly have, like, any time for my boyfriend."

"That's smart of them."

Chloe shrugged.

"What happened after that?'

"Well, the guy left, and Mrs. O'Hare came inside. She'd been crying, and I think she was, like, embarrassed we saw her upset. She yelled at us for coming into the house without her knowing. Amber, was all like, 'You can't talk to us that way, we're just doing our jobs,' and Mrs. O'Hare was like, 'Don't you speak to me in that tone, young lady, I'll call your employer,' and Amber was like, 'Fine. Call her. See if I care.' So, she, like, threw us out of the house! I was scared to death but Amber just, like, laughed about it."

"What happened then?"

"We went outside and sat on the wall by the driveway, waited for the catering van to get there, you know?"

"Did you see anyone else go into the house?"

Chloe hesitated.

"What?" Maggie asked.

"She'll kill me if I tell."

"Amber?"

Chloe nodded.

"She went back into the house?"

Chloe nodded again, her eyes wide.

"Did she say why?"

"She said she left her keys in there."

"How did she get in?"

Chloe shrugged.

"She went around to the back of the house. Maybe, like, the back door was still open? I don't know. I was afraid she would get caught, and we'd both be in trouble."

"How long was she in there?"

"I don't know," Chloe said. "Like five minutes?"

"What did she say when she came back out?"

"She didn't say much," Chloe said.

She wouldn't look Maggie in the eye.

"What is it?" Maggie asked her. "What did she do?"

Chloe sighed.

"You don't know Amber," she said. "After we found out the old lady died, Amber said if I told anybody about her going back into the house she'd slit my throat. I've seen her scare big guys, like, three times her size. She wasn't kidding around."

"Do you think she killed Mrs. O'Hare?"

"Why would she do that? She didn't even know her."

"Then what did she do?"

Chloe paused.

"C'mon, Chloe," Maggie said. "I'm not going to tell Amber you told me. I don't even know her, and she sounds like somebody I don't want to know."

"She stole some stuff," Chloe whispered. "Some perfume, some cash, and jewelry."

"She showed it to you?"

"Yeah, she thought it was funny, like, 'To hell with her, who does she think she is, talking to me like that. I showed her,' you know?"

"Was that the first time you saw her steal something from a client?"

Chloe shook her head.

"Nah, she's done it before."

"What happened after that?"

"She put the stuff in her purse, and then her old boss came up the driveway to talk to her. He's gross, like, a real skeevy perv, so I went down the hill to wait for the van."

"Was Amber friendly with him?"

"At first it was okay, but he was, like, really gross to me? So, I went down the hill. She cussed him out for hitting on me, and they fought. I couldn't hear all of it, but as he came back down the driveway, he told her he was going to give someone a call, and show him some movies. Amber came down the driveway after him. She said if he did she would kill him, and was like, 'Don't think I won't.' He just laughed at her. She was so mad! She said she wished she had her gun with her because she would shoot him."

"Did she tell you what he meant by movies?"

"I knew what he meant. Like, porn movies?"

"She does those?"

"I wouldn't put it past her."

"Does she have sex with men for money?"

"Listen," Chloe said. "Amber will do anything for money. That's, like, all she cares about. She'd kill me for a nickel."

"What happened next?"

"Some lady drove up in an Escalade and went into the house. She came right back out, though, and the little dogs came out with her. She was trying to catch them when the other ladies came."

"Could you identify her if you had to?"

"Sure," Chloe said. "It cracked us up watching her try to catch those dogs. We were sitting in Amber's car watching."

"Then what?"

"More people came. The catering van came, so we walked up the hill to help carry stuff. The dog catcher came and let us all in. We were getting the food ready when the lady who found the body screamed."

"Was the one who found the body the same one who came to the house earlier?"

"Nope," Amber said. "It was the other one."

"What color hair?"

"Dark," she said. "She had a diamond on her finger that was, like, as big as her knuckle. She drives an Escalade, I mean, she's got to be rich, right?"

"Did you catch any names?"

"After they came downstairs, the one who found the body took the one who was in the house earlier into the dining room. They were whispering, but I heard one say, 'what are we going to do now, Candy?' "

"Candy was the one you'd seen go in earlier?"

"I guess."

"Do you think she knew you saw her go into the house before they found the body?"

"Nah, we were in Amber's car, down on the main road. I don't think she knew we were there," Chloe said.

Her eyes widened.

"I thought the old lady had a heart attack or something. Do you think somebody killed her?"

"We won't know until the autopsy results are back," Maggie said. "Until then, Chloe, I think you shouldn't hang out with Amber, or go anywhere alone."

"O.M.G.! Are you for real?"

"You really should talk to the police," Maggie said. "You could be a witness to a crime, and that's dangerous."

"I never thought of that," she said. "This is totes for real scary!"

"Would you talk to the police? I think it might help them solve the case, and they could protect you."

"I don't want to talk to the police," Chloe said. "I'm, like, really scared."

Chloe's eyes filled with tears and Maggie handed her a napkin.

Scott came in the bookstore at the agreed upon time, and Maggie waved him over. As she requested, he wasn't in uniform. She introduced him to Chloe as "her husband, Scott," and asked him to sit down. He shook Chloe's hand and gave Maggie a curious look.

"Chloe was working at Mrs. O'Hare's house the day she died, and she saw some things she's worried about,"

Maggie said. "I told her she should talk to the police, but she's afraid to."

"That's understandable," Scott said. "On TV the police are kind of scary, aren't they?"

He smiled at Chloe, and she smiled back, although she sniffled.

"I don't seem scary, though, do I?" he asked her.

She shook her head.

"You seem nice," she said.

"Well, I work for the police department, and you can tell me what happened, and you don't have to go down to the station or anything."

Chloe looked at Maggie.

"Do I have to?"

"You're just helping me solve a puzzle," Scott said. "Mrs. O'Hare probably had a heart attack or something, but we need to know everything that happened that day."

"Scott won't let anything bad happen to you," Maggie said. "Don't worry."

"Okay," Chloe said, but she didn't sound confident.

"Can we borrow your office?" Scott asked Maggie.

"You go, too!" Chloe said and grabbed Maggie's hand.

"How old are you?" Scott asked.

"Eighteen," Chloe said. "Well, next month, anyway."

"I need one of your parents to be here with you," he said.

"My dad," Chloe said. "My mom would freak."

"Let's go back to Maggie's office and call your dad," Scott said. "We'll just talk about what happened, and I promise it won't be scary at all."

After Chloe and her father left the bookstore, Scott hugged Maggie.

"I don't know whether to kiss you or put you in a jail cell," he said. "I may just kiss you in a jail cell."

"You would never have found her without me," Maggie said.

"I know," he said into her neck. "It just scares me to think of you out there meddling in something so dangerous."

"Who do you think killed her?"

"We don't know for sure it was murder," Scott said.

"Oh, it was murder, and you know it as well as I do. Amber would kill for Chip, I'm sure. Chloe didn't know he was Amber's boyfriend. Amber heard Gigi threaten to disinherit him."

"Jillian might have done it for the same reason," Scott said.

"Jillian may have told Gigi about the affair, thinking Gigi would threaten him, and then he'd drop Amber."

"If she did that, it backfired."

"Maybe her backup plan was to kill Gigi."

"What could she have given her, though, that wouldn't kill her right away?"

"I don't know," Maggie said. "Chloe said her face was puffy and red, but she thought it was from crying. Maybe it was because she had already had contact with something she was allergic to."

Maggie told Scott about Claire's perfume theory.

"I don't remember any perfume on the inventory list," Scott said. "I'll have to look again to be sure."

"Claire saw her put the perfume on that morning."

"I don't know enough about the chemistry involved to know how quickly anaphylactic shock sets in."

"I need to talk to an allergist."

"I know this won't do any good, but is there any way I can convince you to stay out of it?"

"Eugene has an allergist; we can call him."

"Are you even listening to me?"

"Sure, honey, you've been a big help."

Scott sighed.

"Please be careful."

"I will," Maggie said. "I need to call Hannah."

"No way, Nancy Drew," he said. "We have a date night tonight."

"Please," she said. "Give me five minutes on the phone with Hannah, and then we'll go."

"Fine," he said. "While you call Hannah, I'll call Sarah."

"Why does she have to be involved?"

"Because it's her case and I'm just assisting with inquiries."

"Can't you leave her in the dark just a little bit longer? Cats love the dark."

"It's my job," he said. "Now, we can have date night up in Glencora at the Lamplight Inn, or down here in a cell at the station."

They had just pulled into the parking lot of the Lamplight Inn when Hannah called back.

"There's something called Stevens-Johnson syndrome," Hannah said. "The person can be exposed to something and not have a reaction right away. They might feel sick, but not have a dangerous reaction until hours later."

"What can cause it?"

"The doctor said it could be an allergen, a medication, or an infection," Hannah said.

"We need to find out if Gigi ever had this happen before," Maggie said.

"Can't," Hannah said. "HIPAA laws prohibit the release of medical information. I asked her."

"Even when the patient is dead?"

Maggie looked at Scott.

"A legally appointed representative of the family can make that request," Scott said. "Especially if another family member's health is implicated."

"Claire can request it on Eugene's behalf," Maggie told Hannah.

"I'm on it," Hannah said and hung up.

"I think I'm going to have to deputize you three," Scott said.

"You'd be lucky to have us," Maggie said.

"Okay," Scott said. "Who had access to Gigi's medical information?"

"Chip might have known, having lived with her," Maggie said. "Jillian had access, too, from working at the hospital."

"Hospitals are really careful about who has access to medical records," Scott said. "Only medical personnel treating that patient are allowed to access the records."

"But who polices that?"

"The Health Information Systems Department."

"Bingo," Maggie said. "Chip's in charge of that."

"So, Jillian or Amber could find that out what she was allergic to by talking to Chip, and then what? One of them put something in her perfume, her food, her drink?"

"Possibly."

"She couldn't know it wouldn't immediately put her in anaphylactic shock."

"Maybe she experimented. Maybe she gave her small bits over a long period of time, and watched what happened, practiced for the main event."

"That's pretty evil."

"And premeditated."

"What was Candace doing up there, and why hide it?" Maggie asked.

"Sarah will find out," Scott said.

"Unless she's already lost interest in the case."

179

"That's entirely possible," he said. "She didn't sound very impressed."

"So, flirt with her, keep her interested."

"Who are you?"

"Listen, I don't like Sarah, but she's got a weakness for you, so let's exploit that."

"You're a stranger to me in so many ways. It's kind of frightening."

"Listen," Maggie said. "You knew I was nosy when you married me."

"I feel like a piece of meat being dangled in front of a pack of wild dogs."

"Just one cougar," Maggie said. "And now you know what it feels like to be a stripper."

Maggie waited until they were back home, and Scott was in the shower, to call Chloe.

"Did you and Amber bring any food the first time you went in?"

"No," Chloe said. "We were just setting up the equipment. The food came with the van."

"At any time while you and Amber were there the first time, did Amber leave the kitchen?"

"Sure," Chloe said. "She was setting up the dining room."

"Was she gone for a while?"

"I don't know," Chloe said. "I can't remember. I was listening to the fight out back. Amber listened to part of it, but she had to get the room set up before the van arrived."

"Did she get in the refrigerator at all?"

"I don't know."

"Did she prepare any food or drinks?"

"No," Chloe said. "All that came with the van."

"Okay, Chloe," Maggie said. "Sorry to call so late."

"Hey, the other lady came and brought chicken salad," Chloe said. "I forgot about that."

"What other lady?"

"The big lady, the one who was running for mayor."

"Marigold Lawson?"

"Yeah, that's the one," Chloe said. "She said she couldn't come to the luncheon, but she knew Mrs. O'Hare liked her chicken salad, so she wanted to bring it."

"That was so helpful," Maggie said. "Thank you, Chloe."

After Maggie ended the call, she turned around to find Scott, with a towel wrapped around his waist, his hands on his hips.

"I can't leave you alone for five minutes," he said.

"Listen to this," Maggie said and filled him in.

"Marigold?" he said when she had finished. "Why would Marigold want to kill Gigi?"

"I don't think she would," Maggie said. "But I think Amber might have put penicillin in the chicken salad Marigold said Gigi loved."

"I'll call Sarah."

"Tell her I said, hi," Maggie said.

Scott made a rude noise and went to the kitchen to get his phone.

Maggie called Hannah to fill her in.

"Can't talk now," Hannah said. "The motion detectors just went off; someone's trying to get to Eugene."

Maggie interrupted Scott's call to tell him what was going on, and he relayed the new information to Sarah.

"I'll go right now," he told her.

He ended the call and dropped his towel as he ran down the hall to the bedroom to get dressed.

"Nice ass!" Maggie called after him.

Out at Hannah's farm, everything was lit up like daylight. In strategic locations, Sam had rigged up powerful klieg lights that flipped on when the motion detector went off. He and Hannah were in the kitchen playing back the video that started recording as soon as the lights came on.

"Hey," Hannah said as Scott came in.

"Look at this," Sam said.

He backed it up to the beginning, and Scott watched as the lights came on, illuminating someone dressed in black pants and a black hoodie sweatshirt, holding a flashlight, walking toward the barn. The person stopped, frozen in surprise by the lights, and then took off running back through the entrance to the farm.

"Not a lost hiker," Hannah said. "Not in that get-up."

"I didn't see anybody on the road as I came up," Scott said.

"Probably hid in the woods when they saw the car coming," Hannah said.

"What do you think?" Scott asked Sam. "Man or woman?"

Sam studied the playback twice more before he spoke.

"Woman or young man," Sam said.

"Jillian's son?" Scott asked.

"Or Jillian," Hannah said. "I'm going to go check on Eugene."

Claire was lying in bed, looking through her open bedroom window at the moon. A cool breeze blew the curtains this way and that, and although she was cold, she couldn't muster up the energy to do anything about it.

She could easily cry, but she was tired of crying.

Now that Laurie wasn't keeping her company in her head, there was more room for her own self-critical thoughts. It was like her brain had been busy gathering evidence against her all day, and now that she was a captive audience in a quiet room, the trial had begun.

'You've wasted your life.'

'You're shallow and petty.'

'You're too old to have a child.'

'You're going to be old and all alone; everyone you love will die, and you will have no one.'

'You're going to lose all your money, or spend it all on shoes, and it will be your own fault.'

'No one will hire you. You are unemployable.'

'Once Ed really gets to know you, he won't want to be with you.'

'Ed probably wants his own child, and he will leave you for a younger woman who can give him one.'

'Instead of being a help, you're a burden to your mother.'

'You're going to lose your mind like your father, but there will be no one to take care of you.'

'Maggie and Hannah tolerate you, but they don't really like you.'

'You don't belong here in Rose Hill, and there's nowhere else you can belong.'

Claire missed Laurie's voice in her head. At least he was nice to her.

There was a tap on the window, and there stood Ed.

She sat up and scooted over to the window.

"Hey," he said. "Can you sneak out?"

"I'm so tired," she said. "Can you sneak in?"

"For a little while," he said. "I can't leave Tommy alone overnight."

Claire pushed the windowsill up as far as it would go and Ed climbed in. He lay next to her and took her in his arms, her head on his shoulder.

"How was school?" she asked him.

"I like it," Ed said. "I make them put their cell phones in my desk drawer at the beginning of class, and they don't get them back until the class is over."

"They must hate you."

"I don't think they do," Ed said. "I think they like me."

"They should," Claire said. "You're good at what you do."

"I'm glad you think so," he said. "How are you doing?"

"I'm okay," Claire said.

"Don't lie," Ed said. "It doesn't do us any good."

"I'm struggling," Claire said. "But it will pass."

"It's hard to compete with a dead man."

"There is no competition," she said. "There was never anything between Laurie and me but friendship; I just hate the way he died."

"The meth cookers are being charged with his murder," Ed said. "At least there's some justice being served."

Claire thought about this but decided nothing that happened mattered in the context of Laurie's death if it couldn't undo it.

"Are you writing about Gigi's death?"

"I'll have a piece in the next paper about her," he said. "It's more of a tribute than an investigative report. The coroner's report is not back."

"Maggie, Hannah, and I think she was murdered."

"Tell me about that."

Claire told Ed about everything that had happened and all the information they had gathered.

"What do you think?" she asked him when she was finished.

"I think she died from an allergic reaction, but unless the police can prove beyond a reasonable doubt that someone dosed her with whatever killed her, the rest is just gossip and circumstantial evidence."

"Do you mean they could prove that Jillian or Amber had a motive, means, and opportunity, but couldn't prosecute either of them unless someone witnessed one of them committing the actual crime?"

"People have been convicted on circumstantial evidence alone, but nothing beats a good witness."

"So, they're going to get away with it."

"Sometimes that happens," Ed said.

He kissed the side of her forehead.

"I have to go," he said. "I don't want to, but I have to."

"I wish you didn't have to," Claire said.

"Then let's do something about it," Ed said. "Come live with Tommy and me."

"I need to work some things out first," Claire said. "Is that okay?"

"If that's what you need to do, then, of course, it's okay," he said. "I have faith in you, and I have faith in us. Take all the time you need."

After Ed left, Claire was more wide awake than before. She sat up and put her iPad on her lap. She may as well do some research rather than listen to the mean girl in her head.

She started by doing searches on Candy. She looked through her social media sites, saw photographs depicting every event in her family's life: vacations, birthdays, and school events. So much of their private life was on display for anyone who wanted to see it.

Claire wondered about the things that were private, and not on display. Were Candy and Bill happy? There was one picture taken when they were on a vacation where the kids looked happy, but Candy and Bill were obviously faking their smiles.

Did he cheat on her? There was one photo taken at a party they hosted where Bill had another woman sitting on his lap and they were pretending to kiss for the camera. Bill looked kind of into it.

Were her kids really as perfect as she made them out to be online? One of Candy's posts mentioned their son was having some "behavioral challenges," and she was asking for prayers.

Claire found lots of evidence online of Candy's committee work. Several of the committees also featured Jillian, but they never stood together for the photos. If they were close friends, you would think there would be lots of pictures of Jillian on Candy's social media, but there were none.

In contrast, Jillian's social media site had several mentions of a "shout out to my old friend Candy" and some snaps from events where Jillian had her arm around Candy and was taking the photo while Candy looked strained and irritated.

Jillian had several photos of her family, but in none of them did Chip and his son show any sign of affection between them. They didn't touch at all, and in every photo of the three of them, it was Jillian in the middle with an arm slung around each of them. She always had a huge smile plastered on her face, while they looked like they couldn't wait for it to be over. It was plainly evident from her posts that, despite all the chipper quotes on the importance of family, their family togetherness was forced at best.

Claire wondered if people who went overboard posting cheerful quotes and smug advice about being married or parenting children were compensating for something. If you were that happy and well-adjusted, why would it matter what anyone else thought about it?

Sophie Dean's site focused on Trashy Treasures, and there was nothing personal mentioned. There weren't any photos of the daughter who was away at college or any sentimental posts about the joys of being a mother or what having a daughter so perfect meant to her.

Because of a contract she'd had with her employer, Claire hadn't been allowed to have a social media presence. Now that she could, she had no inclination.

What could she write or post?

"So blessed to have known Laurie Purcell, alcoholic, policeman, piano player, and smart-ass extraordinaire. R.I.P."

She couldn't post photos of her cousins, who would make fun of her if she did, or of her father and mother, who were struggling so hard right now. Ed would probably love it if she posted a photo of the two of them, along with the status "in a relationship" front and center in her profile. It would be the only positive thing she could post.

She had nothing else to brag about, humble or otherwise.

Amber's social media site consisted of shot after shot of her in heavy make-up and skimpy clothing, partying with older men and other similarly dressed young women. Even in the shots where she smiled rather than smoldered, her eyes stayed hard and challenging. It was sad to see, and Claire wondered what had happened with her family that she was on her own so young.

Throughout her professional career, Claire had watched several young women just like Amber being used and discarded by the predators who infiltrated the entertainment industry. The ones who broke through and achieved an actual career were ambitious and ruthless like Amber and Claire's former employer, or were extremely lucky, which was rare.

Claire wondered if it was too late for Amber to change her life, or if she even wanted to. Maybe she was happy and felt a sense of accomplishment at what she'd achieved at such a young age. She had money, a little power, and a man who was willing to throw everything away in order to be with her.

But from experience and observation, Claire knew it wouldn't last; not the youthful beauty, the passionate sex, the power, or the money.

If you built anything on how you look: a relationship, a career, or a business; it would only last as long as your looks did. At the rate Amber was partying, she probably only had a few years left to look like she did now.

Then what would happen to her?

CHAPTER EIGHT

Claire was cleaning up the spa room at Pineville Hospice when the door opened, and a tiny older woman walked in. She was dressed in a pink polyester dress suit and a white blouse with a bow at the neck. Her thin legs were covered in dark tan, sagging pantyhose, and her shoes were taupe-colored orthopedic Mary Janes.

"Are you Claire?" she asked.

"I am," Claire said. "How may I help you?"

Claire was used to her customers coming in on gurneys and in wheelchairs.

"I'm Garnet Poudersheldt," she said. "My sister, Gladys, is in here, dying of the cancer. You did her hair earlier this week."

"I remember," Claire said. "She has the prettiest white hair."

The woman patted her own hair.

"Gladdie got the good hair from Mama," she said. "I got this frog fur from Papa."

"How's your sister doing?" Claire asked.

"We've been here five days," she said. "I've been afraid to leave her side for fear she'll slip away without me holding her hand. I don't want her to feel like I've abandoned her. They made me leave her room just now so they could do something to make her more comfortable, so I thought I'd see if you were in."

"I'm so sorry about your sister," Claire said. "What can I do for you?"

189

"There's a full bathroom in her room, so I've been able to bathe and keep tidy," she said. "But I have never done my own hair, you see, and it's getting kind of ratty."

"Let's take care of that," Claire said.

She unfolded a cape and gestured to the woman to sit in the shampoo chair. As was often the case, the woman's scalp was tight with tension, but pretty soon after Claire gently but firmly massaged it, she could feel the tension release. Claire thought that she might have fallen asleep, but the woman surprised her by speaking.

"I don't know what I'll do without Gladdie," she said. "She's 88, and I'm 86. We never married, you see. It's just been her and me since our mother died, back in 1970."

"How wonderful to have a sister you're close to."

"We neither one of us expected to end up this way," Garnet said. "I was always a romantic, but Gladdie's a realist. Once I turned forty, she said that's it, it's never going to happen, and it's been the two of us together ever since."

"They say it's never too late," Claire said.

"My fella died in World War II. His division was crossing a bridge over the Rhine River in Germany. He was shot off that bridge and drowned," Garnet said. "I was sixteen, and he was seventeen."

"I'm so sorry."

"It never seemed real to me," Garnet said. "There was no body, you see, on account of it was never found. His folks had a funeral, but there was no casket."

"That must have been awful."

"Everybody said I was so young I'd get over it, but I never did," she said. "For a long time, I thought maybe he'd survived somehow and would make his way back to me. I didn't care if he was crippled or blind; I was always ready to welcome him home."

"That's so sad."

"We'd been so happy, and in love, you see, and we had all these plans: the house we'd build, the children we'd have. He was going to work in the mill at Lumberton. His daddy worked there and would get him on, no problem."

Garnet seemed lost in her reverie.

"I lived on those memories for so many years," she finally said. "I had a whole life with him in my daydreams that seemed more real than the one I was living."

Claire couldn't think of anything to say.

Garnet looked up at her.

"You ever lose someone?"

"Yes," Claire said.

"I bet you cried your eyes out good and hard for a month straight and then got on with things," Garnet said. "Life is for the living. I wish I'd understood that then. Now, look at me. I'm an old lady about to lose my closest relative, and I have no children and no family to turn to."

"I'm so sorry," Claire said.

"Don't be too sorry," she said. "I'll be with him soon. That's my comfort. Of course, he'll be young and strong, and I'll be this old bag of bones."

"Maybe you'll be young, too."

"Oh, I hope so," Garnet said. "I would love so much to be young again and feel his arms around me."

She was looking ahead, but Claire could tell she was seeing something beyond the spa room in the hospice house. Her eyes shone.

She came to herself, smiled up at her, and Claire could see the young woman she once was. So in love, so optimistic, so sure life was going to bring all for which she'd hoped.

Claire wrapped her tiny head in a towel, helped her up and over to the hydraulic chair.

"Nowadays," Garnet said, "there's the internet you can use to meet people. You ever do that?"

"Oh, no," Claire said. "There are too many scary people out there on the internet."

"That's what Gladdie always says," Garnet said. "Me, if I were a little younger, I might try it. Not too many elderly serial killers about, I reckon."

"You still could," Claire said.

"That's sweet of you to say," Garnet said, and patted Claire's arm. "You ever married?"

"I was once," Claire said. "Divorced."

"Then at least you know what it's like," Garnet said and then sighed. "Still, I think it would be nice to have somebody to hold hands with at the movies."

"It is," Claire said. "It's also nice not to be married to someone you don't like or respect."

"You have a beau now?"

"I do," Claire said. "He's a very nice man."

"Do you have a picture?"

Claire retrieved her phone and showed Garnet a picture of Ed, with his new beard.

"Oh, I like whiskers on a man," Garnet said. "Gladdie never did; she said they tickled too much."

It didn't take long to finish the woman's hair; there just wasn't much to work with.

"Now, you must let me pay you," Garnet said, as she opened her purse.

"I wouldn't accept it," Claire said. "It was a pleasure to talk to you."

"I enjoyed it, too," Garnet said. "I'll tell Gladdie all about it."

Claire knew that Gladys had slipped into a coma the day before, but she didn't mention it.

"Come back anytime," Claire said. "I'll be back on Monday."

"I don't think Gladdie will last the weekend," Garnet said. "At least that's what the doctor thinks."

Garnet took a floral, lace-edged hankie out of her purse and dabbed at her eyes.

"I'm so sorry for your loss," Claire said. "It will be hard."

Garnet took Claire's hand, patted it, and then held it up to her cheek.

"You're a dear girl," she said. "You tell Mr. Whiskers he's a lucky man."

Claire watched the little woman walk out, and then restarted her cleaning efforts. She couldn't stop thinking about Garnet, however, and what it would be like for her to go home after her sister died, to the empty house they had shared.

She wondered again if Laurie was with his first wife. Then she had a thought that stabbed her in the heart: what if Laurie had been able to see her little brother, Liam, and give him a message? What if Liam had a message for her? Why hadn't she thought to ask? It was too late now. She'd never know.

That started her crying, so she sat down and let the tears roll.

Once she'd worn herself out from crying, she texted Maggie.

"I love you," she texted.

Maggie texted back, "Are you drunk?"

Claire laughed.

Next, she texted Hannah.

"I love you," she texted.

"I luv u 2," Hannah texted back, and then: "Who is this?"

Claire laughed.

Lastly, she texted Ed.

"I love you," she texted.

He texted right back.

"Glad my evil plan is working. See you tonight."

Claire smiled.

Out in the garden, Reverend Taylor was seated on the same bench they had shared two days before, reading texts on his phone.

"Sorry I'm late," Claire told him. "I cried all my makeup off and had to start over."

"No worries," he said. "I looked for you after the funeral, but you'd gone."

"After I embarrassed myself and interrupted your wonderful eulogy," she said, "I hid in the bathroom until most everyone left."

"Was it your friend talking to you in your head?"

Claire nodded.

"I thought as much."

"He's gone now, though," Claire said. "While I was hiding in the bathroom, I told him it was time for him to leave me alone. Apparently, he believed me."

"Now, nothing?"

"Not a peep."

"And how is that?"

"I miss him," Claire said. "I feel the lack of him now."

"It's probably for the best," he said. "It was keeping you from moving on with your life."

"I'm so tired of feeling like this," she said. "How do you tell where grief ends and depression begins?"

"I would say if you're worried about it, it might be a good idea to see a doctor. You may just need temporary support and not long-term therapy."

"Anything would be better than this," she said.

"Do you need the name of a doctor?"

"No," Claire said. "When I came back to live with my parents, our family doctor warned me that living with someone who has dementia can make you depressed. He told me if it ever became too much to call him and he'd prescribe something."

"It might help to talk to someone on a regular basis," he said. "I would be glad to see you at my office, or I can give you some names of counselors who are good."

"I'll see the doctor first and then call you," Claire said. "Actually, it feels good just to have made the decision."

"Asking for help can be difficult," he said. "Once you do, though, you can begin the journey back to feeling well again."

"I understand now why they call it mental illness," Claire said. "Mentally, I am not feeling well."

"Everyone could use some help getting through difficult times," he said. "There's no reason to be ashamed. We're human beings; we're all subject to the emotional turmoil that comes with just being alive. Sometimes it overwhelms us, and we need a helping hand, a caring listener, or a renewal of faith."

"I liked what you said at the funeral about the world being a school," she said. "I can't imagine your parishioners all go for that, though."

"What's true for me isn't true for everyone," he said. "The best thing we can do is peacefully coexist."

"I want to thank you for taking the time to listen to me, and for talking me through this," Claire said. "It really has helped."

"I'm glad," Ben said. "Always remember, everyone can teach us something. Sometimes, when you need to learn something, the teacher you need shows up, and if you pay attention, it can change everything."

After Claire left Hospice, she stopped at the depot farmer's market to pick up some vegetables for her mother. She found herself wanting to buy from each stand because she felt sorry for the people who didn't seem to be selling very much. She was buying way more tomatoes than she needed from a forlorn-looking old man when she ran into Sophie Dean.

"Let's have lunch," Sophie said. "I've got some hot gossip to tell you."

Sophie's pickup truck was parked underneath the wide-spread leafy limbs of a maple tree, so they sat in the back of the truck on a quilt and had a picnic. Sophie sliced a huge, red, juicy tomato into fat slices that they ate with salt.

"What's up?" Claire asked.

"I heard more about the day Gigi O'Hare died," Sophie said. "Jillian was there that day, and the police interrogated her."

"Hmm," Claire said. "Is that right?"

"Apparently, they think she might have had something to do with it."

"Really?"

"Gigi was just about to disinherit Chip," Sophie said. "I think Jillian killed Gigi before she could change her will."

"How do you think she did it?"

Sophie shrugged.

"Jillian's clever," she said. "She'll probably get away with it, like everything else she's done."

"That's unfortunate," Claire said.

"I heard Gigi died of an allergic reaction," Sophie said. "That's what clinched it for me. Jillian's a psychopath, but nobody believes me."

"How could she have done it, though? Jillian was locked outside the house when it happened."

"That's what she wanted everyone to think," Sophie said. "She was part of the family. You know at some point she had access to Gigi's house keys and probably had one made."

"That's pretty evil."

"When we were working together at Pineville General, Jillian once played a prank on a coworker who made her mad. The woman was known for eating the other nurses' food and borrowing their bath products out of their lockers while they were on shift. Jillian put oil of poison ivy in her body spray. The woman went into anaphylactic shock and could have died."

"How did she know Jillian did it?"

"She didn't. I figured it out. Unfortunately, no one believed me, and Jillian threw away the body spray before I could have it analyzed."

"Sorry I can't stay," Claire said and jumped down from the bed of the truck. "I promised my mother I'd look after my dad this afternoon."

"Well, call me if you hear anything," Sophie said. "And watch your back!"

Claire found Candy at home, where she was out back, skimming their swimming pool with a long-handled net.

"There was no one at the gatehouse, and the gate was open," Claire said. "I saw your car out front so I thought I'd take a chance you were home."

Candy rolled her eyes.

"I can complain to the Home Owners' Association until I'm blue in the face and nothing will be done about it," she said. "The kid who is supposed to be working the gate this summer is the son of the HOA president."

"Still, it feels pretty safe here," Claire said. "Speed bumps and video cameras."

"We do have real security that patrols the perimeter at night, and they are armed," she said.

"Is there a lot of crime up here?"

"Nope," Candy said. "And that's why we pay the guys with the guns. Between the hillbilly meth-heads and drunken college kids, no one's safe anymore."

"Do you have a minute?" Claire asked.

"Please excuse my poor manners," Candy said as she hung up the pool skimmer. "I needed to get this done before Bill gets home. He absolutely hates to find anything in the pool."

"Remember when we used to swim in Frog Pond all summer? The bottom was so gross and squishy we wore our tennis shoes."

"It's full of venomous snakes, now, apparently," Candy said. "Can I get you a cool drink? I have peach mint iced tea and lemonade."

Claire accepted an icy glass of lemonade, and they settled themselves in the cushy patio chairs.

"This is nice," Claire said.

"We love it," Candy said. "Everyone takes good care of their property, and there is none of that trailer trash drama like in town."

"I heard there was some drama at Gigi's the other day," Claire said.

Candy visibly shuddered.

"That poor woman," she said.

"I guess you saw her earlier in the day?"

Candy's head whipped around.

"Who said that?"

"I'm sorry," Claire said. "I thought it was common knowledge. You hear so much gossip, of course, that I don't remember who told me."

"I went up earlier to talk to her about the pediatric hospital campaign," Candy said. "No one answered the bell, and the door was unlocked. I just peeped in and called for her, but no one answered, so I went right back out. Unfortunately, those little dogs got out when I left. We had a time getting them rounded up, I'm telling you."

"Wasn't the door locked when Hannah went in?"

"Yes, it was," Candy said. "Isn't that interesting?"

"Why do you think that was?"

"I really couldn't tell you," Candy said. "Maybe it locked itself when I went out."

"What were you going to talk to her about?"

"Well, there's no point in being discreet now, is there?" she said. "Gigi had promised to give a very generous donation, big enough that it's going to be named the Eugene O'Hare Children's Hospital. We had the marketing people design the logo, and we needed to print our fundraising materials. I went there to get the check, whether I had to wrestle it out of her or not. Our entire campaign rested on her matching every donation. She had given me her word that she intended to make that donation."

"And now?"

"Well, I guess you know better than anyone that she didn't leave the hospital a dime in her will," she said. "Turns out it wasn't in the will because she planned to give me the check at the luncheon that day. I found the check, funnily enough, sitting on the table in the foyer. So luckily, her wishes are still being carried out."

Claire remembered Gigi saying that morning that she didn't intend to give Candy the amount of money she'd promised. The piece of paper Jillian had given Candy wasn't a note after all; it was a check.

"Was it for the full amount she'd committed to?" Claire asked.

"It was for twice the amount," Candy said with a smirk.

That facial expression struck Claire as inappropriate.

"You deposited it, even though she'd died?"

"Listen," Candy said, as she turned hard eyes on Claire. "It took me months to convince her to underwrite this thing, and the check was just sitting there. I took it so it wouldn't be left lying around, where someone could steal it. Later, it just seemed tacky to bring it up with Chip. I just let him think she'd given it to me before she died, and he seemed happy she fulfilled her commitment. Happy, that was, until after the will was read, and then he wasn't a bit happy. But it was already in the bank by then. There was nothing he could do."

"Lucky for you," Claire said.

"Yep," Candy said. "This has been fun, Claire, but Bill will be home soon and I need to get the house tidied up."

They both stood.

"Do you ever spend much time with Sophie Dean these days?" Claire asked.

"No," Candy said. "It's almost impossible to be friends with someone from a different social class. It can be so awkward. You feel you have to make an effort, of course, not to seem like a snob, but it's always harder on the lower class individual. It only reminds them of their station in life and makes them envious."

"I see," Claire said. "Well, I'll let you get ready for Bill."

"I didn't mean, you, of course. You've lived such a glamorous life it's all of us who should envy you."

Her words were meant to seem flattering, but Claire could see the glint of the knife edge hidden in the compliment.

"What do you think about the check?" Claire asked Maggie and Hannah later after she told them what Candy had said, and what Gigi had said about not giving as much as Candy anticipated.

"I think Jillian went in there, found Gigi dead, and helped herself to the checkbook," Maggie said. "She and Candy are in cahoots."

"Ditto," Hannah said. "It's a Cahootenanny."

"With that much money involved, you should be able to get a forensic expert to look at the check," Maggie said. "If Candy forged it, they will be able to tell."

"I'll have to call Walter," Claire said. "He'll know what to do."

Walter didn't know about the check, but he told Claire he would make a few calls and get back to her.

"I know someone at the bank who will help us," he said.

"What do we do now?" Claire asked her cousins.

"Somebody has got to tackle Jillian," Hannah said. "I was there that day; I can't do it."

"Don't look at me," Maggie said. "I never donate anything to her silent auctions, so she hates me."

"That leaves me," Claire said.

"Just don't be alone with her," Maggie said. "Do it in a public place. Do it in the bookstore."

"But how do I get her to meet with me?"

"Tell her you have some information she might find useful," Hannah said. "She won't be able to resist that."

"What information will that be?" Claire asked.

"Tell her about the strip club," Maggie said. "Tell her what her husband's new business is."

"She may not agree to meet with me," Claire said. "She doesn't even know me."

"Oh, she knows you, all right," Hannah said. "You're Eugene's keeper now."

"How is he?" Claire asked.

"He had a seizure this morning, the first one since he got out of the hospital," Hannah said. "We had to put one of those alert buttons on him and a sensor under his mattress. It's like an intensive care unit up in there. I don't think I'll sleep a wink tonight."

"Poor Eugene," Claire said. "What does the doctor say?"

"They reduced the dosage of his medicine again. He's stuttering more, but he shouldn't have another seizure."

"It seems like this is heading toward him not taking the medicine at all," Maggie said. "Then what happens?"

"Then he's back in stuttering prison," Hannah said, "serving a life sentence."

Claire obtained Jillian's phone number from Candace, on the pretext that she was interested in one of Jillian's charities. She texted Jillian the message Hannah had suggested.

"I have some information you will be interested in."

Jillian texted Claire back within the hour, and they agreed to meet in Maggie's bookstore coffee shop. Claire alerted Maggie, who promised she wouldn't let Claire out of her sight.

Claire was nervous, thinking she might be meeting with Gigi and Cheat's killer. Maggie had rigged up a voice recorder in the napkin dispenser on the table and planned to turn it on as soon as Jillian arrived.

When Jillian came in, the first thing Claire noticed were her pin-dot pupils, a sure sign of some sort of drug use. Jillian was breathless and sniffed three times before she sat down. That explained it.

"Can I get you anything at the coffee bar?" Claire asked her.

"I don't have time, unfortunately," Jillian said, as she scanned the room. "Your message was so intriguing I couldn't very well refuse, could I?"

"I'm sorry we've met under such strained circumstances," Claire said. "I really do have Eugene's best interests at heart."

"But what expertise?" Jillian said. "Why you? Really, I want to know."

"My family has been very fond of Eugene since he was a child," Claire said. "Gigi knew I wouldn't let any harm come to him."

"And I would?"

"I don't know, Jillian. So far, someone has killed his mother and his uncle."

"You can't think I had anything to do with that."

"Of course not," Claire said. "It was Candace who was with her before she died."

"It's appalling that you would think my dearest friend could have anything to do with that."

"Tell me about the check."

"The what?"

"The check you gave to Candace after Gigi was found dead."

"How do you know about that?"

"Ava saw you give it to her."

"It was intended for the committee," Jillian said. "I just put it where Gigi intended it to go."

"Except she told someone that morning that she didn't intend to give Candy as much as she promised, and then, somehow, the check got made out for twice as much."

"She must have had a change of heart," Jillian said.

"What I can't figure out," Claire said, "is why you would let the check be made out for so much money when it would only reduce Chip's inheritance."

"I don't know what you're implying, but I know I don't like it."

"What did Candace promise you in return for turning a blind eye to the forgery?"

"I was already on the short list for that position, if that's what you're implying. I got there on my own merit."

"A pretty important position, I guess."

"Executive Director of the new children's hospital," Jillian said. "I should think so."

"Has it been announced yet?"

"At next week's board meeting, after the vote."

"Which is assured?"

"I have every good reason to anticipate I will be the candidate chosen."

"For a position bought and paid for."

"This is ridiculous," Jillian said. "I don't have to sit here and take this."

"Then go," Claire said. "And I'll just keep my helpful information to myself."

"What do you want?" Jillian asked in a whisper. "Money? A position at the hospital? I could probably get you a clerical position in administration, but with no medical training there's hardly anything else you could do."

"I don't want any favors," Claire said. "I want to know if it was you or Candace who forged that check."

"Neither of us would do such a thing," Jillian said.

"If a forensic specialist takes that check out of the bank, examines it, and compares it with examples of Gigi's handwriting, are you certain he or she will determine that Gigi wrote everything?"

Jillian was trembling, whether with anger or fear, Claire didn't know.

"If Candace did it, you, having been seen to give her that check, will be arrested as her accomplice," Claire said. "How much time do you think you'll both get for that, considering the amount of the check? Maybe they'll put you both in that prison Martha Stewart was in, Camp Cupcake, was it? What will everyone think of you then?"

"You don't know who you're dealing with," Jillian said. "My husband is a vice president at the hospital. He will vouch for that check. He will say that his Aunt Gigi told him it was going to be for that amount. Who are you? A hairdresser from nowhere. Who'll believe you?"

"Your husband, Chippie? The new owner of Tiger Tails Strip Club?"

"What are you talking about?"

"Ask him," Claire said. "Or ask his teenage girlfriend, the one they call Mustang Sally."

"You're lying," Jillian said.

"Ask him," Claire said.

Jillian stood up, almost puffing with indignation.

"You haven't heard the last of this," Jillian said.

"I'll hear about you getting arrested, I'm sure," Claire said. "And your cocaine dust is showing."

Jillian rubbed her nose before she caught herself.

"Go to hell," she hissed, and stalked off, slamming the door behind her as she left.

The bell on the door jangled furiously and then fell off the door.

Maggie came running out of the back office and grabbed the napkin dispenser off the table.

"Oh my God, if we didn't get all of that I will kill myself," she said.

They went back to her office, where they listened to the entire conversation between Claire and Jillian, which was perfectly audible.

"What's wrong with you?" Maggie said. "We've got her! Why aren't you happy?"

"I think I may have just signed Chip's death warrant," Claire said.

"He's a big boy, and he knows what Jillian's capable of," Maggie said. "Besides, he has that serial killer girlfriend on his side."

"I should have asked her about Cheat," Claire said.

"I think Amber killed him," Maggie said. "Jillian killed Gigi, and Amber killed Cheat. Boy, Chip can pick 'em."

On her way to Walter's office, Claire stopped by the station in Pendleton to see Shep, to ask him if there was any progress on the tire-slashing investigation.

"Sorry, gal," he said. "We canvassed the local business owners, but nobody saw our perpetrator in the hooded sweatshirt. There is something I'd like you to take a look at if you have time."

Shep took her in his office and loaded a DVD into a player.

"This is the camera on the corner of Main Street and Lafayette," he said. "Watch this area over here, near the opposite corner. Tell me if you see anyone you recognize."

Claire watched as people came and went, and then saw someone who made her sit up straight in her chair. The video was black and white, but those curly pigtails could only belong to one person.

"It's Sophie," she said.

"Uh huh," Shep said. "And look what she's holding."

He rewound it and played it back a few frames at a time.

"It's something dark, but I can't tell what it is," she said.

"Looks to me like it could be a black jacket of some sort," he said. "It was mighty hot that day for a sweatshirt."

"Let me tell you a new story about our friend Sophie," Claire said.

She told Shep about the intern seeing Sophie slash her own tires so she could blame Jillian.

"Here we have a familiar motive," Shep said. "Slashing tires and blaming Jillian."

"I can't quit thinking about it," Claire said. "She was the only person besides my mother who knew I was coming to Walter's office the next day."

"After I saw this video, I went back over all my notes," Shep said. "She was a young, single mother, barely making ends meet, all because Jillian had run her out of her job. I felt sorry for her. Then Jillian was so uncooperative and ugly about being questioned that it got my blood up, made me want to believe she was the perpetrator. That's just sloppy police work. I'm ashamed of myself."

"But the neighbor said he saw Jillian write on Sophie's garage ..."

"Her so-called witness is currently serving time for possession with intent to distribute," Shep said. "As far as I'm concerned that makes him less than a reliable witness. I'm embarrassed I let her pull one over on me. I need to retire."

Claire clasped his hand.

"My dad said no one can be right one hundred percent of the time, even the police," Claire said. "You're just a person, not infallible."

"I've already told the search committee," he said. "They've got thirty days."

"This is so twisted," Claire said.

"Hell hath no fury, apparently," Shep said. "And that woman carries a grudge like it's her reason for living."

"What are you going to do?"

"Not a thing I can do," Shep said. "It looks like her, but she has every right to walk downtown whenever she wants to. I've got no witnesses that put her in that parking lot, wearing a dark sweatshirt, while you were in Walter's office. If I ask her about it, and she says, yeah, I ran downtown to do x, y, or z, then what do I have?"

"There's nothing we can do."

"Watch your back," Shep said. "I wouldn't get in between these two if I were you."

In her dream, Claire heard voices in the kitchen. Men's voices. She got out of bed but couldn't see very well. She felt her way down the hall to the kitchen, where the light was so bright it hurt her eyes.

'Hey, prom queen,' her cousin, Brian said.

Brian, her dead cousin, the one who had been married to Ava.

He was sitting at the kitchen table with Laurie, Tuppy, and a dark-haired young man she didn't know, playing poker.

'What are you doing here?' she asked Laurie.

He smiled but held a finger up to his lips. He then tilted his head toward the young man she didn't know and raised his eyebrows.

'Tuppy,' she said, turning to her friend and former co-worker, the one who had been killed earlier in the year. 'What's going on?'

'Oh, Clairol,' he said, gesturing to the young man. 'You never were the brightest bulb. Look at him. Don't you recognize him?'

She looked at the young man.

He smiled at Claire, and then she recognized him.

'Liam,' she breathed. 'Oh, sweetie.'

He winked at her and gave her a thumbs up.

'He's perfectly fine,' Tuppy said. 'I don't know what you were so worried about.'

Claire woke up, her heart pounding, Tuppy's words still ringing in her ears.

The next morning, Claire drove down to the depot and was surprised to find Sophie's store closed. Sophie's truck was parked out front, so she knocked on the door of Trashy Treasures until she appeared and unlocked the door.

Sophie's face was a tense mask.

"What do you want?" she asked Claire.

"I need to talk to you about the other day when I was here," Claire said. "Has something happened?"

"Someone tried to burn down my store," Sophie said.

She pushed open the door so Claire could come inside. Her shop was a soggy mess of ruined merchandise, and what wasn't soaked was black from smoke.

"Oh, my goodness," Claire said. "When did this happen?"

"After I left last night, I realized I hadn't taken the deposit, so I came back and saw the smoke," she said. "They must have broken into the store next door and crawled over the partition between us. The fire department said it was arson, no question."

"This is terrible," Claire said. "Who would do such a thing?"

"I'll give you three guesses," Sophie said.

"She'd be the obvious suspect," Claire said. "Have they questioned her yet?"

Sophie shrugged.

"I told the fire chief about her history of harassment and the restraining order, and that they should talk to Chief Shepherd if they had any questions," Sophie said. "So far I haven't seen anyone from the police department. They're probably in her pocket somehow, and couldn't care less."

"I'm so sorry this has happened," Claire said.

Sophie shrugged.

"She's not going to stop until she's locked up. I hope this time they can prove she did it."

"Aren't there video cameras all over the place here?"

"I haven't heard yet if they saw her on the tapes," Sophie said. "They think whoever did it must have gone in one of the stores as a shopper and then hid in there until all the shops were closed and everyone was gone. We have this trouble with birds getting in here and flying back and forth over the shops. It sets the security alarms off, so most of us quit setting them. She could have hidden in any shop and then climbed over the partitions until she got to mine."

"Wouldn't she have needed a ladder?"

"We all have them," Sophie said. "She'd have plenty of time to put one back before she left through the emergency exit. We're all required to have those doors; all she had to do was push to get out. If I hadn't come back when I did, everyone's shops would have burned up."

"I hope you have good insurance."

"Good enough," Sophie said. "I'm not going to let her burn me out, though. I'll rebuild."

"If there's anything I can do to help," Claire said, "please let me know."

"I will," Sophie said. "What was it you wanted to ask me?"

"When I came to see you the other day, I told you I had an appointment at the attorney's office the next morning."

"Yeah, so?"

"Did you happen to mention that to anyone?"

"That you were going to the lawyer?"

"Yes."

"No," Sophie said. "I don't understand why you're asking."

"Someone slashed my tires while I was in his office," Claire said.

"Jillian must have been following you," Sophie said. "It's what she does."

"She's pretty scary," Claire said.

"I've been trying to tell everyone that for years," Sophie said. "Unfortunately, no one ever believes me."

Claire again offered to help her if she could, and Sophie walked her outside.

"One more thing," Claire said, just before Sophie went back inside. "Did you come downtown that day, the morning I had the appointment?"

"No," Sophie said. "I was here all day, why?"

"Just trying to find someone who saw anything out of the ordinary," Claire said.

"Sorry, I can't help you," Sophie said, and went back inside.

Claire sat in her car and thought about everything that had happened and everything she knew. Just because the guy was a drug dealer didn't mean he was lying to Shep about Jillian spray-painting Sophie's garage door. Just because Sophie once slashed her own tires to frame Jillian didn't mean she'd slashed Claire's. Besides, would she really burn up her own shop, her livelihood?

But why would she lie about going downtown? Claire could swear that it was her in the video, but it was far away, and she guessed it was possible someone else could wear funky cat-eye glasses and curly pigtails. If it had been in color instead of black and white, she would have been able to recognize the red-gold hair. Claire had so many conflicting pieces of information churning around in her head that she was starting to get a headache.

She called Hannah.

"The Curious Cousins Detective Agency needs to have a meeting," she said when Hannah answered.

"I've been looking for you," Hannah said. "You need to come out to the farm; we have something to show you."

Claire couldn't help herself; she kept glancing in her rearview mirror the whole way to Rose Hill.

Out at the farm, Hannah and Eugene were setting up his shop in the backroom of the downstairs of the barn. Everything had been swept and mopped, so there was no longer any smelly evidence of animals having been kept there. Penny, the pony, was the only occupant in a stall in the front room, and she was a quiet roommate. Eugene was excited to show Claire how everything was organized. He still stammered, but he didn't let it stop him trying to speak. Claire was careful not to try to finish his sentences for him.

"Th, th, this is my n, n, new plathe," he said. "How d, d, do you like it?"

"It's great," Claire said.

"Hannah th, th, thaid I could th, th, thtay here ath l, l, long ath I like."

"We like having you here," Hannah said. "We needed to put this barn to good use, and you know me, I'd just fill it up with strays."

"I'm your n, n, new th, th, thtray," Eugene said with a big smile.

They left him hooking up his computer and went into the house.

"I'm so glad this worked out," Claire said. "Are you sure you don't mind him staying here permanently? I thought Sam didn't like anyone on his land."

"It was Sam's idea," she said. "I swear."

"He can afford to pay rent, you know."

"We don't want his money," Hannah said. "We just want to help."

"I wish his relatives felt that way," Claire said. "Speaking of which, I've got some new information for you, about Sophie and Jillian."

Claire caught Hannah up on the latest.

"Man," Hannah said. "Those chicks are bat-poop crazy."

"It's hard to know who to believe."

"How about neither of them?"

A tractor pulling a flatbed trailer loaded up with bales of hay rolled through the gates to the farm. There were two young men sitting on the back of the wagon, swinging their legs and laughing.

"Are you getting some cows or horses?" Claire asked.

Hannah's eyes widened for a moment before she responded.

"Ed's having all the vets out to the farm for a movie night," she said. "We're going to hang a sheet on the side of the barn and show movies."

"What a great idea," Claire said. "May I help you set it up?"

"Sure," Hannah said.

With Hannah directing them, the two young men put all the hay bales in several rows parallel to the side of the barn. Hannah then paid the tractor driver, and they left.

"I'm going to cover them with moving blankets," Hannah said.

Hannah and Claire toted stacks of moving blankets from the barn to the driveway and began wrapping the hay bales.

"I thought this would be the easy part," Hannah said. "I should have made those boys do it."

"I haven't run in a while," Claire said. "I could use the exercise."

"People give me a hard time about being skinny," Hannah said. "I'm not going to give you a hard time about it, but I can count your ribs."

"I kind of lost my appetite," Claire said. "I guess Maggie told you."

"If you tell one of us, you've told both of us," Hannah said. "You don't have to talk about it if you don't want to."

"I don't mind," Claire said. "I'm depressed, and I need to take some medication and get counseling. I'll call Doc Machalvie on Monday."

"Do you really have to take something for it?" Hannah asked. "Can't you just ride it out?"

"It's not getting better," Claire said.

"You're not thinking about offing yourself, are you?"

"No," Claire said. "But I am having dreams where dead people play poker in my parents' kitchen."

"That's not good," Hannah said.

They were both silent for a while, wrapping the hay bales.

"Sam gets awfully depressed sometimes," Hannah said, finally.

"What's that like?"

"Oh, he gets down on himself and all the things he can't do," Hannah said. "He gets really quiet and short-tempered. Even the dogs stay away from him."

"That sounds about right."

"He usually goes to visit his buddy, Dave, in Connecticut," she said. "They were roommates in college. After a couple of weeks there, he comes back in better shape."

"How often does this happen?"

Hannah shrugged.

"It used to be every other year or so," she said. "I don't think he's gone up to Dave's since Sammy was born."

"That must have helped."

"Or it could be because I told him if he left me alone with our son for more than twenty-four hours I would advertise his position and replace him within the week."

"I feel like I've let my mom down," Claire said. "She'd probably like to replace me."

"We've got your daddy covered," Hannah said. "Don't you worry about that."

"I keep hoping I'll snap out of it."

"Is there anybody you'd like to go visit? Maybe getting out of town would do you good."

Claire thought about it for a few minutes. She couldn't think of anyone she wanted to visit or any place she wanted to go.

"It's exhausting just thinking about traveling," Claire said.

"You've got everything you need right here," Hannah said. "Plus you've got Maggie and me. We're a whole lot of fun."

"You are, it's true," Claire said.

"Well, that's this done," Hannah said, as she wrapped the last hay bale. "Now I'm itchy and dirty; let's go for a swim."

"You're on," Claire said.

It was relaxing to be out on the pond, drifting on the inner tubes, sipping cold beers and not talking, just floating, and looking at the sky. Minutes passed, and Claire lost track of time. When Hannah finally spoke, it startled her.

"Cold front moving through here this weekend," Hannah said. "Summer's just about over."

"Not already," Claire said. "It's still August."

"We'll have some more warm days," Hannah said. "But this pond won't be warm enough to swim in this time next week."

"Do you think Eugene would mind if I moved in the barn with him?" Claire asked.

"He'd probably die of a heart attack if you asked," Hannah said. "He'd die a happy man, but still, you better not."

"Maybe I could build one of those tiny houses out here," Claire said. "I could get off the grid and go solar."

"You'd need one solar panel just for your hairdryer," Hannah said. "I don't think you're suited to the camping life. I remember the one time you went camping with my family you pouted the whole time and cried to go home."

"Your brothers kept throwing spiders on me," Claire said. "Then when we tried to sleep, they made bear noises to scare us."

"They haven't changed," Hannah said. "Now they just throw spiders on their own wives and children."

"Do they ever come to visit?"

"Not very often," Hannah said. "They mostly do stuff with their wives' families. You know my mom, she hates having company. Every fall my dad goes to Canada, fishing with the boys. I have nieces and nephews I haven't met yet. Only Owen's met Sammy."

"You could visit them."

"And leave the farm, the dogs, Sam's work, my work, and let Sammy destroy someone else's house? Connor's wife, Sherri, collects porcelain figurines. She has them sitting all over the house. Evan and Debbie have white carpet. Can you imagine? No way."

"What about Sam's mother?"

"She who must not be named?" Hannah said. "She stays in Florida, and we stay out of Florida. She calls on Christmas and Sam's birthday. She's never met Sammy."

"How could she stay away from that darling child?"

"She's still mad at Sam for marrying me," Hannah said. "Sammy's mine, so he must also be punished."

"That's so sad."

"Fine with me," Hannah said. "Suits me down to the ground."

"We should have a big family picnic and invite everyone who lives away," Claire said. "It's a shame for everyone to lose touch and not have some kind of relationship."

"You want all those people in your backyard?"

"There's no room at my mom's."

"Well, don't look at me, and Maggie sure as hell doesn't want them," Hannah said. "Our family's full of drama queens, and it's never more apparent than when we're all together. If you want us all to love each other, then good Lord, don't make us spend any time together."

"It was just an idea."

"Let's keep it that way," Hannah said and then shuddered. "You didn't come to your parents' fortieth anniversary party, or you wouldn't suggest such a thing."

"What happened?"

"Crying, shouting, fistfights," Hannah said. "And that was just my mom and me."

"You're exaggerating."

"Ask Maggie," Hannah said. "We swore an oath never to do it again."

Sam came walking down the hill, holding Sammy.

"Mama!" Sammy yelled. "Come home! Me hungry!"

Hannah sighed.

"Coming!" she called out.

They both paddled back toward the dock. Sam took Sammy back up the hill while they got out of the water.

"You should adopt a kid," Hannah said.

"What?"

"Why not?" Hannah said. "Kay could tell you how to do it. There are lots of kids who need a home."

"I'd be a terrible mother," Claire said. "Plus, don't those kids have lots of problems?"

"You'd be a great mother. Look at how you're taking care of Eugene," Hannah said. "And all kids have problems. Don't you remember being a kid?"

As Claire walked down Possum Holler, she thought about what it was like being a kid. After Liam died of leukemia, her parents grieved so hard that she felt forgotten. Her cousins had pulled her into their dysfunctional families, where she always felt like an outsider, and the conflicts in their households made her long for her own home. Unfortunately, her devastated parents could hardly cope with their grown-up responsibilities. By the end of the day, there was little energy left for their daughter.

Claire tried to imagine what it would have been like to lose both her parents at that age. She would have been absorbed into one of her uncle's families. What about kids who didn't have families to absorb them?

'I'm in no shape to take that on,' she thought to herself. 'But what if I felt better?'

The thought of taking care of a child who had experienced the kind of heartache she had known, or even worse experiences, might strengthen her resolve to do something about her depression. If she could get straightened up enough to find her own place to live, get a job, and get her life back on track, maybe she could eventually make room in that life for a child that needed a home. Ed would be all for it, she knew.

By the time she got to her parents' house, she not only felt better, she felt like she had something to work toward.

CHAPTER NINE

Ed was waiting when Claire got home. He was sitting in the living room with Claire's father, talking about a fishing trip they had planned.

"Claire Bear," her father, Ian, said. "Curtis, Calvert, Ed, and I are going fishing this Sunday."

"That should be fun," Claire said.

"Calvert knows where there's some trout, he says, and we aim to fly fish them out of their beds and onto our dinner plates."

"I love trout," Claire said. "Be sure to catch one for me."

"With your permission," Ed said, "I'd like to take your daughter out for dinner and dancing tonight."

"Well, she knows her own mind, I reckon," Ian said. "If she doesn't mind, I don't mind."

"Thanks, Pop," Claire said.

"It's a school night, though, so don't you two be staying out late."

She checked on her mother, who was reading in her room.

"Everything all right?" Claire asked her.

"You go on," Delia said. "If he wants to know where you spent the night, I'll say at Maggie's."

Outside on the front porch, Claire turned to Ed.

"Dancing?"

"I couldn't think of a euphemism he wouldn't object to."

Claire laughed.

"Where's Tommy tonight?"

"At an all-night gaming session at Grace's house," he said. "They've been playing over the internet with Elvis and some of his new college friends."

"Sounds like we'll have the place all to ourselves."

"I thought you might want to re-establish your territory, just in case some college girls get funny ideas about their professor."

"Sounds like a plan."

"Please restrain your enthusiasm."

"I'm sorry," she said. "I haven't been the best company lately. Thanks for putting up with me."

"Claire, I know you've been down, and you haven't wanted to talk about it, but I'd like to know more about it. I've been so preoccupied with this new job I'm afraid I've been neglecting you."

"I don't feel that way," Claire said. "I've wanted to be alone, not to contaminate anyone with my misery."

"You should talk to someone, even if it's not me. I'd understand."

"I had a long talk with Maggie," Claire said. "I'm going to go see Doc Machalvie next week and see if there's something I can take that will help."

"I'm glad to hear that," he said. "I'm going to ask this because it's been bothering me ... is this still about Laurie?"

Claire paused and gathered her thoughts. How much information was too much information, where Ed was concerned? More than anything, she didn't want to hurt him, but they had agreed to be honest with each other.

"Partly," she said. "I think it's also coming to grips with this big left turn my life took this year; quitting my job, Tuppy dying, what's happening with Dad, and not knowing what to do about a job. I was so excited about the possibility of the position in the theater department at

Eldridge, and when that fell through, it kind of knocked the stuffing out of me."

"Is there anything I can do to help?"

"Just knowing you're there for me helps a lot," she said. "You're the best."

"Keep telling yourself that," he said. "I'm like a cult, and you have to continually be indoctrinated."

"Is that a euphemism, too?"

"Absolutely," he said.

That night, while Ed snored lightly in his sleep, Claire was awake and staring out the window at the crescent moon. There was no music in her head, and she did not feel Laurie's presence. It was sad, but she didn't feel the sharp pain she had felt when she thought about him. She guessed she would always miss him, but that she had found a way to get on with her life and to enjoy the people who were still alive, who loved her and understood.

The next morning Walter called Claire.

"I touched base with some contacts I have on the board at Pendleton General Hospital," he said. "Sophie Dean was beloved by the staff and administration, and they had no trouble with her until Jillian started working there. Jillian's personality was difficult, and she was combative when criticized, but no one could fault her work. The consensus seems to be that while both women were good at what they did, when they were pitted against each other for the hand of the fair Chip, it brought out the worst in both of them."

"I have a feeling he egged it on."

"It seems that for a little while, at least, he was involved with both women."

"Why doesn't *he* have a bad reputation?"

"Because he's a man."

"I know that's true, but I still hate being reminded," Claire said. "What about Jillian's previous job?"

"My friend in HR is on vacation," he said. "But I shook some other trees, and something fell out. It seems our Jillian left rather than be fired from another hospital. She worked in the Labor and Delivery unit at Fairview General in Montgomery County for several years, and had an exemplary record up until just before she left."

"What did she do?"

"She had an affair with one of the OBGYNs," he said. "The wife found out about it and forwarded his and Jillian's torrid emails to everyone with a hospital email address."

"Oh, that's juicy."

"The doctor kept his job, but Jillian was asked to leave."

"Of course," Claire said. "Because he's a man."

"A man who brought in hundreds of thousands of dollars to the hospital," Walter said. "He was disciplined, and put on probation, but nothing else happened, so he's still there."

"Or he got better at hiding it."

"You've grown cynical," Walter said. "I thought only attorneys and law-enforcement thought the worst of everyone."

"How's our petition to see Gigi's health records going?"

"Slow moving through the hospital bureaucracy," Walter said. "There is a formal process that cannot be circumvented. It may take months."

"Oh well, there's only so much we can do."

"Let me know what else I can do. I'm enjoying this endeavor."

"You are an asset to the Curious Cousins Detective Agency," she said. "What's the word on the forgery?"

"I'm setting up a meeting with a bank representative I know very well. He was very interested in the recording of the meeting with Jillian that you shared with me. Can you meet me at my office, oh, say elevenish?"

"With bells on."

Maggie woke up with a start.

"Scott, look at the time!" she said, as she shook him awake.

He had come home for lunch, and one thing had led to another, as it frequently seemed to do since they got married not quite two months previously.

"Relax," he said. "Skip will let me know if something happens."

"I thought we were supposed to have less sex after we got married," she said.

"We're still in the honeymoon period," he said. "We've still got months to go before we get tired of each other."

"Jeanette asked me about your house," Maggie said, as she got dressed. "Are you still interested in selling it?"

"I hate to think how much work it needs, or how much it will cost to get it in shape to sell," he said. "Is she the one buying?"

"She and Fred are looking for something smaller, for retirement."

"Well, it's small," he said. "It also still has Laurie's stuff in it."

"Don't tell Claire," Maggie said. "I don't want her having to deal with that."

"It might help," Scott said. "Give her some closure."

"I need to get downstairs and help clean up from lunch," she said.

"That reminds me," Scott said. "Floyd called; he wants to talk to you about those complaint calls."

"Floyd," Maggie said when she finally got the health inspector on the phone. "Scott said you called?"

"Yeah, Maggie, I got a number for you," he said. "I called in a couple of favors down to the shop and got the number from the complaints about your café and your mother's place."

"It was the same person?"

"Same number, anyways," he said. "Now, I know I can count on you not to tell anybody how you come to have this."

"My lips are sealed."

Maggie wrote down the number as he read it off. When she called it, it rang and rang, but no one answered. She called Hannah.

"Hannah," she said when her cousin answered. "What's it called where you can look up a number and see who has it?"

"Reverse look up," Hannah said.

Maggie told her what information she had.

"Keep me on while you look," Hannah said.

Maggie used her office computer to open a browser, find the website, and enter the phone number.

"What's 'Trashy Treasures?' " Maggie asked her.

"That's the shop owned by Sophie Dean," Hannah said. "She's Jillian's archenemy. Claire's been working that angle; you better call her. I'm on my way over."

Maggie hung up and called Claire.

"Oh my goodness," Claire said. "These people are all crazy."

"Don't say anything more," Maggie said. "You're on your cell."

"I'm coming over," Claire said.

Claire met Hannah and Maggie in Maggie's kitchen. Sunlight streamed through the east-facing windows, and Scott's big tabby cat, Duke, was reclining on his back in the recycling bin on top of a stack of newspapers, soaking up the warmth. He opened one big gold eye to see who was disturbing his sleep, then stretched and turned over.

"Sorry," Claire told him.

They sat at the kitchen table and sipped iced tea while they brainstormed.

"So, this Sophie chick sees her opportunity to cause Jillian some grief by framing her for slitting your tires and trying to get our businesses shut down," Hannah said.

"Looks like it," Claire said. "She made the health department calls after I visited her for the first time, she was the only one who knew I had an appointment at the attorney's office, and she lied about being downtown that day. I know it was her in the video."

"Should you confront her about it?" Maggie asked.

"I'm afraid to," Claire said. "And what good would it do?"

"Maybe she'd stop if she knew we were on to her," Hannah said.

"How far would she go?" Maggie asked. "Would she try to frame Jillian for Gigi's death?"

"You mean, kill Gigi and frame her?" Claire asked.

"That's pretty extreme revenge," Hannah said.

"No, probably not," Claire said. "It's malicious mischief, but I don't think she'd kill Gigi. She sounded as if she was fond of the family. I think she just saw this as an opportunity to cause trouble for Jillian."

"Okay, then, what's next?" Maggie asked Hannah. "We've got Amber, Candace, and Jillian all with opportunity and motive. We've got Marigold supplying the chicken salad, but I can't imagine why she'd want to kill Gigi."

"Let's start with Amber," Hannah said. "She's my first choice. She had access to the chicken salad and the perfume, and she stole the perfume afterward."

"But she didn't get rid of the chicken salad," Maggie said.

"If you weren't allergic to penicillin, it wouldn't harm you," Hannah said. "No one who ate it would know."

"Gigi had an argument outside with Chip," Claire said, "and while Chloe is busy listening, Amber puts penicillin in the chicken salad or the perfume."

"Or both," Hannah said.

"But then she would have to count on Gigi putting on more perfume or eating the chicken salad before she went back in to steal stuff," Maggie said. "There's no way she could guarantee that."

"You think she put it in the chicken salad, but not in the perfume, assuming Gigi would eat the salad at the luncheon?" Claire said. "And she just stole the perfume because it was expensive?"

"Let's say that's true," Hannah said. "Where was Gigi when Amber went upstairs into her bedroom and stole the perfume?"

"Hmm," Maggie said. "Could she have been dead already?"

"Only if she ate the chicken salad or put on the perfume as soon as Chloe and Amber left," Hannah said.

"She was probably just in the bathroom or something," Maggie said.

"Okay, how about this?" Claire asked. "Amber puts the penicillin in the chicken salad, knowing Gigi will eat it at the luncheon. Let's assume all goes as planned and Gigi goes into anaphylactic shock during the luncheon. She'd have guests there who could call the paramedics; it may not have killed her."

"She'd want the penicillin to be in something she was sure Gigi would have contact with while she was alone," Maggie said.

"But there would be no guarantee she would put on more perfume that day," Claire said.

"Maybe it was set up to happen the next time she put on her perfume, whenever that was," Hannah said. "Maybe Amber didn't expect it to happen immediately, but the next morning."

"Then why steal the perfume?" Maggie asked. "She'd leave it there."

"I'm as confused as a fart in a fan factory," Hannah said.

"We're running in circles," Claire said. "I think she stole the perfume just because it was expensive and she was mad at Gigi."

"There may have been more than one bottle of perfume," Hannah said.

"What if she didn't put penicillin in anything?" Maggie asked. "What if it wasn't Amber?"

"Candace is next," Hannah said. "She was in the house after Amber."

"She went in and came right back out, according to Chloe," Maggie said. "Unless she ran upstairs, injected her with penicillin, and left ..."

"She's not the nurse," Hannah said. "She needed Gigi alive to give her the check."

"Which she probably forged," Claire said.

"That leaves Jillian," Hannah said. "She probably had a key or could have come and gone at any time through the back door with no one seeing her. She could have tainted the chicken salad and the perfume, or, she could have given her an injection."

"With no witnesses," Claire said.

"She was the first one to get to the body afterward," Hannah said. "She could have taken anything before I got up there."

"True," Claire said. "We know she took the check and gave it to Candace."

"What does Scott say?" Claire asked Maggie.

"He won't tell me much," Maggie said. "He's going to interview Marigold today about the chicken salad."

"That should be fun," Hannah said.

"What's Sarah doing?" Claire asked. "This is her case."

"Not much," Maggie said. "Unless the coroner's report suggests Gigi was murdered, it's not worth her while. It could be weeks."

"Meanwhile, someone's getting away with it," Hannah said. "On our watch."

"Let's go back to this check thing," Maggie said. "We now know Candace gave Jillian a job to keep her quiet about the forgery."

"Yep," Claire said. "Director of the new children's hospital."

"What if Candace killed Gigi, knowing the check was not going to be for what she said it would be and bribed Jillian with the job to help her cover it up?" Maggie asked.

"I have a hard time seeing Candace as a cold-blooded murderer," Claire said. "An opportunist after the fact, yes, but not a killer."

"I hate this," Maggie said. "How are we going to get any of them to confess?"

"I'm meeting with Walter later on today," Claire said. "I'm hoping that if Jillian and Candace are threatened with jail time over the forgery, one of them will rat the other one out."

"How can we get to Amber?" Hannah asked.

"I've been thinking about that," Maggie said. "I think she may confess to Ingrid."

"Who's Ingrid?" Claire asked.

"Oh," Maggie said, realizing she was just about to spoil the surprise party. "She's Amber's boss at the catering company. I met her, and she told me all about Amber's sad run-away life. She loves the little beast, but even she says Amber's capable of just about anything."

"Lovely," Claire said. "Are we of the same mind about Sophie Dean? She's an angry, jealous nut but she was nowhere near Gigi's house the day she died so she couldn't have done it."

"Agreed," Maggie said.

"Agreed," Hannah said.

"What do we do next?" Claire asked.

Everyone was silent for several moments.

"You and Walter will work on Jillian and Candace," Hannah said. "Maggie will talk to Ingrid again, see if she can find out something more about Amber, and I'm going to grab a tiger by the tail."

"What's that supposed to mean?" Maggie asked.

"I'm going out to Tiger Tails to apply for a job."

Maggie and Claire exchanged looks.

"Not as a stripper," Hannah said. "They advertised for a cleaner, and I'm going to apply."

"Be careful," Claire said. "Amber's armed and dangerous."

"I'll be sure to wear my bulletproof G-string," Hannah said.

Claire met Walter in his office, where he introduced her to a distinguished-looking, gray-haired man in a suit and tie.

"Call me Jeremy," the man said and shook her hand in a warm, gracious manner. "Walter has gone on and on about you; I'm so glad to finally meet you."

Claire must have looked confused because Walter and Jeremy exchanged smiles.

"Jeremy is my partner," Walter said. "We've been together for over twenty years."

"Oh, I see," Claire said. "How wonderful! Congratulations. Are you planning to make it legal now that you can?"

Jeremy laughed, and Walter winced.

"We talk about that a lot these days," Jeremy said. "I'd like to do it, but Walter thinks we're safer leaving it as it is."

"We're more committed than most legally married couples I know," Walter said. "I don't see what we would gain from exposing ourselves to the negative attitudes that surround the issue right now."

"So many people worked hard to earn us this right; some lost their lives," Jeremy said. "It seems ungrateful not to exercise it."

"That's admirable but not very romantic, Jeremy," Walter said.

"It would be romantic, Walter," Jeremy said. "And I'm just saying my mother isn't going to be around forever."

"Sorry I started this," Claire said.

"Don't be sorry," Walter said. "I'm sure we will talk about it again before the day is over."

"Walter confided in me about the check," Jeremy said. "I brought a copy for him to see."

Jeremy handed the photocopy to Claire, who went to stand by the window, where the light was better.

There was no question the handwriting on the middle of the check was different from Gigi's on the top and bottom. Whoever had done it had not even bothered to disguise the difference in the style of zeroes added to the number.

"This is pretty blatant," Claire said and looked up at Walter.

"I don't think we need an expert," Walter said. "The question is what do we want to do about it?"

"Shouldn't you call the police?" Claire asked. "Aren't you obligated to report something like this?"

"Come sit down with us," Jeremy said. "I want to give you my perspective on behalf of the bank."

Claire sat down at the conference table, and Jeremy and Walter joined her.

"Right now the check is being held at the bank pending further due diligence," Jeremy said. "Unless I approve it to be deposited in the Children's Hospital Fund account, it won't be. We have a little time to figure out the best course of action. If we get the authorities involved, it has the potential to embarrass the bank, the hospital, and quite possibly put two women in prison. If they had forged the check for personal gain, I wouldn't hesitate. I think this was more a case of good intentions and poor impulse control."

"What can you do?"

"I've called both women, and invited them to meet with me to discuss it," Jeremy said.

"Here in this office?"

"They should be here any minute," Walter said.

"What's the plan?"

"We'll show them the photocopy of the check," Walter said. "We'll communicate our concerns, and then give them the opportunity to do the right thing."

"Jeremy will suggest that they allow him to shred the check," Walter said.

"I can withdraw it from that day's batch as a mistakenly deposited check," Jeremy said. "The auditor will have questions, but I think we can discreetly handle those."

"What if they won't admit it's forged?" Claire asked.

231

"Then I will inform them that I, as the estate's executor, will contest the check, subpoena the bank to seize it, and have it analyzed by the F.B.I.," said Walter.

"I would love to be a fly on the wall for that meeting."

Walter and Jeremy exchanged pleased looks.

"As Eugene's guardian you have every right to be here," Walter said. "As long as our bank representative doesn't mind."

"I'd be delighted for you to stay," Jeremy said. "Afterward, we'll go to lunch."

Jillian and Candace arrived separately, and both were surprised by Claire's presence. Candace covered her fear with politeness, but Jillian was a raw nerve.

"What's she doing here?" she asked.

Walter explained Claire's presence and invited Jillian to take a seat. Claire could see they were both nervous. Candace kept touching her hair and her face. Jillian was visibly trembling, could not sit still, and her pinned pupils were once again on display. More interesting to Claire was the fact that the two "dear friends" didn't greet each other or even acknowledge each other's presence.

Walter introduced Jeremy. Instead of speaking, Jeremy took two copies of the check and handed one to each woman. His stern face did all the talking.

Candace kept her cool, but Jillian could not.

"Why show me this?" she asked. "This has nothing to do with me."

"I understand you gave this check to Candace at Mrs. O'Hare's house just after you found her body," Walter said.

"It was made out to the Children's Hospital Fund and Candy's in charge of fundraising. There's nothing wrong with what I did," Jillian said. "If you accuse me of breaking any laws, I'll call my attorney."

Her tone was contemptuous, but Jeremy maintained his poise.

"Unfortunately," Jeremy said, "the check seems to have been altered. You can see that zeroes have been added to the numerical portion, and someone other than Mrs. O'Hare has finished filling out the middle line."

"Looks fine to me," Jillian said. "I certainly didn't tamper with it. I guess someone else could have."

At this point, she threw such a shade-filled look of contempt at Candace that it almost took Claire's breath away. To Candace's credit, she kept it together.

"What are our options?" Candace asked Walter.

"I would suggest that, since there is a question as to the authenticity of the check, it be withdrawn and destroyed."

"I already told the committee about it," Candace said. "They're preparing marketing materials based on its existence."

"You're sure to suffer some embarrassment," Walter said. "But wouldn't that be preferable to the alternative?"

All the color drained out of Candace's face. It stood in stark contrast to the red which suffused Jillian's.

"I had nothing to do with this," Jillian said. "I want that on the record."

"Jillian," Candace said. "Pay attention; if we cooperate, there will be no record. You don't need to say anything else. It's over."

"I was promised a job," Jillian said. "You can't go back on that now just because the check didn't pass inspection."

"That will be up to the board," Candace said, wearily. "Since I plan to resign my position as chair of the committee, I won't have any influence over that."

"That seems the wisest course," Walter said.

"I will see that the check is destroyed," Jeremy said.

"Fine," Candace said. "May I go?"

"Certainly," Walter said. "Thank you both for coming in."

Candace left, with Jillian close behind her, haranguing her about the job she was promised. Jeremy and Walter waited until they were safely out of hearing distance before chuckling.

"Nicely done," Claire said.

"We still have one important matter to discuss," Walter said.

"What's that?" Claire asked.

"Where shall we go for lunch?" he said.

Maggie went to the catering company and found Ingrid working in the kitchen.

"I don't have time to talk," Ingrid said, as she checked the status of several dozen mini quiches in the oven. "I'm short-handed and down to the wire."

"May I help?" Maggie asked.

"Actually, that would be great," Ingrid said.

Maggie scrubbed her hands and put on the clean apron Ingrid offered. For the next hour, she was Ingrid's assistant, and when they were done, Ingrid handed off the results of their labor to two college-aged boys, who loaded them in the catering van and headed out to a venue.

Maggie helped Ingrid clean the kitchen, and then they sat at the island and drank lemonade.

"I'm exhausted," Maggie said. "But you seem fine."

"I thrive on the chaos I create," Ingrid said. "I'm never happier than when I have more to do than I can get done and not enough time to do it. Makes me feel alive."

"I don't see how you can do this every day with no days off," Maggie said.

"You just haven't worked at the bakery for a while," Ingrid said. "I hope this doesn't seem rude, but what will happen to it when your mother can't work anymore?"

Maggie shrugged.

"We don't talk about it," she said. "First of all, my mother doesn't think she'll ever be too old, and everyone else is too afraid of her to suggest she might already be."

"I'll buy it," Ingrid said. "If it ever comes up, I would find the money somehow and buy it. I wouldn't change the name, either, as long as the recipes come with it."

"I'll keep you in mind."

"What did you come to see me about?"

Maggie told her about Gigi's murder and their suspicions about Amber.

"I'm not going to lie, I can imagine her doing it," Ingrid said. "I hate to think what she's been stealing from all my other clients."

"Is there anywhere here she might have hidden the evidence?" Maggie asked. "The perfume and whatever else she stole from Gigi's house."

"I'll look around," Ingrid said. "I'll call you if I find anything."

After Maggie left Ingrid's place, she saw that she had received several texts of the S.O.S. variety from Hannah. She threw the Jeep into gear and flew down the frontage road to the strip club, where smoke was billowing out of what was left of the building, and a group of barely dressed women and a few fully dressed men were watching from a safe distance. There were also the remains of a burned out car parked at the back of the lot.

Maggie's heart didn't stop pounding until she found Hannah, sitting in the bed of her pickup truck, accepting a cigarette and a light from a curvaceous blonde dressed and made up to resemble a famous, busty actress.

"I thought you quit," Maggie said.

"You never really quit," Hannah said. "You just take long pauses that sometimes seem to go on forever. Man, this is good. I can actually feel the nicotine flowing through my body. It's like a warm bath for my nerves."

"Did you do this?" Maggie asked her, gesturing to the fire.

A fire truck came wailing down the frontage road to join two others already fighting the fire. There were state, county, and local police milling around.

"I was here when it started," Hannah said, grinning.

Maggie hopped up to sit next to her.

"What happened?"

"Well, it was like this," Hannah said.

When Hannah arrived at the Tiger Tail Strip Club, there was no one parked outside, so she backed her truck up under the only shade tree available and made herself comfortable. Sammy had been up the night before with a tummy ache, and she needed to catch up on her sleep.

She woke up to two men arguing in the parking lot behind the strip club. One was Chip, and the other was an older, overweight man wearing, despite the heat, black pants, a black shirt, and a black tie. He had slicked back thinning hair dyed jet black, an intricately shaved goatee, and wore lots of gold jewelry. The gist of the argument seemed to be that someone wanted to buy the club, and Chip did not want to sell it.

"I'm suggesting to you, in a friendly way," the man said, "that it would be in your best interest to sell the club to us, or pay for my employer's protection, rather than lose your investment in a sudden and most unfortunate way."

"I'm not afraid of your threats," Chip said. "There are laws against extortion, and I will call the F.B.I."

"The fact of the matter appears to be that you do not know with whom you are dealing," the man said. "If you had been apprised of this information beforehand, in regard to the things of which we are capable, you would not hesitate to do as I am now kindly suggesting."

"Some small-town mob boss is not going to crowd me out," Chip said. "This is my club, I paid for it, and I'm going to run it clean, despite whatever you threaten to do."

"I am warning you, one last time, as a courtesy, in regards to this matter, that it would be advisable to cooperate with my employer. If you do not, I am afraid you will be left with the sort of a mess that will not be easy to redd up."

The man gestured to a big black Lincoln Continental that was idling at a distance.

"He is not a patient man. What's it gonna be?"

"Tell him no dice," Chip said. "I'm not going to bend over for a bully."

"It is with great sorrow that I must inform you that, because of your unwillingness to cooperate with my employer, I am now forced to blow up your club. You have five minutes to get everybody out."

"You're bluffing."

The man took what looked like a remote control out of his pocket.

"How's come younz never believe me?" he asked.

"That's fake," Chip said.

The man pushed a button and Chip's newly repaired BMW, parked back at the edge of the parking lot closest to the highway, blew up in a ball of fire. Hannah ducked down in her seat and speed-dialed 911.

"My car!" Chip yelled.

"I would suggest that you make the most of the four minutes you got left to evacuate the building," the man said.

237

Chip ran to the back door, and soon after, employees spilled out into the parking lot from every exit. They congregated well away from the man with the remote control and the idling black car. When a group wandered close to Hannah's truck, she got out and mingled with them, looking for Amber. She didn't see her.

Chip ran out the front entrance and raced toward the group. Behind him, there was a rumbling sound, and then flames shot out of the roof.

"My best good wig is in there," one woman said.

"I knew this was too good to be true," another said. "It was nice while it lasted."

Chip fell to his knees in the parking lot, and several people ran forward to help him up. He was crying, in an ugly, pathetic way.

"They destroyed it," he said. "All my dreams, everything I worked for."

"Did you clean out the safe, man?" one man asked him.

"There wasn't time," Chip said.

"Anybody else would have let us burn and saved the money," the man said. "You did the right thing."

"Maybe it's fireproof," Chip said.

"Yeah, well," the man said, "I'm not going to wait around to find out."

"Wow," Maggie said. "What did the guy with the remote control do then?"

"He got in the big black car, and they drove away, but not even fast. And here is the best part: as they passed Chip, the back window rolled down, and who do you think was in the back seat with Mr. Big?"

"Amber?"

"The one and only," Hannah said. "She waved at Chip and smiled. It was so evil it gave me goosebumps."

238

"What did Chip do?"

"He just stared," Hannah said. "I think he was still in shock."

"Where is he now?"

"He went with the state police," Hannah said.

They watched as the firefighters continued to douse the club with water. The roof had collapsed, and all that was left were the blackened walls and broken windows.

"That's a total loss," Hannah said. "Let's hope he has good insurance."

"How brazen just to do that in broad daylight with witnesses all around," Maggie said. "Won't the police be looking for the car?"

"The license plate had black tape over it," Hannah said. "They're probably halfway back to Pittsburgh by now."

"There's mafia everywhere," Maggie said. "We've got them in our state, too."

"Yeah, I know," Hannah said. "But this guy had 'the burg' way of talking."

"Have the police questioned you?"

"I told them I didn't see anything," Hannah said. "Whatta you think I am, nuts? I gotta kid. Fuggedaboudit."

When Maggie got home, there was a message on her landline voicemail from Ingrid.

"I found some things I think you might be interested in," Ingrid said. "I'll bring them with me tomorrow to Claire's party."

"How was your interview with Marigold?" Maggie asked Scott, who was eating cereal at the kitchen table.

"Brutal," he said. "She screamed at me and threatened to have me fired."

"Did you find anything out?"

"She bought the chicken at the IGA, and nobody touched it but her until she delivered it into the caterer's hands."

"Did she say where Gigi was when she delivered it?"

"The caterer said Gigi was meeting with someone, so Marigold didn't stay."

"Hmmm," Maggie said.

"Have *you* got anything you'd like to share with the class?"

"Not really," Maggie said. "My day was kind of boring, actually."

"Good," Scott said. "Let's keep it that way. It's much safer."

When Hannah got home, Eugene was sitting on the floor in the kitchen, playing a card-matching game with Sammy. Sam was cooking dinner, which smelled like chili, his favorite. The two little dogs were curled up with the two big dogs. Hannah used her phone to take a picture of the scene to send to Maggie and Claire.

"Hello, family," she said as she walked in.

When Eugene looked up, she saw a bruise on his forehead.

"What happened?" she asked him. "Did you have a seizure?"

He nodded and shrugged.

"Genie fell off the bed," Sammy said. "Me telled him it's okay, me's fallen off the bed lots of times."

"Why didn't someone call me?"

"We went to the emergency room, they looked him over, ran some tests, and Dr. Schweitzer called in orders to take him off the meds completely," Sam said. "Eugene asked me not to bother you. We men took care of it ourselves."

Sammy ran out of the room and returned with a blown up blue latex glove that had been tied to make a balloon.

"Look what's they's gave me at the hops pedal," he said.

He batted it over to Hannah, and she batted it back.

"Eugene, are you okay?" she asked.

He nodded and smiled sadly.

"Is your stutter bad?" she asked.

He nodded again.

Hannah crouched down on the floor and hugged him.

"We love you," she said. "It'll be all right, no matter what."

Eugene was overcome momentarily and wiped his eyes.

"Th, th, th, thankth," he said.

Sammy came over and patted his shoulder.

"Genie be all right," he said. "You wants to play with my hand bloon?"

Eugene accepted the balloon, and Sammy sat down on his lap.

"Genie's my new brudder," Sammy said. "Me takes care of him, and he's takes care of me."

Eugene gave Sammy a squeeze and smiled at Hannah.

"Welcome to the family," she said.

Later that night, when Sam came to bed late, Hannah was waiting up.

"Can't sleep?" he asked her.

He sat on the side of the bed and took off the two lower leg prosthesis he wore.

"I never in a million years would have expected you to accept Eugene into our family," Hannah said. "Every step of the way I kept waiting for you to say, 'He's not our responsibility' or 'Don't get too attached.' "

He stopped what he was doing but didn't look at her.

"You never leave an injured brother on the battlefield," he said.

Hannah touched his back, and he flinched. She pulled her hand away and rested it on her stomach. Sometimes, when he was remembering things, he couldn't bear to be touched. After all these years, it was still hard not to take it personally.

"Anyway," she said. "I'm sorry for thinking less of you."

He shrugged. He took off the stockings he wore over the nubs of his legs, took the lotion off the nightstand, and rubbed it in.

"Eugene is good with Sammy," she said.

"Sammy is good for Eugene," Sam said. "He doesn't see his limitations, he just sees someone to love and play with."

"I love you," she said. "Even though you're often a dick."

He laughed softly and turned to her.

"Apology not needed but accepted," he said. "Permission to approach the wife?"

"Permission granted," she said and took him in her arms.

CHAPTER TEN

Hannah called Maggie at noon.

"Ingrid hasn't shown up or called," she said. "Patrick and Scooter are here setting up the stage and sound system for the music. I hate to tell ya, but it looks like our small, quiet party is going to look more like Woodstock."

"If you would quit telling people about it," Maggie said.

"I can't help it, I'm that excited," Hannah said. "I'm going to the IGA now to buy everything just in case Ingrid's a no-show."

"It's not like her to bail," Maggie said. "I'll follow up with her."

When no one answered her repeated calls, Maggie decided to drive out to the catering company to see what the hold-up was on Claire's party food.

The front parking lot was empty, and the front door was locked, so Maggie drove around back.

Out in back of the building, Ingrid's van was backed up to the open kitchen door.

"Hello," Maggie called as she walked in.

It took a moment for her eyes to adjust from the bright sunlight outside, to see Ingrid lying face down on the floor of the kitchen, her frothy blonde hair matted with bright red blood. She knelt down and lifted Ingrid's hair to find her neck, felt for a pulse, and was relieved to find she was still alive.

Maggie's heart raced as she pulled her phone out of her pocket and speed-dialed 911. Having notified the emergency operator of her location and situation, she set her phone on the kitchen island and again knelt down by Ingrid.

She had to search through her thick hair to find the wound, which was on the back of her head and was already clotting. She stood back up and grabbed a handful of clean kitchen towels out of a basket on the counter, and then carefully slid them under Ingrid's head. There was a huge knot on one side of her forehead, from falling onto the tile floor, but other than that and the back of her head, Maggie couldn't find any other obvious wounds. She carefully rested Ingrid's head on the dish towels so she could breathe easier, but did not dare move her body for fear of additional, unseen injuries.

Just beyond Ingrid's body, Maggie saw a piece of paper on the floor. She reached over and retrieved it. It was a flyer from Tiger Tails featuring Amber as Mustang Sally.

As Maggie stood back up, she heard what sounded like metal chairs falling over in the room in front of the kitchen. All the hair stood up on her arms and neck. Scanning the kitchen for a weapon, she spied a lethal looking butcher knife and picked it up.

The interior kitchen door was a swinging door, so there was no way to lock it. She considered her options, including piling up things to block the entrance, but considered whoever was hiding in the next room could just pull the door inward. There was no help for it, she was going to have to try to scare the person out the front entrance.

Maggie pushed as hard as she could so that the door swung open with a crash.

"Stop! Police!" she yelled, in as loud and deep of a voice as she could muster.

She heard the shot, but before she could duck, the bullet zinged past her head and embedded in the door of the refrigerator in the kitchen behind her. Maggie cursed and hunched down, then reached up with her hand to search the wall for the light switches. She flipped the lights on in the outer room and just caught a glimpse of a person retreating behind several tall stacks of chairs. The shooter no longer had a clear shot, but Maggie was afraid one look would reveal she was neither the police nor armed, so she reached back up for the light switch.

On the wall above the light switch was a steel hook to which a stalwart rope was wound and tethered. Following its path upward, Maggie could see it was holding the huge, rolled-up marquis tents against the pulleys attached to the steel joists that supported the roof. Maggie turned off the lights, stood up, and sawed the ropes with the butcher knife until the weight of the marquis tents pulled it loose. There was a loud banging crash as the tents hit the chairs, then a heavy thump, and silence.

Maggie heard the sirens, dropped the knife, ran to the front door, unlocked it, and waved her arms at the ambulance and county squad car. It was Sarah, of course, but she was all business.

"In there," Maggie told her. "I dropped the tents on someone who shot at me. They knocked Ingrid out; she's in the kitchen."

"Is there another way in?" Sarah asked her.

Maggie pointed around to the back.

"Ingrid's on the floor in the kitchen," Maggie said.

Sarah directed the E.M.T. team to stay back until she gave them the all clear. Maggie went with them to stand on the other side of the ambulance.

Sarah sent her deputy around back and waited until she heard him come through the swinging kitchen door. He turned on the lights, and then they both disappeared into the room.

Maggie braced herself for shots to be fired, but it was silent. Her heart was pounding, and her mouth had gone dry. While they waited, she described Ingrid's injury and the E.M.T.s prepared their supplies.

Sarah came out and told the E.M.T. team to go ahead with Ingrid first, and called for backup for the person inside the front room. They got back in the ambulance and drove it around the building, leaving Maggie standing in the middle of the parking lot.

Sarah came forward and held out her hand as if to shake Maggie's. Maggie reluctantly took it, and Sarah squeezed it as hard as she could. Maggie responded by gripping the smaller hand in hers and channeling all her fear and anger into a grip she felt sure would break the smaller woman's hand.

Sarah grunted and let go first.

Maggie could feel her whole body flush with anger but took a deep breath instead of slugging an armed county cop.

"Knocked out cold but still alive," Sarah said, as she massaged her hand. "You have damn fine instincts for a civilian."

"Who was it?" Maggie asked.

"I'll let you see for yourself," Sarah said, and led the way back into the front room of the building.

They had rolled back the tents to uncover the body of the person and had rolled the body over so it was face up.

The woman was wearing black clothing and black shoes, and her black head scarf had been pulled back to reveal her face.

"I don't know her," Maggie said.

"Her ID says she's Sophie Dean," Sarah said.

"Oh, my Lord, I do know her," Maggie said and filled Sarah in.

Maggie followed the first ambulance to the hospital, and she was at Ingrid's bedside in the E.R. when she woke up. Ingrid gingerly touched her bandaged head and the bump above her eye.

"Ingrid, it's Maggie," Maggie said. "You're in the hospital."

"My head hurts," Ingrid said. "I'm thirsty."

Maggie fetched some ice chips and informed the charge nurse that her "sister," Ingrid, was awake. When she returned to the curtained cubicle, Maggie raised the head of her bed so Ingrid could sit up.

"They think you have a concussion, but your skull's not cracked," Maggie said.

"That's good news, I guess," Ingrid said.

A nursing assistant came in, checked her blood pressure, her pulse, and her IV. She also checked all the sticky patches that linked her to the beeping, monitoring machines.

"A doctor will be in to see you soon," she said.

After she left, Ingrid eyed Maggie.

"Did they catch her?"

"Yeah, I dropped the tents on her, and it knocked her out," Maggie said. "They took her to Morgantown, on account of you being here. What happened? Why was she there?"

"She was looking for Amber," Ingrid said. "I told her Amber no longer worked for me, and she got really agitated. She accused me of lying to protect Amber from her."

"She must have found out it was Amber who had taken up with Chip, her ex-fiancé," Maggie said. "That woman's quite the stalker, and she never gets over a thing."

"Sophie is Amber's mother," Ingrid said.

"Wait a minute," Maggie said. "What?"

"They had a huge falling out before Amber ran away. Amber said she was crazy and violent, but she seemed pretty harmless to me, until today."

"You've seen her often?"

"Oh yeah, about once every few months for the past couple of years. The last time was about a week ago," Ingrid said.

"The morning of the O'Hare luncheon," Maggie said. "What happened?"

"She showed up, and she and Amber argued, as usual. Sophie wants her to take her GED and go to nursing school, and Amber told her to get lost. I made them go outside. When Amber came back in, she acted like nothing had happened. When I asked her about it later, she just shrugged it off."

"What was it you found that you thought I might be interested in?"

"I broke the lock off of Amber's employee locker. It was stuffed full of things she must have stolen from my clients. There was a lot of money, some drugs, and a gun, but after the story you told me, I thought you'd be most interested in the perfume bottle, the antibiotics, and the epi pen. They're locked up in my safe at the office."

Scott came through the curtain to the emergency room cubicle, white-faced and big-eyed.

"Hi," Maggie said, as she stood up. "Ingrid, this is my husband, Scott."

"Hi, Scott," Ingrid said. "Your wife saved my life today."

"My wife is going to give me a heart attack," Scott said, as he embraced Maggie.

"I guess Sarah called you," Maggie said.

"No," Scott said. "Skip saw it on the blotter and told me. I didn't know until just now whether you were hurt or not."

"I'm sorry," Maggie said.

248

"Let's go outside," Scott said. "Ingrid, it was nice to meet you."

Out in the hospital parking lot, Scott took a deep breath and wiped his face with both hands.

"I don't know what to do," Scott said. "I don't ever want to be scared like that again. I could have lost you."

Maggie felt terrible, but she didn't know what to say, except, "I'm sorry."

He grabbed her, hugged her, and Maggie could feel him trembling.

"I'm sorry," Maggie said. "I'm okay. Really."

"Why were you there?"

"I went to see why Ingrid hadn't shown up to the party," Maggie said. "Sophie Dean had knocked her out and left this strip club flyer to make everyone think Amber had done it. I think she was looking for the evidence Amber had stowed in her employee locker. Sophie is Amber's mother; can you believe that?"

Maggie told him everything happened and didn't leave anything out, even though hearing about the bullet zinging by her head made the color drain from his face again.

"Maggie, I can't bear this," he said. "How can I convince you to quit putting your life in danger?"

"I didn't go there intending to get shot at," she said. "It just happened."

"This kind of thing will break me, Maggie, I'm telling you; I can't go through this again."

"I'm sorry," she said. "What more can I say?"

"Say you'll quit investigating things with Hannah."

"But that would be a lie," she said. "You don't get this about Hannah and me: investigating things is not just a hobby, it's something we have to do. We can't not do it. When we're in the midst of figuring something out, I'm using all of my brain cells and relying on my intuition at the same time. There's no other feeling like that. It's invigorating. It's addictive. I love it."

Scott sighed.

"Then we're getting you a gun permit, and I'll take you to get trained."

"I don't want a gun," Maggie said. "They're too dangerous."

"If you're going to keep getting yourself into situations where people shoot at you, wouldn't it be better to be armed and trained?"

"I'm not getting a gun, period," she said. "That's not what this is about. This is about outsmarting criminals, not fighting with them."

"It wouldn't hurt for you to take some self-defense courses," he said. "Just as a precaution."

"Hannah's going to get her Private Investigator license," Maggie said. "I'd rather do that."

"God help us all," he said.

Maggie picked up Claire at her parents' house and drove down the street.

"Have I got a story for you," she said.

After Maggie finished, Claire sat in dumb silence.

"Sophie is Amber's mother," Maggie said.

"I got that," Claire said. "She told me her daughter was in college."

"She's a liar," Maggie said with a shrug.

"Sophie sent Amber to kill Gigi?" Claire asked.

"Or just gave her the idea and means," Maggie said. "What better way to frame Jillian one last, brilliant time?"

"Did she know Amber was sleeping with her ex-fiance?"

"What better way for Amber to get back at her mother?"

"This is seriously twisted."

"Oh," Maggie said. "Here's another update straight from a cop I happen to sleep with: the coroner's report says that Gigi died of anaphylactic shock due to an overdose of penicillin and that Cheat was killed by an injection of epinephrine straight to his heart."

"Both killed by Amber?"

"Here's my theory," Maggie said. "Amber's mother finds out she's involved with Chip. She's furious, but more importantly, she sees a way to use her daughter to frame Jillian for murder. She's a former nurse, and she knows about Gigi's allergy from being close to the family years ago. When she finds out Amber is working Gigi's luncheon, she appeals to her daughter's insatiable appetite for money, tells her what to do, and Amber agrees to do the deed. Sophie gets the penicillin; Amber takes it with her.

"While Gigi is fighting with Chip out back, Amber sneaks upstairs, doses the perfume, finds Gigi's epi-pen, and hides it in her purse. After they're thrown out, she goes back in to steal something because she's mad about being kicked out, finds Gigi dead, steps over her dead or dying body, and takes the perfume bottle so no one can test it. She then uses the epi-pen to kill Cheat."

"Wow," Claire said. "Just, wow."

"I know, right?" Maggie said. "It's diabolical."

"What does Scott say?"

"That it's all circumstantial evidence. If they can trace the epi-pen in Amber's locker back to Gigi's prescription, and the perfume bottle has penicillin in it, then that will be compelling evidence against Amber. But Amber will just say her mom did it, and Sophie will say Amber did it. Sophie was trying to frame Amber for Ingrid's assault, so it's only a hop, skip, and a jump to her framing her for Cheat and Gigi's murders."

"You think they'll get away with it?"

"Well, Sophie will go to jail for attacking Ingrid," Maggie said. "What do you want to bet she'll throw her daughter under the bus to get a shorter sentence?"

"If they ever find Amber," Claire said. "She's protected by the mob now, remember."

"She'll do well there," Maggie said. "They promote psychopaths in that organization."

"So, Jillian didn't do anything wrong?"

"She conspired with Candace to forge a check for several million dollars."

"And got away with it."

"Not completely," Maggie said. "She's lost her cushy job offer, and it's just a matter of time before Chip's misadventures get her disinvited from every committee and social event."

"She lost control," Claire said. "Her worst nightmare."

"Thanks to you," Maggie said.

"Where are we going?" Claire asked. "We're just aimlessly driving around Rose Hill."

"I'm killing time before I take you out to Hannah's."

"Why?"

"There's a party for you brewing out there."

"Oh, no," Claire said. "I was hoping nobody would remember. I don't want a party, Maggie."

"I know, hon," Maggie said. "It was supposed to be a small, family-only thing, but it's kind of expanded out of control."

"Please tell me you're kidding."

"Scooter Scoley and the Snufftuckers are going to play," Maggie said.

"No," Claire said. "Make it stop."

"They spread the word to their fans, and between that and Hannah's big fat mouth, half the town is up at the farm waiting for you to arrive."

"Is there any way out of this?"

"Not out," Maggie said. "Just through."

"Please kill me now."

"I know," Maggie said. "That's why I'm telling you first, so you can prepare yourself."

"I need a drink or a cookie."

Maggie reached into the back seat, flipped open a cooler lid, and handed Claire a beer.

"I thought of that," she said. "Poor you."

"Poor me? Poor Eugene," Claire said. "This will scare the bejeezus out of him."

There were so many cars that Maggie had to park halfway down Possum Holler, and they walked up. As they walked past the dozens of cars parked on the side of the narrow road, they could hear the mandolin and banjo music echoing off the hills.

"It sounds like a festival," Claire said.

"Claire-a-palooza," Maggie said.

Up at the farm, Scooter and the band were blazing through a fast-paced number. Patrick had set up a bar on the sunporch, and Sam was supervising a line of ten barbecue grills being tended to by vet buddies of his from the community center.

Claire's mother, Maggie's mother, and several of their friends were doling out food from a potluck collection on white-paper-covered tables, and folks were congregating to eat at one of the many picnic tables that had been borrowed from the Whistle Pig Lodge.

When Scooter spotted Claire, he stopped playing and shouted, "There's the birthday girl!"

Everyone turned and hollered at Claire. Scooter's band began to play "Happy Birthday," and everyone sang. Claire could feel her cheeks burn with embarrassment.

He invited her onstage to sing, but Claire shook her head.

"You'll be up here singing before the night is through," Scooter said. "Mark my word."

She accepted many hugs and handshakes on her way to the sun porch, where her cousin Patrick handed her another beer.

"Great party, cuz," he said.

Ed came out of the kitchen with Sammy in his arms. Sammy had been crying, and he showed Claire his skinned knee. He held out his arms and Claire took him.

He rested his head on her shoulder and said, "Too loud."

"I know," Claire said. "Let's go see Eugene."

She kissed Ed and said she'd be back soon. They made their way to the barn, which had a sign on the door that read, "Do Not Enter. Vicious dogs." She let herself in, closed the door behind her, patted Hannah's big dogs, and went up the stairs to the loft.

She knocked on the door.

Sammy said, "Genie, me's Sammy and Claire Bear; we comes in."

Eugene opened the door.

Bunny and Chicken danced around Claire's feet, delighted to see her.

Eugene looked haggard. There were dark circles around his eyes, and his cheeks were sunken in. His clothes hung off him due to the weight he'd lost. Claire put Sammy down, and he ran to Eugene, who had to use great effort to pick him up.

"Sorry about the party," Claire said. "If it's any consolation, I didn't know about it, and I didn't want it, either."

Eugene shook his head and smiled without showing his teeth. He put Sammy down and took him by the hand, showed him what he was working on. He was tumbling rocks in a polisher, and he let Sammy help him.

"Look at me, Claire," Sammy said. "Me's doing it!"

254

"It's amazing how insulated this room is," Claire said. "I thought it would be much louder in here."

Eugene gave Sammy a bag of brightly swirled marbles, and Sammy sat down on the floor to play with them. The little dogs chased the marbles and made Sammy laugh.

Eugene took a white dry erase board off the table and wrote something on it. He then turned it toward Claire.

"Too much work to talk. Worse than before," he'd written.

"If you want to see a specialist, we'll take you anywhere you need to go. Someone may be able to do something for you."

"No more doctors," he wrote. "I just want to stay here and do this."

He gestured to his work behind him.

"Hannah had said you always wanted to move to South America," Claire said. "Wasn't that your dream?"

"I used to want that," he wrote. "Now I have a family."

"That's good," Claire said. "Family is the most important thing."

"Are you going to marry Ed?" he wrote.

"Probably. But you and I are family now, too."

"No kissing then," he wrote and pantomimed laughing.

"No," Claire said. "Sorry."

He shrugged.

"I want to pay for Sammy to go to college," he wrote. "Set up a trust for him. Can you do that?"

"Walter can do that," Claire said. "Anything you want, we will do."

He nodded and mouthed, "Thank you."

"Genie, play with me," Sammy whined.

Hannah appeared in the doorway and said, "There you are. Sorry about the Burning Man thing, Claire. Things got a little out of hand. Come on, Sammy. Papaw has the tractor out, and he's going to take the kids on a hayride."

"Pretty clever getting me to set up for my own party," Claire said.

"I had to think fast," Hannah said.

Sammy jumped up, hugged Eugene's legs, looked up at him, and said, "Me's play with you's later. Me's gotta go."

Hannah picked up her son and went down the stairs.

"I guess I should at least attend a party thrown in my honor," Claire said.

Eugene nodded and smiled.

"I'm so glad you're all right," Claire said. "If you feel like coming down later, find me, and we'll sit together."

Eugene held up a finger and wrote something, then held it up for Claire to see.

"Thank you, Claire," it said.

Outside, children were running and screaming, the music was loud, and everyone kept touching her as she passed through the crowd. Claire felt an overwhelming need to escape, but instead, she just kept smiling and thanking everyone for coming.

Her Uncle Curtis was down in the lower field, loading up the hay wagon with children and adults. Claire sat down on the front porch steps to watch. Scott came out of the house and sat down beside her.

"I guess you heard about Sophie Dean getting arrested," he said.

"It's sad," Claire said. "All that fuss over a man who didn't even love her."

"Don't you think it was more of a power struggle between her and Jillian?"

"I guess so," Claire said. "Nobody won, of course."

"I was out of my mind for a few hours thinking Maggie might be hurt," he said. "The Neanderthal in me wanted to lay down the law and forbid her from investigating things with Hannah."

"How did that go over?" Claire said.

"I calmed down as soon as I saw she was okay," he said. "When we got married I promised not to try to change her. That's easier to say than to put into practice."

"She won't change, anyway."

"No," he said. "I did convince her to get some self-defense training; at least then it will be a fair fight. I suggest you do the same."

"I think my detective work days are behind me," Claire said. "I want to settle down, get my life in order, and adopt a kid."

"That will be a relief to Ed," Scott said. "He is still in that picture, isn't he?"

"Definitely," Claire said.

"I'm sorry about Laurie, but I'm glad you're going to give Ed a chance. You couldn't find a better man."

"It was always going to be Ed," Claire said. "Even if Laurie had lived."

They were quiet for a bit, watching Curtis's tractor pulling the hay wagon around the pond while Hannah tried to keep Sammy from falling off.

"Eugene seems to be doing well out here," Scott said.

"He's not well at all," Claire said and told Scott about the complications from the medicine. "He might even be worse off than before."

"Poor little guy," Scott said. "He just never catches a break."

They watched as Sammy took wads of hay and rubbed them in someone's hair.

"Hey, Claire," Scott said. "I need to clean up my Sunflower Street house, and Laurie's things are still there."

"Hmm," Claire said. "Did you call Daphne, his ex?"

"She said donate whatever it is because she doesn't want anything."

"Maybe that's what you should do, then."

"There are papers, personal things, and a journal," he said. "I didn't read it, but I thought you might want to have it."

A journal.

She didn't know Laurie kept a journal.

"I'll do it tomorrow," she said. "Thanks for asking me."

"He was a good guy," Scott said and handed her a key.

"I know," Claire said.

Scott stood up, rested his hand on her head for a moment, and then went back into the house.

Claire watched the tractor pulling the hay wagon, and listened to the music echoing off the hills on the other side of the valley.

Ed came around the side of the house and paused at the bottom of the steps.

"Care for some company?" he asked.

"If it's you, always," Claire said.

The next morning, Claire woke up before the sun came up, dressed, and left the house before her father woke up. The air outside was downright chilly, so she ran to warm herself up. It felt good to run, breathing the cool air down into her lungs and exhaling steam. She crossed Rose Hill Avenue, which looked deserted, cut through the alley behind PJ's Pizza, and ran up the alley behind Sunflower Street.

Her hands were trembling as she unlocked the back door. Scott had stacked some boxes in the kitchen for her to use. It was cold inside, so she lit the gas fire in the fireplace and made some coffee. After she felt warmed up, she took some boxes down the hallway to the bedroom, the one in which she had slept with Laurie, both in her dreams and in reality.

Memories flooded back, and she let herself drown in them.

His bathrobe hung on the back of the bedroom door; she held it to her face and inhaled his scent. She took his clothes out of the drawers and closet, carefully folded them and placed them in a box on the bed. She got a plastic bag out of the kitchen to put his toiletries in before she placed them in the box. The spare change he had left on the dresser she put in her own pocket.

She opened one of the bedside tables, but it was empty; the other held the journal. It was a plain, ring-bound notebook with a blue cardboard cover, on which the year was written. She riffled the pages; it looked as if half the pages had been written on in Laurie's spidery black penmanship. She set it aside while she finished cleaning and packing up his things.

She took the notebook back to the living room, where she could sit by the fire and stay warm. She held it in her hands, listening for him in her thoughts.

"Should I read it, Laurie?" she asked out loud.

No piano music played, no pithy quips popped up in response.

"I could just burn it," she said.

But there was no answer from Laurie.

He was gone.

Acknowledgments

Thank you to my mom, Betsy Grandstaff and my dear sister, Terry Hutchison, my most excellent first readers.

Thank you to P.A. and Sarah for giving me the best day job a person could hope for, and for being such good friends.

Thank you to everyone who bought and read the books, took the time to write reviews on Amazon, and sent me sweet emails.

Thank you to Tamarack: The Best of West Virginia, for selling my paper books in your beautiful building.

Thank goodness June Bug is still here, and George has turned into the nicest dog.

If you liked this book, please leave a review on Amazon.com (Thank you!)

More info on RoseHillMysteries.com

Made in the USA
Monee, IL
08 July 2021

72468247R10146